THE
STOLEN LAKE

OTHER YEARLING BOOKS YOU WILL ENJOY:

THE
STOLEN LAKE
JOAN AIKEN

A YEARLING BOOK

Published by
Dell Publishing Co.
a division of
The Bantam Doubleday Dell Publishing Group, Inc.
1 Dag Hammarskjold Plaza
New York, New York 10017

This work was first published in Great Britain by Jonathan Cape Ltd.

Yearling ® TM 913705, Dell Publishing Co., Inc.

ISBN: 0-440-40037-6

Reprinted by arrangement with Delacorte Press

Printed in the United States of America

March 1988

10 9 8 7 6 5 4 3 2 1

CW

A NOTE TO THE READER

This book forms part of the series begun in *The Wolves of Willoughby Chase* and continued in *Black Hearts in Battersea* and *Nightbirds on Nantucket*. It is set in the reign of King James III, supposing that he had been king of England in the nineteenth century instead of Queen Victoria, and it follows the adventures of Dido Twite after she sets sail for England, at the end of *Nightbirds on Nantucket*, and before she gets there, in *The Cuckoo Tree*. But this is a separate story, and you don't need to have read any of the others to understand it.

Everybody knows that the ancient British *didn't* migrate to South America when the Saxons invaded their country; this is just my idea of what it would have been like if they had. But Brazil did get its name from the old Celtic belief that there was a beautiful magic country called Breasil's Island, Breasail, or Hy Brasil, somewhere out in the Atlantic, west of Ireland, where the sun sets.

J.A.

THE
STOLEN LAKE

1

The new captain of H.M.S. *Thrush*, who had come on board at Bermuda, was very particular in his views as to what a young female passenger on a British man-o'-war might or might not do.

"How old are you, child?" he sharply demanded when he first set eyes on Dido.

"I dunno."

"You do not *know* your own *age*? You do not *look* like a stupid child."

"O' course I ain't stupid," said Dido, nettled. "But before I came on board this here ship I were asleep a plaguey long time aboard a whaling vessel—months and months—Davy Jones alone knows how long."

"A fine skimble-skamble tale!" said Captain Hughes incredulously. "Well, however that may be, a young person of your age—and I doubt if that can be more than twelve—should remain belowdecks and learn lessons. I cannot have you skylarking with the midshipmen or continually getting under the men's feet.

Needlework would be a more proper occupation. Have you no piece of embroidery—no sampler to sew on?"

"Sampler? Not blooming likely!" said Dido. "Needlework's a mug's game."

Captain Hughes peered at her disapprovingly over the logbook of the *Thrush*.

"It says here," he pursued, "that you were received on board, for passage back to England, off the isle of Nantucket, after having been instrumental in uncovering a Hanoverian plot against his Majesty King James III." He read aloud these last words with patent disbelief, and added, "How, pray, could a young person such as yourself have come to be concerned in such matters?"

"Oh, that's a long story," said Dido. "That'd be several long stories."

She had been studying Captain Hughes, and her first impressions of him were no more favorable than his of her. Captain Osbaldestone, who had invited her aboard the *Thrush*, had been a lively, imperturbable little man, on cordial terms with all his crew. But shortly after Dido's arrival on board, the *Thrush* had encountered, first, a pirate vessel, and then a Hanoverian merchantman. There had been a couple of sharp sea battles; the pirate had been sunk, the Hanoverian captured, manned with a prize crew, and escorted by the *Thrush* to the island of Bermuda, where both vessels needed a good deal of repair after the engagement. And while that was going on, Captain Osbaldestone had been promoted to command a larger British naval ship, and Captain Hughes had come to take his place on board the *Thrush*.

It was a change for the worse, Dido soon decided.

"Pray remember, Miss Twite, that I do not wish to

see you outside your own quarters," the captain said severely.

"*What?* Mayn't I go up on deck, even?"

She stared at him, wondering if he could be serious. He certainly looked it—he was a tall, stern individual with a thick, upstanding brush of gray hair and bristling gray brows. His mouth was exceedingly firm. He replied, "You may take the air twice a day on the foredeck. But no unseemly frolicking with the ship's company, if you please!"

"Mayn't I even climb the *rigging*?"

"Certainly not!"

"What the dickens shall I *do* all day, then?"

"I shall instruct my steward, Holystone, to take charge of your education. Which, so far as I can make out, has been wholly neglected. You appear to know nothing about *anything* except navigation and how to cut up whales. During the passage to England you may at least learn to spell, and the basic rudiments of arithmetic."

Mr. Holystone, the steward, however, preferred to teach Dido logic, astronomy, the use of the globes, trigonometry, ancient history, and the rules of war. His company was the one thing that consoled Dido for the arrival of Captain Hughes, and since she was no longer allowed to frolic with the midshipmen, she spent most of her time with the steward and his cat, assisting him with various of his tasks while he gave her instruction. Mr. Holystone had come on board with the captain at Bermuda. He seemed fitted for higher employment, but performed his duties calmly and capably, was on friendly terms with the crew, and entrusted with the captain's confidence to a considerable degree. He was a very silent man, so quiet sometimes that he seemed like a hole in the air—as if, Dido thought, he were trying to remember a dream that had sunk down to the bottom of his mind. But at other times he could be talkative enough, and had passed on much useful information to his young companion: why the Black-Browed Albatross is known as the Hollyhawk; how to make Dandyfunk and Crackerhash; that you should never drink the first cup of liquid offered you by a stranger.

Dido was sitting on the foredeck, cross-legged, polishing up the captain's silver spoons and forks with a piece of sharkskin and a little pot of powdered hartshorn during the second of her two daily airing periods. Above her in the sky hung a great pale moon which had been following the ship all afternoon. It was like a drum, Dido thought, made of silvery parchment, dangling up there over the stern, waiting for someone to climb up the mizzenmast and give it a bang.

Must be nearly dinner time, she reckoned.

In confirmation of this, she saw Mr. Holystone picking his way neatly among the marlinspikes, belaying pins, coils of rope, capstans, and windlasses.

"Just done the last spoon, Mr. Holy!" she called, shuffling them all together.

The captain's steward was a slight man, of medium height, with regular features and so calm an expression that he looked like a figurehead, carved from pale brown wood. His hair had bleached and his skin had weathered to the same beech-brown color. His eyes were gray and thoughtful; he had an air of sober dignity at all times. Despite this he was not very old, Dido thought—nothing like as old as the captain.

He held out a hand for the silver, then paused, glancing in some surprise over Dido's shoulder.

"What's up, Mr. Holy?"

Dido looked round too; then, exclaiming "Caramba!" she scrambled to her feet. For the moon, instead of floating behind the mainmast, had glided all the way round the horizon and established itself on the ship's right-hand side, where it was beginning to glow pink in the rapidly darkening sky. The fresh following breeze had shifted round to the starboard quarter and was ruffling Dido's short brown hair and making her square midshipman's collar stand on end. The smoke from the *Thrush*'s stern funnel streamed away to port.

"Hey!" said Dido. "We've turned round!"

Staring back along the rail she saw that the ship's wake, which all day had carved out an arrow-straight line of creamy froth, stretching southwest behind them, was now an enormous curve, like a giant question mark across the deep-blue ocean.

"What's amiss, Mr. Holystone? D'you reckon one o' the crew fell overboard? I didn't hear nobody yell out."

"It is indeed singular. A most unforeseen occurrence."

"D'you reckon Cap'n Hughes suddenly remembered summat he'd left behind in Bermuda?"

Dido sighed, remembering how many months she had already been away from her family and friends in Battersea, London. Her family were not particularly lovable—indeed her mother and elder sister had often been extremely unkind to Dido, and her father, though he could be larky when the spirit took him, frequently forgot his younger daughter for weeks on end. But still, she wanted to see them again, if only to tell her adventures—how she had been all round the world on a whaler, and had helped rescue a girl called Dutiful

Penitence from a wicked aunt who turned out to be no aunt at all but a Hanoverian rebel, planning to blow up St. James's Palace with a long-range cannon.

There was also a friend of Dido's called Simon whom she wanted to see very much indeed.

"Maybe Cap'n Hughes just slipped a mite off course," she suggested hopefully.

But the *Thrush* sailed on along her new course; the moon, now large and pink as a peony, remained obstinately on the right-hand side, casting a pearly path over the dark water.

"I will take these below," said Mr. Holystone. "It may be that I can discover what has caused the change."

His cat, El Dorado, who had come on deck with her master, stretched elaborately, first her front paws, then her back.

"Come on, Dora," said Dido. "Let's us go too, and find out what's happening."

She picked up the copper-colored cat. Dora's immensely long tail instantly went twice round Dido's neck.

The big three-masted man-o'-war was breasting large Atlantic waves; the deck rose, dipped, and rolled from side to side in a long, continuous, corkscrewing glide. But Dido crossed it with practiced ease, making for the captain's companionway. As she passed them, several sailors nodded to her in a friendly manner, but they did not speak. Captain Hughes was a strict disciplinarian. One or two of the midshipmen gave her cautious grins. A man called Silver Taffy (on account of his impressive, shining, hallmarked dentures) cast a malevolent look at both Dido and the cat, making a figure-eight sign with fingers and thumbs as he spat over the side.

"Pair o' Jonahs!" he muttered as Dido passed him. "I know what I'd do if *I* had charge o' this vessel."

Dido scowled at him. He had been one of the crew aboard the *Queen Ettarde*, the vanquished pirate ship, and had elected to become a member of the *Thrush*'s crew rather than go to jail in Bermuda. He'll bear watching, Dido thought, as she climbed down the companion ladder. I'd as soon not run across *him* on a dark night.

She passed the door of the officers' wardroom, from which came a strong smell of fried onions and salt pork. The officers—except for those on watch—were at supper. Dido as she passed could hear what they said, for it was very hot belowdecks, and the door was braced open.

"Plaguey tedious change of course," said Mr. Windward, the first lieutenant. "I wanted to get home to Blighty and spend my prize money. What possessed the captain to turn south?"

"Maybe he had an order?" suggested Bowsprit, the second lieutenant.

"Who gave it? Where the deuce could it have come from?"

"The admiralty, of course. Where else do orders come from?"

"How did it get here, sapskull?"

"Sealed, maybe," suggested one of the midshipmen. "You know: not to be opened till two months out at sea."

"We'd have heard about it before," said Lieutenant Windward.

"Not from old Mumchance. He'd not tell you it was Tuesday."

Dido went on to her own cabin, a tiny box next to

the captain's big day cabin ("so that I can keep an eye on you and see you don't get into trouble," he had said severely, supervising her removal from a much more comfortable cabin farther off). She took her meals with Mr. Holystone in his galley, where he prepared food for the captain. This was two doors farther on, beyond the captain's sleeping quarters. She went to the galley now, and found Mr. Holystone thoughtfully paring off thin curls of coconut and laying them on a silver dish. Captain Hughes was partial to tropical food.

"Here," said Dido, "lemme do that." She took the knife from Mr. Holystone, inquiring, in a lower tone, "What's to do? Cap's up on the quarterdeck—walking to and fro—looks as pothered as a flying fish that's forgot how to swim."

"He had a message." Mr. Holystone gave a stir to a cauldron of shark soup, turned a mutton ham on its roasting spit, then began kneading a pan of dough and breaking it into rolls.

"He did have a message? From the admiralty?"

"No, from Admiral Hollingsworth at Trinidad."

"How the blazes did it get here?"

"By carrier pigeon." Mr. Holystone put his rolls in the oven.

"Hey—was it that pigeon that Dora nearly caught this morning?"

"There it is."

Now Dido noticed the same pigeon perched on top of the dish rack, with its head under its wing. Must be tuckered out, she thought, if it's flown all the way from Trinidad—wherever that is. "Best watch Dora don't get it, Mr. Holy?"

But the cat, El Dorado, was engaged in gnawing

some shark scraps on a tin pan which her master had put down for her.

"Lucky Noah Gusset caught the pigeon afore Dora got to it, or Cap'n Hughes'd never have got the message," Dido remarked.

"And we would have been spared much trouble."

"Why? What was the message? Did you find out?"

"*Sí, sí.*" Mr. Holystone sometimes absently lapsed into Spanish or Latin. When he was fifteen his adopted father had sent him to be educated at the University of Salamanca, in Spain. He was so fond of learning that he had remained there for ten years. In consequence he knew a great deal about almost everything, and spoke nine languages fluently.

"Talk English, please!" said Dido, who did not.

"Excuse me! Captain Hughes has been instructed to sail down the east coast of Roman America to the port of Tenby, in New Cumbria."

Mr. Holystone did not look particularly happy about this change of plan.

"Is that a long way?" asked ignorant Dido.

"I should say so! Two thousand miles, I daresay. We must cross the equator."

"Two *thousand* miles?" Dido gasped. "But I thought we was on our way home, bound for London river."

Her mouth drooped. Mr. Holystone looked at her with sympathy.

"Poor young miss. It is a sad feeling—to be so far from home."

"Where's your home, Mr. Holy?"

"Hy Brasil?" The steward sighed. "It is not so far from where we are going. But I have no friends there anymore. I cannot return."

"So why do we have to go to this New Cumbria?"

"Admiral Hollingsworth had a message from the queen of that country, asking for help."

"Why should the British Navy help *her*?"

"She has sustained some wrong at the hands of a neighbor country. There has been some attack, some invasion—the message did not say. Something has been taken from the queen."

"Captain Hughes has to get it back?"

"So he was told."

"But why should we help this queen?" asked Dido. She folded the captain's table napkin into a neat cockade. "Why can't the queen's own army do that job?"

"Really you are a remarkably ill-informed young person," Mr. Holystone said rather severely. "Have you never learned the history of your own land?"

"Oh, come off it, Mr. Holy. Don't preach at a person! It ain't *my* fault I never got no schooling."

"No, that is true," he apologized. "And it is true, too, that all *my* education has done me little good. What is the use of being able to read Sanskrit, Homer, and Machiavelli, if you end up as a ship's steward?"

"You're ever such a good steward, Mr. Holy," Dido said kindly. "Never mind about Mucky Velly. Tell me about the queen of Cumbria. What's her name?"

"The message did not intimate. Her country is Britain's oldest ally. There have been links of friendship between Britain and New Cumbria since the year 577."

"Coo!" Dido counted on her fingers. "More than twelve hundred years. What happened in five seven seven?"

"A battle—the battle of Dyrham. Here, take the

tablecloth." He handed her a heavy white damask square and followed her into the captain's cabin, a big, handsome room which contained a massive mahogany table, as well as a desk and several armchairs. The walls were paneled in walnut and covered with maps, charts, and diagrams of the flying machines which were the captain's passion. He had a theory that ships could be constructed to fly like birds. Up to now, no one at the admiralty had taken him seriously.

Big, slanting windows let in the moonlight and followed the line of the ship's side.

Dido spread the cloth on the table, and Mr. Holystone laid out a single place setting of knives, forks, spoons, plates, and glasses for wine and water.

"Who won the battle of Dyrham?"

"The British lost. You never heard of the Bath Brigade? Or the Glastonbury Guards? Or the Mendip Diehards?" Dido shook her head. "The British and Romans were fighting together against a lot of invading Saxons. When the battle was lost, a number of British and Romans escaped to the coast. There they took ship—in fact the ships that the Saxons had arrived in—and set off across the sea with their wives and families. The first land they reached was New Cumbria, so there they settled."

"And they've been there ever since?" Dido was greatly struck. "Didn't they *never* go back?"

"Some of their descendants went back. And by that time the Saxons had settled down in Britain and made friends with the natives. So there has always been a link between the two countries."

"And that's why this queen thinks poor old Cap'n Hughes has got to come running two thousand miles to pick up her knitting when it drops off the needles? If you ask *me*," said Dido, "I think she has a sauce!"

Mr. Holystone looked a little baffled—some of Dido's language was beyond him. But at this moment they heard Captain Hughes coming along the passage.

"It's lucky," pursued Dido, without heeding this, "that the *Thrush* is one o' these newfangled steam sloops, or it'd be Blue Moon Habbakuk Day afore we ever gets to London. How long'll it take us to sail down the coast of Roman America, Mr. Holy?"

"A week or two—depending on the wind."

Picking up his tray, the steward gestured to Dido to follow him as Captain Hughes appeared in the doorway. The captain, however, halted her with an uplifted hand.

"One moment, Miss Twite."

Oh, blimey, now what? wondered Dido. She searched her conscience for misdeeds. Captain Hughes had a decidedly gloomy expression, as if he had swallowed a sea lemon.

Mr. Holystone had gone to his pantry, and now returned, carrying a bowl of shark soup and the pan of freshly baked rolls.

Captain Hughes said, "Lay another place for Miss Twite, Holystone. I have instructions to give her."

Mr. Holystone was far too well trained to betray surprise. He had attended butlers' school in London; part of the course consisted of half an hour's poker-face work every morning. So now he said, "Certainly, sir," with perfect calm, and retired to reappear next moment with silver, plates, napkin, and glasses for Dido. She, however, gaped at the captain, startled out of her wits by this unexpected honor.

"Sit down, Miss Twite," said the captain.

"Ay, ay, Cap."

Captain Hughes did not go so far as to pull out her chair. He eyed her morosely, as if she were some small obstinate piece of grit that had fallen into his chronometer. Dido herself, now that the initial surprise was over, endeavored to appear quite at her ease. She sat down opposite the captain as if she dined at his table every day, while Mr. Holystone supplied her with a plate of soup and a hot roll.

"It has become my duty, Miss Twite—" said Captain Hughes after a fairly lengthy pause, while he eyed his own plate of soup as if wondering how to navigate a vessel across it. "Ahem!—it has become my duty to change course and make passage to the kingdom of Cumbria."

He paused, as if expecting to be questioned, but as Dido continued quietly spooning up her soup, he demanded in a tone of some asperity, "I daresay you will tell me you have never heard of the place?"

"No I shan't," replied Dido with aplomb. "It's Britain's oldest ally, in the middle o' Roman Ameriky; been that since the Battle o' Dickerydock in the year 577."

"Ah. Ho-hum." Captain Hughes was taken aback. "Yes—er—that is, in fact, the case. Ships of the New Cumbrian Navy have been of assistance to us in attacking the Hanoverians. And their ports are at our disposal for watering, refitting, and taking on food."

"Mighty obliging of 'em," said Dido.

"So we are bound to go to the help of the present ruler, who has sent an appeal to His Britannic Majesty King James III."

"Crumbs," said Dido, wondering what sort of help a ruler would need. "I mean, natcherly we are." She also wondered why Captain Hughes was taking pains to explain all this.

Mr. Holystone removed the soup plates and brought in a roasted mutton ham, which the captain proceeded to carve.

"Since it is not yet perfectly clear what the queen wants," said Captain Hughes, handing Dido a plate of meat, "I shall disembark at the port of Tenby and travel inland to wait on her at her capital."

"Is that far?" inquired Dido. It would, she thought, be very boring if the *Thrush* had to lie at anchor for many days, waiting for the captain.

"Over two hundred miles, I understand. The capital, Bath Regis, lies in the Andes Mountains, which range forms the western boundary of the kingdom."

Dido sighed, chewing on a piece of gristly mutton. He'll be weeks at it, she thought. But then the captain astonished her by saying, "I intend taking you with me, Miss Twite."

"Me?" Hastily Dido gulped down her piece of gristle.

"Don't gape, child! It is most unbecoming. Yes, you," said the captain irritably. "You have been committed to my custody; it would be a shocking dereliction of duty if I were to leave you on board without somebody to watch over you."

"I've managed without custard whatever-it-is plenty o' times before," said Dido ungratefully. "'Sides, I reckon Mr. Holystone'd keep an eye on me."

"I intend taking him as well."

"Oh."

"Do you not *wish* to see New Cumbria?" demanded the captain. "I had thought I was doing you a favor."

(In fact he had thought nothing of the sort.

"We have Reason to Believe," the British agent in Trinidad had written to Admiral Hollingsworth, who had passed on the letter, "that the Queen of New Cumbria is somewhat crack'd in her Wits. She insists, among other things, that she is the rightful Ruler of the British Isles; & asserts that she would set Sail to Make Good her Claim had she not Pressing Reasons for remaining in her Domain of New Cumbria. But she threatens to withdraw her Friendship, including Use of her Ports by British vessels, unless we Come to her Assistance. Do, Pray, Admiral Hollingsworth, send one of your most Trusted Officers to Settle the Old Lady down—for it wd be a most Disastrous Inconvenience to lose those Roman American Bases. Very likely the Whole Affair will prove to be No Great Matter. —By the bye, I hear the Queen is devotedly Fond of Young Female Children & likes to have one or two such Youthful Protégées always at hand. If any of your Officers shd chance to have a Wife and Young Family, the addition of these Persons to the Mission might well serve to Butter Up the Queen & win her Goodwill, should there prove to be any Difficulties about carrying out her Wishes.")

I only hope the queen does not prove to be a *cannibal,* thought Captain Hughes rather uncomfortably.

"I never said I didn't want to come!" retorted Dido to his last observation. "All I said was 'oh.' I don't mind coming along. Is this here Bath Regis a grand town—big as London?"

"I doubt that," said Captain Hughes shortly. He was feeling guilty and anxious—not to say deceitful—about Dido's part in the business, and this made him sound sharper than usual. He added, more mildly, "Yet it is said that some of these cities in the Andes Mountains are very magnificent—the Cities of the Kings, or Caesars, they are called; it is believed that the streets are paved with gold and silver, that the rivers run with diamonds. Even their plows and farm implements are reported to be made of precious metals."

"Fancy," said Dido. Even she was impressed at the thought of silver cobblestones. "Is Bath Regis like that, then—silver cobbles and all?"

"I do not know. We shall see."

Dido began to be reconciled to the prospect of breaking her journey.

Mr. Holystone removed the meat and brought in a gluey conserve of quinces in syrup. Captain Hughes absently spooned out a ladleful of this delicacy for Dido and added, "Ahem! Miss Twite! Since your manners and conduct appear to have been scandalously neglected (indeed I cannot imagine *how* you have been brought up or who has had charge of you), I shall instruct Holystone to bring all your other studies to a halt, and concentrate, during the next week, on teaching you ladylike deportment and elegance of bearing."

"Croopus!"

"You must learn to curtsey—"

"Blimey!"

"You must learn to walk with a book on your head—"

"*Why?*"

"And," continued the captain, beginning to recall disciplines under which his sisters had suffered, "you will lie each day on a backboard, and will recite 'Papa, potatoes, prunes, and prisms' a hundred times, to give you a more refined diction."

Luckily at this moment—for Dido seemed about to burst—the midshipman of the watch knocked and came in with the day's sextant readings giving the ship's position. Captain Hughes exclaimed with satisfaction over these.

"The *Thrush* certainly has an excellent turn of speed. It is that steam screw—a remarkable invention, to be sure. Now, if only it could be harnessed to *wings*. . . . Thank you, Mr. Multiple; you may return on deck. And you, Miss Twite, had best retire to your cabin; you have much to learn before we reach the port of Tenby."

"Ay, ay, sir," said Dido in rather a stifled manner. She walked slowly toward the door.

Noticing her glum looks, Captain Hughes remarked sharply, "And no sulks, if you please! I shall expect a livelier obedience than *that,* when we are ashore in New Cumbria! The country is excessively dangerous; there are jaguars, giant owls and bats, spiders seven inches in diameter, which can, I am told, leap thirty feet in one spring; there are alligators, poisonous snakes, hostile savages in the forest armed with poisoned darts, besides huge hairy tusked birds, larger than horses, which can snatch up a grown man in their talons and fly off with him to their eyrie in the mountains."

"Blister me!" muttered Dido, startled out of her gloom. "What are they called—them big birds? Lucky we don't have *them* in Battersea, or it'd be short commons for the sparrows."

"Their correct designation is *rocs*," said Captain Hughes. "But I understand the Cumbrians refer to them as *aurocs*—because of the tusks, presumably. So you see it is imperative that, while we are in that land, you behave yourself obediently—let there be no quirks or foolish capers, I beg!"

"Reckon there won't be time," said Dido. "We'll be too busy dodging the snakes and alligotamoses—not to mention them awe-rocks. G'night, Cap."

She quietly shut the door behind her and glanced into the galley, hoping to find Mr. Holystone. One thing—I'm glad *he*'s coming along, she thought. He's a right handy cove; daresay he'll be a regular oner when it comes to dealing with giant spiders and bats and awe-rocks.

But Mr. Holystone was not in his galley.

And, strangely enough, Dido thought she recognized the back view of Silver Taffy, walking away along the corridor.

What was *he* doing in Mr. Holystone's galley? she wondered.

The cat, El Dorado, emerged fom a place of concealment in the galley coal scuttle, and came to wrap her long tail twice round Dido's ankles.

"Hey, puss!" said Dido. "Lucky Taffy didn't see you or he'd likely have poured a pot of shark soup over you. Are you coming to New Cumbria too? I'd not give a groat for your chances if you stayed on board without Mr. Holy to keep an eye on you. How about coming to share my bunk?"

The kitchen slate was hanging on the wall. It contained the notes: "Weevils in flour. Tell Quartermaster. Fish for Cap brek. Shark again?"

Dido added at the foot: "Hav tuk Dora to bedd. Cap sez you gotta lern me Maners. D."

Then she retired to her tiny cabin, scrubbed her teeth with a rope's end, and clambered into her bunk, where Dora was already purring.

"Well," she yawned, "I guess us'll have some fine larks in New Cumbria, hey, Dora? With the silver cobbles and the hairy spiders—maybe the cobbles'll come in handy for beaning the spiders."

Presently the door opened softly, and Dido felt the blanket twitched off her feet.

"Hey," she muttered, "you're tickling!" Then she was suddenly wide awake, bolt upright. "*Murder,* is it one o' them spiders? . . . Oh, it's you, Mr. Holy! What the blazes are you doing to my toes?"

"We are in cockroach latitudes," replied Mr. Holystone, who held a little bottle of dark green liquid and a paintbrush. "They swim out from land. So you must paint your toes every night, and your fingers, with this cactus oil. I thought I might do it without waking you." He passed her the bottle.

"What if you don't?" inquired Dido, industriously painting away at her toes.

"Cockroaches come into bed and nibble; you wake up next day with half a dozen toes missing."

"Oh."

"Good night, Miss Dido," said Holystone, and took the bottle from her.

"Mr. Holy, Silver Taffy was in your pantry—why? What'd he come there for?"

"He came to steal the pigeon," Mr. Holystone replied. Dido could feel anger beneath his calm.

"The pigeon? What for? To *eat?*"

"No, no. He sent it off—Mr. Multiple saw him toss it over the side."

"With a message? Who's he want to send a message to?"

"How can we tell? To some of his piratical friends, maybe."

Frowning to himself, Mr. Holystone withdrew, and closed the door.

Dido went back to sleep, and dreamed of hairy cockroaches, bigger than horses, with tusks thirty feet long.

2

Even with the added power of her steam screw, it took the *Thrush* a week to make her way down the coast of Roman America as far as Tenby. For three days, while they were crossing the equator, the weather became outrageously hot, and, as Mr. Holystone had prophesied, cockroaches came on board in large numbers. They were a great nuisance, turning up in wholly unsuitable places, the crow's nest, the captain's bath, the compass, and the quartermaster's molasses jar.

Dido had a busy and aggravating week.

"Love a duck! Why did I ever let myself in for this lay?" she grumbled, when obliged by the exacting Mr. Holystone to walk up and down outside the wardroom door with a copy of the heavy King's Regulations balanced on her head, in order to acquire a more dignified and ladylike posture.

"Plenty of girls would give their eyeteeth to meet a queen," observed Mr. Holystone. He was sitting in his galley, so that he could keep an eye on her through the open door, while he stuffed half a dozen flying fish with a mixture of minced barnacles and powdered hardtack. "When I did my butler's training in London there was a young ladies' finishing school in the same building. All the girls talked about was the day when they would make their curtsey before His Majesty King James III."

"Finishing school?" growled Dido. "That's a right good name for it. It's liable to finish *me*, I can tell you."

"Now curtsey," said Mr. Holystone calmly. "Do not let the King's Regulations slip off your head. Point the right toe—swing the leg slowly to the side, then back—bend the left knee—hands move slowly backwards, spreading the fingers wide—"

The King's Regulations thudded to the floor, narrowly missing the feet of the first lieutenant, a fair-haired young man with a long, earnest face, who came by at that moment. He gave Dido a sympathetic grin, and went into the captain's cabin, where they heard him reporting:

"Thirteen volcanoes sighted ahead on the starb'd bow, sir."

"Thank you, Mr. Windward. You may give the order to slacken sail. We shall heave to, a safe distance out to sea from the port of Tenby, in case the state of hostility between New Cumbria and its neighbor should have worsened. I hope to receive further information and instructions from the British agent in Tenby."

"Ay, ay, sir." Lieutenant Windward saluted and returned on deck.

Dido replaced the King's Regulations on her head.

She pointed her right toe and announced, "How do you do, Your Majesty?" Then she shakily lowered herself on a bent left knee, continuing, "It was kind of you to invite me to your palace. . . . Oh, fish guts!" as the heavy book crashed to the floor once more.

"You had better come in here," said Mr. Holystone, "and practice taking tea. Thumb and three fingers together on the handle—small finger extended. . . . Good. Let me hear your tea table conversation."

"No sugar, thank you, Your Majesty. Merely a drop of cream. There; that is just as I like it. Pray, ma'am, from which Tradesman do you obtain your tay?"

"No, Dido, *no*! Not 'Pry, from which tridesman dew yew obtine yer tie?' 'From which *place* do you ob*tain* your *tay*?' "

"From which plaice dew yew obteeyne yewer teeaye?"

Mr. Holystone threw up his eyes to heaven.

At this moment a sudden shudder through the ship indicated that the *Thrush* had hove to; they heard the creak of windlasses and the thud of feet on deck as the sails were lowered.

"Oh, please lemme go up on deck, Mr. Holy!" begged Dido. "I'll practice ever so hard tonight, cut my throat and swelp me, so I will!"

Mr. Holystone shrugged and let her go. To his mind, the chances of Dido's acquiring the manners of a polite young lady seemed about as probable as a mouse's nest in a cat's ear. Besides, he thought, how do we know what is considered polite behavior in Bath Regis?

Up on deck, Dido glanced eagerly about her.

The Cumbrian coast was visible as a line of black cliffs, about two miles to westward of the *Thrush*. Those cliffs must be tarnal high, Dido thought, to be so plain from here. But at one point they dropped to a V. And a pinnace, which had put out from the *Thrush*, was steering for this cleft.

Beyond the cliffs, and a good deal farther inland, Dido thought, a line of mountains could be seen—a cluster of peaks, very high and spiky, like the teeth of some great trap. Wonder if Bath Regis is up in them mountains? If so, it's going to be a scrabblish climb getting up there. Oh, scrape it! Dido sighed to herself; don't I just wish it was the Kentish flats, and that there port was Gravesend!

A considerable bustle was going on about the decks and rigging, as the sailors spread sails over the yards to act as awnings, bundled other sails tidily into canvas cases, coiled up the shrouds, and generally prepared the ship for a spell of inactivity. Dido, on the foredeck, had to duck and dodge several times, as men dashed past her or ropes whistled over her head.

All of a sudden she heard an angry yell and the outraged squall of a cat. Spinning round, she was just in time to see the sailor known as Silver Taffy grab hold of El Dorado, who had been perched on one of the main-deck eighteen-pounders, minding her own business. Twirling the cat by her long tail, Taffy tossed her over the side. Not, however, before Dora had avenged herself by slashing with all her claws at Taffy's face. She whirled through the air, turning over a dozen times, and would certainly have fallen prey to the sharks had she not struck the anchor cable. With despairing strength the poor animal managed to twine her long, sinuous tail several times round the cable, and so dangled there, swinging and wailing, as she scrabbled frenziedly to grasp the rope with her paws.

"Hang on, Dora—I'll get you!" shouted Dido, who was not far off. She flung herself over the rail and slid down the anchor cable. Grabbing El Dorado round the chest, she hugged the cat against her and began to work her way upward again—no easy matter, as the frantic Dora bit, struggled, squalled, squirmed, and did all in her power to hinder the rescue. Luckily, a couple of midshipmen had witnessed the incident and leaned over to take the cat from Dido; Dora was a general favorite with all the crew except Silver Taffy because of her prowess as a mouser.

"Thankee, Mr. Multiple," panted Dido, scrambling back over the rail. "Dang it, ain't she a Tartar, though! Reckon my face looks like Blackheath Pond after a week's skating!" and she wiped the blood from her eyes.

"It just about does, Miss Dido," said the red-haired Mr. Multiple with a grin. "You'd best take puss below and get Mr. Holystone to bathe those scritches. That was a right nimble job you did there, miss—anyone'd think you'd spent your life at sea."

"Well, I justabout have," said Dido. "Here, Dora, you'd best come along of me. Seems you ain't welcome on deck."

With a darkling glance at Silver Taffy she picked up El Dorado—who had resumed her usual calm and was haughtily putting her ruffled copper fur to rights—and carried the cat below.

"What in the world have you been at, child?" exclaimed Mr. Holystone. "Captain Hughes will hardly think you fit to attend the queen's court if he sees you like that. Here—" and he anointed Dido's countenance with a most evil-smelling paste of shark's liver and seaweed, ordering her to lie in her bunk for three hours, and meanwhile occupy the times usefully by reciting a litany that went:

We clean three tweed beads a week with Maltese seaweed;
Lady Jane Grey, pray do not stray to Mandalay on market day.

Dido found this very unfair. She flung herself crossly on her bunk.

"We clean three tweed beads a week . . . Oh, butter my brogans, what rubbish!"

Luckily, before she had time to become too annoyed, Dido fell fast asleep; the cockroaches had been particularly troublesome the previous night, rustling around with a noise like toast crumbs being shaken inside a paper bag; they had kept her awake for hours.

When she next woke, evening had come; the air was cooler and the light was dim. Yawning, she rolled off her bunk—the weight that had settled on her chest proved to be El Dorado—and went up on deck with the cat for a breath of fresh air, keeping a wary eye out for Silver Taffy.

She found Mr. Holystone on the foredeck, scraping mussels, which he took from a wicker hamper and dropped, when clean, into a cauldron. Dido squatted down to help him, and he exclaimed with satisfaction on the healing work already accomplished by the shark paste.

"Miss Dido," he went on in a lower tone, "I cannot sufficiently express my obligation to you for saving my poor Dora from that ruffian. Young Multiple told me the whole while you were asleep. I had thought you must have been teasing Dora—I might have known I was wrong."

Dido kindly forgave his unjust suspicions. "Anyhows, if you thought I'd been pulling Dora's tail, Mr. Holy, it was right kind of you to doctor me. But why is that Silver Taffy so down on poor Dora?"

"When we were at Nombre de Dios a fortune-teller came along the dock, telling fortunes by dropping a spoonful of soot into people's hands. She told Taffy that the lines in his hand foretold that a cat would be the end of him. He is a very superstitious fellow," said Mr. Holystone, shrugging.

"No wonder he's so tarnal mean to Dora. I'm surprised you let her up on deck."

"Oh, she can usually look after herself. The El Dorado cats have a superior degree of intelligence."

"Are there others like her, then?"

"Indeed yes. Where I come from in Hy Brasil and in Lyonesse such cats are not uncommon."

"With such long tails?"

"Many longer still. They can swing on trees as nimbly as any ape. I have heard it said that there were such cats in the lost garden where our forefathers walked with the gods."

"Fancy!" said Dido. Looking thoughtfully at Mr. Holystone, she asked, after a moment, "Is it a nice place, that land of Hy Brasil? Where you come from?"

A cloud appeared to pass over the steward's brow. He began to say something, checked himself, and, after a moment, merely remarked, "Yes; it is a pleasant place." Then he stood up, easily lifting the heavy cauldron of cleaned mussels.

"Captain Hughes has invited the British agent to dinner. See, there is the pinnace, putting out to fetch him. Bring down the basket, Miss Dido, if you will be so kind."

Mr. Brandywinde, the British agent, proved, when he came on board, to be a blotchy-faced, wandering-eyed, seedy-looking individual. He wore a tricorne hat, snuff-colored suit, silver-buckled shoes; his sandy, thinning hair was dressed in a style long out of date, tied at the back with a small grosgrain bow. Dido, peering through the galley doorway as he passed, thought how untrustworthy he looked, and she guessed that Captain Hughes felt the same, for his voice, when he greeted Brandywinde, was noticeably quiet and dry.

"Claret, sir, or ship's grog—or would you care for a cup of tea?"

"Grog, sir—grog will do capitally, thankee, Captain," Mr. Brandywinde replied, in a tone that was both eager and creaking, like a rusty handle cranked at an uneven rate. "Grog, now, is excellent, if it is well mixed—on shore, I must tell you, we combine it with a little orock—cane spirit, you know! Then, if at the same time you smoke a pipe or two of abaca—hangman's weed, that is—why, you could believe yourself a veritable pasha. I believe even the White Queen herself—"

Then the captain's door was shut, and the two voices died to a murmur.

"Jemima!" said Dido. "What a havey-cavey cove. He looks as if he'd sell his own ma for cats' meat. Don't you think so, Mr. Holy?"

"Very likely his life is a lonely one," said Mr. Holystone guardedly. "The port of Tenby is a small place, cut off by a great forest from the interior, and the capital."

"What's the forest called?"

"Broceliande."

"So how do we get through? If we're going to Bath to see the queen?"

"By boat. Tenby lies at the mouth of a great river, the Severn. It is the captain's intention to hire a boat and travel by water."

Dido was rather disappointed. Having been at sea for most of the last eighteen months, she had hoped for a spell on land. But Mr. Holystone assured her that there would be plenty of that. Halfway along its course the Severn River was interrupted by a formidable series of cataracts dashing down from the Andes Mountains in the west of New Cumbria; these falls were not navigable, and so the party must take to land at that point.

The captain's bell rang, and Mr. Holystone went off to remove the bowls of mussel shells and replace them with fresh mutton and hearts of palm, brought out from shore in the pinnace. Dido, busy decorating a chocolate cake with babassu nuts, judged from the voices coming through the door that Mr. Brandywinde was becoming garrulous from drink and the unaccustomed company.

"You ask what the queen is like? The White Queen? My dear sir, she's rum. Rum as they come. How do you do, sir, what's your game? Rum, Rum, Rumplestiltskin is my name," he caroled. "The White Queen, they call her. Because of her hair, you know. Et cetera, et cetera. Sits at her embroidery all day long. Says she's waiting. Waiting for what? you ask. And may

well ask! But as to that, mum's the word. Both rum
and mum. Her Royal Mercy ain't confidential."

"If the queen is so unapproachable," persisted Captain Hughes, "does she have reliable ministers, advisers
round her, to whom one may apply?"

"Oh, ay, there are some villainous-looking old scala-
wags with beards down to their shins—the vicar general, the grand inquisitor, the accuser, the advocate of
the queen's tribunal—each more slippery than the
next, if you ask me. Besides them there is the queen's
jester—or soothsayer, if you prefer the term—"

"*Soothsayer*? What is *he*?" demanded the captain in
a tone of disgust.

But before Dido could catch the answer, Mr. Holystone emerged with a trayload of plates, and the door
was closed.

During the rest of dinner it remained shut, and no
more of Mr. Brandywinde's disclosures could be heard.
Dido—who had finished decorating the cake—was told
to run up on deck and take the air. "For," said Mr.
Holystone, "you have done more to help me than is
fitting, though indeed I am very much obliged."

"Oh, pho!" retorted Dido. "You know your conversation's always an eddication, Mr. Holy. I'm a-learning
all the time I'm a-helping you. Deportment and manners too!"

She put out her tongue at him teasingly and skipped
out on deck with a small cake, which he had baked for
her in a separate pan.

Dusk had fallen by now, and large southern stars
were beginning to twinkle out in the deep blue above
the *Thrush*, though the Cumbrian coast and the snow-
covered western peaks were still outlined against a sky
of pale phosphorescent green.

Earlier that evening Dido had, without asking permission, removed from the captain's cabin an exceedingly powerful telescope, which was one of his most valued possessions, for when carefully focused it had the power to render clearly visible objects which might be fifty or even a hundred miles off.

"*He* ain't about to use it while he's a-giving dinner and doing the civil to old Brandyblossom," calculated Dido, "so there's no harm in *my* borrowing it for a couple of hours."

When she had eaten her cake, she drew the glass from its case and, with its help, studied various features of the twilit shore. She could see the small town of Tenby clearly enough—its wharves, quays, the shipping at anchor in the river mouth, the tall black-and-white houses with feathery palms above them on the hillside. Then there came a belt of dense green, presumably the forest of Broceliande, full of pythons, pumas, alligators, and aurocs. Beyond that again, much farther off, hardly visible to the naked eye but clear enough through the powerful glass, lay a line of silvery foothills, below the higher peaks. Dido stared at these hills, trying to discover the point at which the Severn River tumbled over them in its majestic series of cataracts. She thought she had found the right spot—a white zigzag line against the gray of the hills—when she chanced on an even more interesting sight—what looked like a long procession of camels moving very slowly southward across the lens of the telescope.

Were they camels? If not camels, then what else could they be? They were shaggy, long-haired beasts, long necked too, with heads like those of sheep. Each bore on its back a large bulging pack. Each was led by a drover, and the procession crept at a snail's pace, as if the loads were a tremendous weight. As they toiled along, they were outlined clearly, some against the green sunset sky, some against the rose-flushed snow-clad peaks.

"Blow me," muttered Dido. "Ain't there a right lot of them, jist?"

She began to count, but counting was not Dido's strong point, and she gave up after four sets of twenty.

"Reckon they must use camels in New Cumbria where we'd use carriers' carts," she decided. "Maybe they finds it best to shift goods at night when the aurocs has gone to roost. Them aurocs must be a plaguey nuisance, if they can scrag a sheep or a cow like Dora nobbles a mouse."

The last of the line of loaded camels disappeared into a dark cleft among the hills. It was now becoming really dark. Following Mr. Holystone's instructions for doing so, Dido found the Southern Cross; then she heard the pinnace being whistled for, so she tucked the telescope under her duffel jacket and went below. As she descended the companionway, Mr. Brandy-winde and the captain came out of the dining room.

"Perhaps by tomorrow," the captain was saying, "you will have received more information as to this—this *loss* that Her Majesty has sustained."

"Oh, what she has lost she refuses to say," caroled Mr. Brandywinde. "It seems to have vanished like last Wednesday!"

"Let us hope not!" retorted Captain Hughes acidly, "or my mission is but a sleeveless errand."

"A fool's errand—what a shocking thought! A fool in the forest of Bro-cel-iande, one foot on the water and one on the land."

At this moment Mr. Brandywinde laid eyes on Dido, who was politely waiting in the galley doorway for the two men to pass by. The agent's bloodshot eyes bulged until it looked as if they would burst from their sockets like horse chestnuts—he gulped, gasped, and fell into such a fit of coughing and choking that, if he had been on deck, it seemed highly probable that he would have fallen overboard as he staggered about.

"Deuce take the fellow!" exclaimed Captain Hughes impatiently. "Here—Holystone—thwack him on the back! Give him some hartshorn or spirits of tar—otherwise the man will take an apoplexy!"

Restoratives having been administered, Mr. Brandywinde was presently able to mop his streaming eyes and apologize.

"It is nothing—nothing—a trifling infirmity," he panted, still staggering. "Takes me thus at times—but it is nothing at all, I assure you! A slight disability resulting from the quantity of pepper in the diet hereabouts—nothing, sir, nothing, nothing! You must try the pepper-pot stew, Captain—I do *urge* you to try the pepper pot."

"Yes, yes, very well," replied Captain Hughes, not at all interested in pepper-pot stew. "Now, I shall be obliged, Mr. Brandywinde, if you can arrange for beds in Tenby for my party tomorrow night—since we must board the riverboat so early. Unless you can accommodate me and my men in your residence?"

"*Quite* out of the question," said the agent hastily. "Only two bedrooms—one for me and m'dear wife, one for our little angel. No, no, sir; rooms shall be bespoken for you at—*hic*—The White Hart. Fair tap there, but don't trust the gin. But, Captain, you never

informed me, you never gave me to understand that
you had a young female person—a child—among your
crew. I was not apprised of this!"

"Why in the world should you be?" snapped the
captain. "It is of very little import! And she is not a
member of my crew—good heavens, I should hope not,
indeed!—merely a—a supercargo, a kind of passenger
whom I am escorting back to England. And I intend
taking her to wait on Queen Ginevra; but she will
require more suitable apparel." The captain glanced
with disfavor at Dido's jacket and trousers. "Is there,"
he asked Mr. Brandywinde, "a dressmaker in Tenby—
or—or a milliner, haberdasher, needlewoman, who
could supply miss there with an outfit to wear at
court?"

If Mr. Brandywinde could have become more flab-
bergasted, this announcement, it seemed, must have
rendered him so. He gaped at Captain Hughes, feebly
flapped his hands up and down, opened and shut his
mouth several times, before at length replying, "You
intend taking miss to visit the queen? Indeed! And
you require some apparel—?"

"Petticoats! A gown! A sash! What about your good
lady—Mrs. Brandywinde—perhaps she might know
the name of some sempstress?"

"Oh . . . ah . . . really I am not . . . that is to say
she does not . . . or at least—"

"Perhaps I and young miss could wait on your good
lady at your house, sir," cut in the captain, as the
agent's replies did not seem to be tending in any useful
direction. "We will bestow our luggage at the inn,
tomorrow, leave my first lieutenant to make arrangements for our trip upriver, and then call at your house

—*if*," he added with some irony, "if this will suit your convenience, Mr. Brandywinde?"

Mr. Brandywinde almost threw himself into another paroxysm in his efforts to assure the captain as to his zeal to be of use. There would not be the least difficulty in the world about finding some suitable person —"*suitable*, ha, ha, for she will supply the young lady with a *suit*," he concluded, with a burst of almost hysterical merriment. "And I wish you good night, dear friend—dear friend; would that such evenings might never, never end!"

So saying, he bounded over the rail with such agility that, had there not been a coxswain waiting to receive him in the boat, his evening would most probably have ended in the jaws of a shark.

Captain Hughes went forward to the quarterdeck. From the irritable haste of his steps as he paced to and fro, the state of his mind could be guessed at.

Dido availed herself of this chance to restore the telescope to its place on the captain's desk.

Next morning Dido was up soon after dawn, roused by the fresh scent of trees and grass from the land, and the shrill cries of seagulls, which sounded like a great many tin spoons being scraped on a large number of china plates.

Hastily she tumbled her small handful of belongings together and stuffed them into a canvas bag. This done, she went hopefully on deck and stared at the land; she could not borrow the captain's spyglass now, for he was in his cabin writing a report.

"What time does we get to go on shore?" she asked Mr. Holystone when she went below for her breakfast.

He had his absentminded expression; he looked as if his mind were a hundred miles off, almost out of reach. But at Dido's question he sighed, pulling his mind back into place, and handed her a mug of hot coffee with molasses in it.

"When the captain has decided which men to take and who shall be left in charge of the ship."

Soon after breakfast the captain sent for Dido.

"Mr. Holystone informs me that you have made fair progress in your deportment, and that your politeness is greatly improved, Miss Twite."

"Old Holy is a regular brick, ain't he? He never gets miffed or skiffly, even when I gives him a bit o' lip." Dido then recalled herself and added, "Ay, ay, sir."

"Let me see your obeisance."

"Eh?"

"Curtsey, child!"

Dido looked round for a copy of the King's Regulations, but the first lieutenant had borrowed it. Without this handicap, she managed quite a creditable curtsey.

The captain, however, remained dissatisfied.

"You certainly cannot appear before the queen in *that* rigout. We had best go on shore directly and set about finding a sempstress. Send Holystone to me, and tell him to have Mr. Windward summoned."

Dido ran out joyfully.

"You're to go to the cap, and we're all to start for land so's I can get some gals' togs in Tenby," she called to the steward, grabbing her bag of needments, and she bounded up on deck.

Mr. Windward was supervising the stowage of provisions in the pinnace, and the embarkation of the shoregoing party. To Dido, leaning on the rail and watching, it came as a most disagreeable shock to discover that Silver Taffy was to be one of the shore crew. The others were a big cheerful lad called Able Seaman Noah Gusset; a sailor known as Plum because of the color of his nose; Mr. Midshipman Multiple, who was freckled, blue eyed, quick-witted, and, if of a somewhat teasing disposition, on the whole friendly to Dido; and the first lieutenant. The second lieutenant, Mr. Bowsprit, was to remain in charge of the *Thrush*.

"Oh, croopus," Dido muttered, when she saw Silver Taffy climb into the pinnace. "If *he*'s along, there'll be nothing but trouble!"

Assembling all her resolution, she ran down the companionway and tapped on the captain's door.

"Come in!" he called impatiently.

Dido slipped in and carefully closed the door behind her.

"Sir," she said rapidly in a low tone, "*please* don't have Silver Taffy along in the lot that's going ashore! There's bound to be no end of shenanigans if you do— it'll bring a whole peck o' trouble—acos he can't abide Mr. Holystone's cat—or me—and if we're all a-going to be traveling in a boat up the river, it'll be hokus-mokus all the blessed time, don't you see?"

In her urgency she grasped hold of the captain's blue superfine broadcloth lapels, tarnishing the gold lace. Captain Hughes stepped back sharply, regarding her with amazed disapprobation.

"Miss Twite!! Pray, who do you think you are? Remember that I am the captain!"

"Lud love you, sir, that's jist what I does remember! Jeeminy, you're the one as has got us into this mux, and you're the only one as can get us out. *Do* tell Silver Taffy as he ain't wanted arter all!"

"I shall do no such thing," said Captain Hughes. "David Llewellyn is a strong, useful seaman—one of the strongest men on board—which is one of the reasons why I chose him. He will be a capital member of the party should we chance to encounter wild beasts or hostile savages. Furthermore, he is familiar with this country—another advantage. He has an old aunt residing in Bewdley and he particularly requested permission to form one of the party so that he might visit her. But I do not know why I should be required to explain my reasons to *you*, Miss Twite, after all! How dare you enter my cabin uninvited, and speak to me with this—this unheard-of effrontery? Return on deck at once, if you please!"

"Oh, blimey!" said Dido despairingly.

Entering Mr. Holystone's galley, she found him putting up a hamper of the captain's favorite delicacies, and a set of plate, glass, knife, fork, spoon, and linen napkin.

"You'll never guess what, Mr. Holy," said Dido in deep dejection. "That there perishing Silver Taffy is a-coming ashore with us. I tried to persuade Cap'n Hughes agin it, but he's so sot in his judgments there's no talking to him."

Mr. Holystone did not appear too discomposed. He replied calmly enough, "Indeed? It was very forward of you, child, to argue with the captain."

"Yes, that's what *he* said," Dido replied glumly, kicking at a basket of damp seaweed in which Mr. Holystone was packing hard-boiled gulls' eggs.

"But how'll you keep an eye on Dora, with Silver Taffy along?"

"I can leave her here on board, which will be a great

advantage. Mr. Bowsprit will look after her, I am sure."

"Ay, that's so," said Dido, sighing. "But it's spoiled *my* pleasure, I can tell you."

"Fiddle-de-dee! Now, take this pail on deck, if you will be so kind, and hand it to Able Seaman Gusset."

Once aboard the pinnace, Dido found her spirits lifting. It was such a fine day, after all! The eight oars raised in salute, the captain descended the ladder; then, when he was seated, all the rowers cleft the sea together and shot the boat forward. The hot sun blazed overhead, the sea underneath was brilliantly blue and clear. In it, however, huge dark shapes roved about, sometimes looming uncomfortably close to the pinnace. One of them rose out of the water and snapped at the oars, revealing a ferocious triple row of teeth.

"Tiburone, he is," Able Seaman Gusset told Dido— he had a slow, country voice, and a pleasant blue-eyed open face. "Best not trail your hand in the water, missie. You might bring it up less a few fingers!"

"I don't reckon as a few fingers'd be much use to *him*," said Dido with a shudder; and after that she took good care to keep her hands well inside the boat.

The land, which from a distance had looked like a frieze cut from blue and silver silk, acquired clearness and detail as they moved closer. Dido saw that the black-and-white timbered houses of Tenby each had an upstairs gallery, overhanging the street, glassed in with big windows, doubtless for protection from Atlantic gales.

On the quayside lay piles of fish, stacks of crates and barrels, and mounds of gaily colored nets. The houses of this small port were grouped on either side of the river, which flowed deep and swift between two headlands. About a quarter of a mile upriver, an island, built over with houses, divided the Severn, and bridges spanned each arm of water.

"It looks a right nice little place," Dido said to Noah Gusset, "but it's mighty quiet, ennit? There bain't many folk about. You'd think they'd be keen to see chaps from a British man-o'-war?"

"Maybe 'tis work hours," suggested Noah.

The streets of Tenby did seem peculiarly empty. Dido looked with interest to see if the cobbles were made of silver—but they were merely the usual sort, smeared over with fish offal. And the houses looked remarkably like those of Southwark or Battersea. Dido could not avoid a slight feeling of disappointment as she climbed up the steps and onto the quay. She had hoped for something more foreign and surprising.

Captain Hughes was the one who seemed surprised —and not agreeably. Apparently he had expected Mr. Brandywinde to be there to meet them; but there was no sign of the British agent on the harborside.

"Plague take the fellow," Dido heard the captain mutter. "I only hope he is not touched in his wits. He seemed half dickey in his cups. It is a fine thing to set out on such a difficult and delicate mission with no better counsel than the word of such a dibble-dabble fellow."

"You think he's a rabshackle, Cap'n?" said Dido. "So do I."

Captain Hughes cast her an impatient glance.

"Mind your own business, child! Speak when you are spoken to, not before!"

Thus snubbed, Dido applied herself to studying the

streets of Tenby. A tall, skinny fellow now approached them, who, briefly bowing, without any particular look of civility or goodwill, announced himself as Sandai Bando and said that he had been directed to lead them to the inn.

"Where is Mr. Brandywinde?" demanded Captain Hughes.

Sandai Bando shrugged, shook his head, and spread out his hands; then, turning his back, he led them off along the harborside at a rapid pace. He was bronzed, hook-nosed, had on a suit of black worsted, much the worse for wear, yellow stockings, black slippers, and very short trousers. His black hair was tied back in a queue.

The distance to The White Hart Inn, where they were to leave their bags, was not great; quitting the harbor, they turned up a steep hill and soon saw the inn sign ahead of them. On this street there were a few people about: the men, in general, rather short, dark, stern-looking, clad like Sandai Bando in suits of black worsted, the women equally small of stature, wearing black stuff dresses, white aprons, and steeple-crowned hats over white caps. These people glanced at the party of foreigners with what seemed like distrust and ill will; they did not smile at the strangers, or make any attempt to engage them in talk.

"What a set of dismal churlish bumpkins," Dido muttered to Mr. Holystone. "They stare at us as if we was rattlesnakes. Not very civil, are they?"

Several of the people they passed stared at Dido, in particular, with apparent astonishment. What's so odd about me? she wondered. Is it because I've got on boys' togs? Are ain't gals allowed on the streets here?

Certainly no girls were to be seen, and very few boys.

In the windows of some of the houses they passed, placards were to be seen, often carrying a picture of a person. *"Puella perdida"* or *"Niña perdida," "Infans absens,"* were the messages printed under these pictures; about to ask Mr. Holystone what this meant, Dido saw one that had the inscription in English: Lost child.

"Rabbit me," she muttered in perplexity. "Has *everybody* in this town lost a child? They must be a rare careless lot. No wonder they're all so down-in-the-mouth."

Now the ship's party passed a few little stores, chandlers' shops displaying flour, candles, twine, eggs, soap; and some poverty-stricken market stalls with bright yellow potatoes (Mr. Holystone told Dido these were yams), yucca roots, cassava bread, onions, and green pineapples.

The White Hart was a decent-looking establishment with an arch for coaches to pass under, and flowering cactuses in stone pots on either side of its main door. No coaches were to be seen in the yard behind, however, and the inn appeared to be doing very slow business, to judge from the alacrity with which the captain and his party were received by Don José Jones, the innkeeper. He was a small bustling red-faced man, who promptly escorted the captain to his best suite, and promised to have dinner for the party at five o'clock sharp.

A sour-faced chambermaid led Dido to a small chamber next to that of the captain, but she had time to do no more than drop her duffel bag on the bed before Captain Hughes summoned her to accompany him to Mr. Brandywinde's house.

"Did you expect to find Mr. Brandywinde a-waiting

here, sir?" asked Dido, observing that the captain looked rather put out.

"Never mind that, miss!" snapped Captain Hughes. He added under his breath, "I daresay if we were to wait for that bag of wind to do anything useful, we might wait until the forty-second Tuesday in Trinity Week."

It's too bad the captain's such an old gruff-and-grum, thought Dido, for there's nought amiss with his sense.

Captain Hughes had instructed Sandai Bando to lead them to the agent's residence, but it was plain he did this with no good grace; scowling, with his lower lip thrust out, he took them round such a number of corners that Dido began to be positive he was leading them a long way round on purpose.

At last the captain exclaimed, "Come, come, my man! Do not try to pull the wool over our eyes, if you please! We have been past that market stall once already. I distinctly remember those wizened little cassava loaves. I shall not pay you one bezant more, I warn you, however far you take us!"

And he hailed a passer-by, a respectable-looking man in black broadcloth who carried what looked like a Bible under his arm, and inquired the way to the British agent's residence.

"Well, it is not far from here, but you are going in exactly the wrong direction," replied this man. "You should climb the hill to the monument, turn right, and it is the first house along the new road. You cannot mistake, for there is a monkey-puzzle tree in front, white palings all round, a cactus by the steps, and the name *Mon Repos* on the gate."

As Captain Hughes thanked the stranger, Sandai Bando fairly took to his heels and scudded off up the hill as if the devil were after him. Since the monument was plainly visible at the top, Captain Hughes did not call him back; all their breath was needed for climbing.

The hill was excessively steep, and the little thatched houses continued up it, each one three steps higher than its neighbor, until just before the monument, where there was a patch of rough, open, thistly grass, on which a few donkeys grazed. There were also two tall, shaggy beasts, breathing in a rather supercilious manner over the dusty herbage, unable to move away because their front and back feet were hobbled.

"Oh!" exclaimed Dido. "They are the same as—" "—As the animals I saw last night," she had been about to say, but then recalled that this would reveal her unauthorized use of the captain's spyglass, and quickly shut her mouth. The captain briefly informed her that they were llamas, large sheeplike animals much esteemed in these parts both for their wool and as beasts of burden. "A llama will not travel alone, but only in company with his fellows; and it will never carry a load of more than one hundred pounds avoirdupois."

"How do they know?" Dido asked, but the captain did not answer.

The monument, when they reached it, also excited Dido's curiosity; it consisted of a sword stuck in a large granite rock, on top of a high plinth. On the plinth were engraved the words: *Vide ut supra.*

"What's that mean, Cap?" panted Dido, glad of the chance to stand still for a moment. After so long a spell at sea, her legs were not prepared for such a steep climb.

"It means 'See what is written above,'" briefly replied the captain.

"Well, what *is* written above?"

"Blest if I can see anything. Oh—there—on the handle of the sword, I suppose."

Dido instantly scrambled up onto the rock and reported that the words on the sword handle read, "*Non in aeternum moriar.*" "What's that mean, sir?"

"It means 'I shall not die forever.' Do, pray, for heaven's sake, child, come down off that rock directly! What *will* people think?" irascibly demanded the captain.

Dido jumped nimbly down, informing the captain that there was a crown carved on the other side of the rock, and a tiptop view to be had from its summit. "You can see the old *Thrush*, sir, her own self. And there's a ship putting into port; one o' them Biruvian trading scows."

Captain Hughes merely urged Dido to make haste and not dusty her breeches any more; so they walked on to the white gates of the house called Mon Repos. Beyond the house, the earth road came to an abrupt stop, barred by a pair of locked gates set in a high palisade fence made of thick, strong palm trunks; it seemed that the town of Tenby was carefully fortified. Beyond the palisade, the tops of forest trees could be seen.

"Heyday, what have we here?" exclaimed Captain Hughes. A large cart, already half-loaded, stood in front of Mon Repos. Furniture was being carried out to it. "This looks like a move. Are they leaving?"

So it appeared. Servants were running to and fro, bearing trunks, portmanteaux, bandboxes, and all manner of bundles, besides toys, blankets, and cooking utensils; in the midst of all this bustle was Mr. Brandywine himself, directing the stowage in the cart.

At the sight of Captain Hughes the agent halted his activities, evidently somewhat embarrassed and discomposed.

"Ah, there you are, my dear Captain! What a charming surprise. 'Oh, what a surprise, doth gladden my eyes, What a vision of joy your admirer descries!' "

"Are you moving house, then, Brandywinde?" demanded the captain, interrupting these transports.

"Why—why yes; yes, that is so; in the joy of welcoming *you*, Captain, it had slipped my memory, but such indeed is the case."

"By hokey! Why the deuce didn't you tell me so? It is fortunate that I reached Tenby yesterday, and not next week," indignantly answered the captain. "Or are you merely removing to another quarter of the town?"

"Ahem! Well—in fact—that is to say—"

Mr. Brandywinde's answer was cut short by the emergence of a slatternly-looking woman clad in a tattered satin wrapper, which had a great many frills, and dangled about her in a highly insecure manner, as if it might slip off altogether at any moment.

"Order them to make haste, my ducky diddlums, or we shall miss the packet!" exclaimed this personage, and then, observing Captain Hughes, she changed her expression to a simper and added, "Oh, la, I declare! Well, for shame, Ludovic! You never told me that you were expecting company!"

"Did I not, my angel? It must have slipped from my mind in the press of business. Allow me, my love— my dear old messmate, Captain Hughes of His Majesty's sloop *Thrush*. And this is little Miss Pittikin-Pattikin," Brandywinde added vaguely. "I told you that the captain wished to consult your views, my honeycake, as to where the young lady could best obtain suitable raiment in which to make her curtsey before Her Mercy."

As he pronounced the latter words, Dido noticed that both he, his wife, and all the servants looked nervously about, as if fearful that he might be overheard. And several of the servants made figure-eight signs with thumb and fingers.

"Of *course* you told me about the matter, my love-kin," shrilly replied Mrs. Brandywinde. "And I writ a note about it, not this half hour since. Do you return to The White Hart, Captain, directly, and before you can say 'Pop goes the weasel,' my dear sir, I can assure you, two of the best needlewomen in New Cumbria will be in attendance on you— *Mind* that chiffonier, blockhead! You nearly had the legs off it!" And she aimed a thump with her palm-leaf fan at the head of a passing servant. This had the effect of dislodging her wrapper, and she turned to retreat indoors, hoisting it together with a hurried hand.

"Are you quite certain of that, ma'am?" Captain Hughes called after her doubtfully. He sounded as if, judging from her own untidy apparel, he wondered whether she was the best person to recommend a dressmaker.

"Sure as sharks is sharks," replied Mrs. Brandywinde, stopping in the doorway to give the captain such an extremely wide smile that she was able to display every one of her thirty-two teeth, all made of well-polished silver. "Why, I may tell you that both semp-stresses have been in the employ of Lady Ett—of Her Mercy's own mistress of the wardrobe." Dido noticed the agent give his wife a scowl at these words.

The captain said, "Oh, well—in that case—I am

much obliged to you, ma'am. And I shall not dis-
commode you further at this time. Are you being replaced, sir, by another agent, may I inquire?" he added
to Mr. Brandywinde.

Dido missed the agent's answer, if there was one,
for at this moment there sidled out of Mon Repos the
most unattractive small child she thought she had ever
laid eyes on.

Young Miss Brandywinde had the protruding eyes
and lank sandy hair of her father, added to the bulging
girth and sly expression of her mother; her face was
covered in spots, and she was stickily sucking a length
of sugarcane which had dribbled down the front of
her frilly red sarcenet dress. She might be about five
years old.

"Oh, my eye! Who's *this*?" she demanded, removing
the sugarcane from her mouth just long enough to put
the question, then popping it back in again. She gestured at Dido with her elbow.

"Why—why—why, it is Cap'n Hughes's little friend
—that's who it is!" indulgently but somewhat nervously replied her father.

"I reckon you come from Greenland?" The child
fixed her mud-colored eyes on Dido.

"Greenland? No, why'd you think that? I comes from
London."

"What you doin' here, then?"

"What do you suppose? She is visiting New Cumbria,
my pipkin." And, smiling in a somewhat sickly way at
the captain, Mr. Brandywinde explained, "This is our
little angel, sir! It is for her benefit, indeed, that we
are removing from Tenby. The air hereabouts is—is—
is insalubrious for young females between the age of
five and fifteen. *Decidedly* insalubrious. They—"

"Ludovic!" shrilled his wife. "If those papers are not placed in the hamper directly they will be left behind. And if we are not out of the house in ten minutes, we shall miss the packet!"

"Yes—yes, my angel—I am coming, I am coming!"

"Well, I reckon you *must* be from Greenland," persisted Miss Brandywinde to Dido. "Acos otherwise you'd never be sich a peevy clodpole as to come here. Why, it's bezants to breadcrumbs as you'll never—"

"Quiet, you little dev—angel!" exploded her father, and with something less than fondness Mr. Brandywinde picked up his daughter and plunked her into the cart, jamming her so tightly between a copper cauldron and a bundle of butter pats that she let out an indignant squawk.

"What d'yer do that for, Pa? It's bezants to breadcrumbs as the aurocs'll—"

But Mrs. Brandywinde, coming out at that moment in a bright pink India muslin which she must have donned at great speed, deposited a large roll of cotton quilts right on top of her child, which had the effect of silencing the little angel, as a canary is silenced by having a wrapper put over its cage.

The driver cracked his whip, and the loaded cart started off at a gallop. The agent and his wife had meanwhile jumped into a light chariot which had come up behind. Just before this rolled off, Dido thought she heard Mrs. Brandywinde inquire of her husband, "Did you collect the dibs from Mrs. M?" and his reply, "What do you think I paid the passage with, my honey tart? I am not made of coleslaw, I assure you!"

Then the chariot clattered off downhill toward the harbor in a cloud of dust.

"Well!" muttered the captain in a tone of gloomy satisfaction. "I am never wrong in my judgments. The moment I laid eyes on Brandywinde I knew him to be a dem'd unsatisfactory, dilly-dallying, fossicking, freak-ish sort of fellow."

"*I* could have told you that, anytime these last twenty-four hours," said Dido.

"*Will* you be quiet, child, and not speak unless you are required to?" Captain Hughes added crossly, "We had best make all speed back to The White Hart, in case that slattern was telling the truth."

He started off at a round pace, and Dido was obliged to trot in order to keep up with him.

3

On his return to The White Hart Inn, Captain Hughes was informed by a waiter that two modistes had arrived and were waiting in the young lady's bed-chamber to take measurements.

"Aha! Then that frowzy female spoke the truth; so far so good!" he exclaimed. "I will step upstairs and give them their orders. Meanwhile you may have a nuncheon prepared for me and serve it in the coffee room. Is there a mayor in this town?"

"Yes, sir, the *jefe*—Don Luis Pryce."

"I will wait on him as soon as I have finished my repast. Come along, child, make haste," he added to Dido, gesturing her to precede him up the shallow, polished wooden stairs. The White Hart appeared to be a very old building; the floors were black with age, and the upper story was a maze of small dark rooms and passages, with steps up and steps down, and very little light coming from very tiny windows. There were thick cobwebs hanging from the rafters. Dido, not fond of spiders, recalled that the captain's catalog of New Cumbrian fauna had included seven-inch ones able to leap thirty feet; she hoped there were none of that kind in The White Hart.

In Dido's room two ladies were waiting, seated on a wooden chest by the window. An enormous pincushion, the size of a saddlebag, lay between them on the chest, together with a massive, glittering pair of scissors, and a two-yard mahogany rule.

The sempstresses stood up and curtsied respectfully to Captain Hughes. They were dressed alike, in the black stuff gowns that seemed to be standard garb for the women of Tenby, with white fichus and white frilled caps, but in other respects they were as different from each other as possible. Dido took an instant dislike to both. One was small, aged, skinny, and wrinkled, the other big and buxom with a thick shock of coarse curly black hair escaping from under her cap and hanging halfway down her back. Each had a velvet pincushion fastened to her fichu, and a tape measure attached to her belt. Both looked very attentively at Dido.

"You are the needlewomen recommended to me by Mrs. Brandywinde?" inquired the captain.

"Yes, Capting. I am Mrs. Morgan," said the little old one, smiling—when she did so, she revealed the fact that she had no teeth at all, which made her smile rather like that of a lizard. "And this here's my daughter, Mrs. Vavasour."

The younger woman also smiled.

"So this is the young lady who needs fitting out?"

Her pitying, disdainful glance swept over Dido's

salt-stained breeches, frayed collar, darned socks, and scuffed brogans, one of them with a loose buckle.

"Ah! Pretty as a pink palm blossom she be!" cooed Mrs. Morgan, in a voice that did not match the expression in her sharp little black eyes.

Dido was resigned to her own looks. She knew that she had a pale, pointed face, freckled like a musk flower; pale, observant gray eyes; and short, stringy brown hair. They're a-trying to gammon me, she decided, but I'm not a-going to let them. She stared coldly back at the two dressmakers while Captain Hughes gave them their instructions.

"The young lady will be among the British party attending the court of Queen Ginevra to pay their respects to Her Majesty. I wish the child to be fitted out with two gowns, suitable for a young person of her—ahem—age and station—to wear at court—besides slippers, sashes, kerchiefs—whatever is needful. Can you do that?"

"Certingly, certingly, Capting." Mrs. Morgan curtsied again.

Mrs. Vavasour said, "Both gowns oughter be white. Mull for daytime wear—a round gownd over a silk pettingcoat, ingbroidered with cattails in turkey-work—"

"—and," struck in her mother, "French knots round the neck, and the border round the sleeves ingbossed—"

"—a pink sash—"

"—then, for evening wear, a white silk taffety gownd, pinstriped with cream, and a lace pettingcoat—"

"—a sash of the same, ingbroidered with silver sequing fronds!"

"She'll look like a hangel from heaving, that she will!"

"Very well, very well!" said Captain Hughes testily. "That sounds suitable enough—I know little of such matters. So the cut be plain and neat—nothing fussy or overtrimmed. Can you have both gowns ready by tonight? We leave on the dawn riverboat tomorrow morning."

Another glance passed between the two.

"Why, surely, surely, Capting," cooed Mrs. Morgan. "By midnight the work shall be done. The young lady will be fine as a bird of paradise—willn't she, Nynevie?"

"Gracious to goodness, yes indeed!" smiled the younger woman. Dido could not decide which smile she disliked more—the bare gums or the flashing silver teeth.

"How much will the two gowns cost?"

"One hundred bezants, Capting—and cheap at the price."

"Good God! Furbelows are costly in New Cumbria, it seems."

He glanced at Dido, as if wondering whether the outlay was worth it; she glanced back with equal resentment. "Well, well—you shall be paid tonight."

"Beg parding, Capting," said Mrs. Morgan respectfully but firmly. "We has to be paid in advance. Mull and silk and taffety and lacings—them's costly stuffs. Let alone the floss and ribbing and trimmings. Pay us *now*, if you please, Capting."

"Oh, very well! I will send Mr. Windward up with the money directly. Be a good child now, miss!" he said to Dido.

"What about when they're through measuring me?" said Dido. "Can I go out to see the sights?"

"We shall be wanting you all afternoon, missie," said Mrs. Vavasour. "For trying and fitting."

"What? Don't I get to see the sights, not at all?"

Both sempstresses shook their heads.

"The streets of Tenby ain't safe for little misses," said Mrs. Morgan. "Little gels has got lost and never come home to their own kitchings."

"Even in their gardings they ain't safe."

"You'd do best to stay with us, dearie!" Mrs. Morgan shook her head warningly.

"Do as they say, child," said Captain Hughes. Then he was gone.

Dido felt much aggrieved. Captain Hughes had not offered *her* a nuncheon! And she was decidedly hungry. Furthermore, she was by no means enthusiastic about the sound of her court apparel. White mull embroidered with cattails—I shall look a right Charley in it, she thought glumly. And what possible use would it be on board ship?

Might as well get it over with, however.

"Ain't you a-going to measure me?" she demanded of the two women, who were indeed looking at her measuringly, but who made no move to take out their tape measures.

"In a twinkling, dearie. Just a-waiting for the wampum."

"Wampum?"

"The mish, the ready, spondulicks, mint sauce! Us don't work on credit, lovie."

What a havey-cavey pair, thought Dido. I wouldn't trust them as far as I could toss an eighteen-pounder.

"Going to see the queen, is she? There's a lucky young lady," said Mrs. Morgan, grinning.

"Indeed to goodness, *yes*!" agreed her daughter.

"Many young ladies'd give their eyes—wouldn't they, Nynevie?"

"The eyes out of their heads!"

At this moment Mr. Windward entered the room, bearing the captain's sharkskin money bag, from which he carefully proceeded to count out a hundred gold bezants. The two women stopped laughing and watched him with close and avaricious attention; their eyes wistfully followed the bag when, having passed over the ten little heaps of ten coins, he tightened the strings, knotted them again, and took himself off.

"Hey—Mr. Windward!" called Dido, as he was about to leave the room.

"Well, young 'un?"

"Is Mr. Holystone downstairs? Is he busy?"

"He is supervising the captain's repast. Do you wish me to give him a message?"

"Jist—when he's free—I'd be obliged if he'd get someone to fetch me a bite of prog. I'm nibblish sharp-set," Dido said disconsolately.

Mr. Windward's long, serious face broke into a sympathetic grin as he looked at the two dressmakers waiting to start operations on Dido. He said, "Very good, young 'un, I'll tell him to have a bite sent up to you." The door clapped to behind him.

"Well, now! Listen to Miss Throw Her Weight Around!" said Mrs. Morgan, with strong disapproval.

"Acts as if she were Lady Ettarde herself!"

"Little gels oughter be seen and not heard!"

"Us had best waste no time."

"Not a blessed minute."

"Just you step thisaway, dearie."

Drawing their tape measures from their belts, both women urged Dido toward the window.

"Come here where the light's better," cooed old Mrs. Morgan, and Mrs. Vavasour said, "See that pincushion, sweetheart? See all those pins in it? Can you make out what's writ there?"

A quantity of brass-headed pins were stuck into the fat cushion; they spelled out some word with a large number of *x*'s in it. Dido, no great reader at best, shook her head.

"Study it a mite closer, dearie—see if you can't make it out."

Both women had her by the shoulders now; they were forcing her head down on to the pincushion. As it came closer to her face, she discovered that it had a strong, sweet, musky odor, somewhat resembling camphor, but much more powerful.

"Hey! Lemme go!" she said, struggling; but already her head was swimming, her voice seemed to come not out of her throat, but faintly, and from a long way off.

"*That*'s the dandy! Now then, us'll jist oping this lid . . ."

With immense indignation, Dido realized that Mrs. Vavasour had tied her hands behind her with a tape measure, while Mrs. Morgan opened the lid of the chest. Surprisingly, this proved to cover and surround a kind of stairhead; a flight of narrow steps led down steeply from it into blackness.

"Now, us'll jist help the liddle dear over the side . . ."

"I'll not! I'll not go! Cap'n Hughes'll have your guts for garters when he hears of this!" gasped Dido, doing her best to fight the two women, who were half lifting, half dragging her over the side of the chest.

"Ah, but he won't hear, lovie, not till you're as lost as Lucy's pocket. You step down, Nynevie, hold her legs—lucky she's sich a skinny one, her 'on't be no trouble to fetch to the boat. . . ."

Dido was rolled down the steps; Mrs. Vavasour made no attempt to break her fall, and she lay half-stunned at the bottom of the fairly long flight. A moment later she felt a thick, blanketlike sack pulled over her legs and body; a string was drawn tight at the top, catching some of her hair painfully, and tied in a knot. Then she felt herself being dragged along the ground over rough, uneven planks full of splinters, many of which pierced through the fabric of the bag, and also through Dido's skin. Her head and limbs were banged and thumped against the edges of boards; she was shaken and scraped and jounced and battered.

One good result of this unpleasant exercise, however, was that, after a few minutes of it, Dido, who had been at the start almost unconscious from the fumes of the pincushion, was jolted back into full, angry, and wary intelligence. Blister them, the old bags, she thought; I'll not yammer to let them know I'm awake—but what a gull I was! How could I be sich a nodcock as not to twig their lay from the first minute? Any addlepate could see they was a pair of downy ones. Guess I'd best look out for myself in New Cumbria; Cap'n Hughes ain't used to sich goings-on. He'll be no more use here than a thread-paper parasol in a thunderstorm.

She had to bite her lip several times not to cry out. As she was ruthlessly dragged along, she wrestled against the tape that bound her wrists until it cut into them. She thought she felt it give a little, and so persisted in spite of the pain.

"Lay aholt with me, Ma, and pull her down here," said Mrs. Vavasour's voice.

The bag was given a sudden vigorous jerk. Again, Dido felt herself rolling helplessly, over and over down a long bumpy slope. By the time she came to a stop she was too dazed and bruised to do anything but lie motionless. To her joy, though, the tape round her wrists had finally broken. She was able to move her hands.

"Where'll we lay her?" came Mrs. Vavasour's voice.

"There, on the dried fish."

"What about rats, Ma? Wouldn't do if her was to turn up gnawed. *She* 'on't have 'em if they ain't complete."

Something in the woman's voice made Dido's skin crawl; also, she did not care for the reference to rats.

"Oh, very well. On the ax heads, then."

The sack was hoisted up, and dropped heavily on to a pile of sharp edges and hard corners.

"When's the boat leave, Ma?"

"Midnight. Best you stay and keep an eye on the kinchin. Do she stir, give her another whiff of guayala."

"I stay here? Not on your oliphant! She'll not stir. Give her another whiff now, to make certing."

"Not too much, then! *She* don't like 'em if they're droopy."

The camphor fumes came close again. Dido tried to hold her breath; she pressed her lips together, wrinkled up her nose, and squeezed her eyes tight shut.

Then, suddenly, she heard a man's voice raised in

song, not far away; the sound was muffled, as if heard through a thin partition or a pile of objects.

"*My heart goes pink!*" he sang:

> "*My heart goes pink, the very minute I see her!*
> *My heart goes rose pink, like the rrrrrising sun!*
> *When she is nigh, this unmistakable feeling*
> *Tingles in all my senses, every one!*
> *I feel she is close, I know she is nigh,*
> *If I were in Paris, Geneva, or Rye,*
> *I'd quickly perceive her,*
> *My cherished Nyneva—*"

"Oh, no!" Dido heard Nynevie exclaim in a horri-fied whisper. "That's Bran!"

And Mrs. Morgan snapped, "How the pest did *he* get here? I thought he were in the mountains?"

"Oh, who ever knows where he'll turn up? Quick— let's get outa here. Make haste, Ma! Never mind the liddle varmint. She'll be right enough—"

"A-right, a-right! Don't hurry me, gel!"

From the sound, it appeared that Mrs. Vavasour was pushing her elderly parent up a flight of steps; there was a stumble and a smothered curse. Then a door closed with a rattle of bolts. This was followed by silence.

Dido found herself in no great hurry to make a move. For one thing, she was not certain as to the whereabouts of the singer. The fact that this Bran, whoever he was, seemed to strike alarm into the dress-makers did not, Dido thought, necessarily mean that he would be prepared to help *her*; she was not going to risk being found by him. She would wait awhile.

She occupied the time by enlarging a hole in the

sack, which had been torn as it was dragged along. At
last she managed to get her head out, but could see
little of her surroundings, for the light was very dim.
She thought she must be in some cellar or storeroom
of The White Hart. They sure got a big store, she
thought; seems big as Covent Garden.

By cautious rolling and slithering she worked herself off the ax heads, which were very uncomfortable,
and onto what felt like a pile of sacks, or sails. That's
better, she thought. Now I'll jist rest me a few minutes, then I'll wriggle out of the sack. Croopus, how
those old harridans did thump me along. . . .

Her head dropped back against the dusty sackcloth,
and she slept.

When Dido next woke, it was with a feeling of deep
anxiety and apprehension. How long had she been
asleep?

Addlehead! she told herself. For all you know, it's
nigh on midnight, and those old carrion crows'll be
coming back any minute. Why the pize did I have to
go and fall asleep?

Trying to make as little noise as possible, she wriggled clear of the sack and looked around her. Although
it was darker now, her eyes were more accustomed to
the dimness. She seemed to be in a very large warehouse stacked with many kinds of goods: farm implements, fodder, tools, seeds, bales, barrels, and crates.
Narrow alleys threaded between the high piles; it was
like a maze, and Dido tried several alleys before she
found one that led her to a wall, in which she saw
two or three small window squares high above her
head.

They were too small and too high to be any use for

escape; she edged her way along the wall, hastened
on her way by certain squeaks and scurryings close
by; there ain't no shortage of rats here, she thought,
and was glad not to be still fastened in a sack with
her hands tied behind her.

At last she reached a wide loading space by a pair of
big double doors, plainly the main entrance to the
store. But the doors were fastened, as was a little
wicket cut through them.

Dido began to feel annoyed. She was hollow with
hunger too. Old Cap'll be real mortallious when he
wants to catch that boat and finds I'm missing, she
thought. Peering up in the gloom she discovered that
the fastening of the double doors consisted of a long
iron bar, held in place by four massive staples. All I
have to do is knock that out, she thought. But what
with? It's out o' my reach. But among all this mollux
of goods there must be summat I can use.

Her luck had changed. She discovered a pile of hay
rakes not far away in the murk—fell over them, in
fact, and grazed her shin on the sharp tines. Just the
job, she thought joyfully, rubbing her leg, and she
pulled one free and returned to the door.

It was impossible not to make a good deal of noise
pushing the bar along through the staples. In for a
penny, in for a pound, Dido decided, bashing away
with her rake head. At least, if those two hear and
come back, I've got me summat to thump *them* with.
They won't put me in a bag so easy next time!

The bar fell to the ground with a clang. Of their
own accord, the two great doors began to open
slightly, disclosing a twilit scene outside. Inching her
way through the narrow gap, Dido looked cautiously
round her. She was amazed to find herself down on

the quayside. Fancy! she thought. There must be a passageway right from The White Hart to that storehouse. Underground, maybe. Likely there's a bit of smuggling goes on in these parts.

Dusk was falling fast—she must have slept for two or three hours. The quay was empty and silent, except for an occasional seagull, pondering on a bollard. But—Dido was delighted to notice—only a couple of hundred yards from the building in which she had been imprisoned floated the pinnace belonging to H.M.S. *Thrush,* still moored alongside the quay.

Glancing both ways, Dido broke into a fast run. I'll ask one o' the crew to see me back to The White Hart. Reckon that Vavasour was right in one thing she said—this don't feel a healthy town to loiter about the streets alone.

A couple of sailors were in the pinnace, doing something to the rudder; she hailed them, panting, as she came alongside.

"Hey-o, Solly and Tad! Can I come aboard?"

"Why, 'tis the supercargo—little Miss Dido. What be you a-doing down on the dockside? Thought you was with the cap'n, dining on roast goose and gravy!"

"He's a-calling on the mayor," Dido replied. "And I'm not supposed to be in the street by myself. Would one o' you coves be agreeable to walk me back to The White Hart?"

"The bosun'd have us over a gun barrel, duck, if he come back and found us missing—he's in the town buying nails. You'd best come on board till he gets back."

Dido was about to accept this invitation when a man who had been limping slowly toward them came up beside her and said, "The young lady wishes to be

escorted to The White Hart hostelry? I shall be glad
to accompany her. I am going that way."

The sailors had been working by the light of the
two lanterns that hung in the rigging. Their yellow
glow illuminated the face of the newcomer. Swelp me,
he's a rum gager, Dido thought. Dare I trust him?

He was indeed a very strange-looking individual:
tall, deathly pale, even in that gold light—as if he had
been in prison fifty years—with great cavernous eye
sockets, a long curved nose, a thin wide mouth, and
a shock of snow-white hair. His clothes were black. A
large white cockatoo sat on his shoulder, and he
carried a triangular stringed instrument. He had a
wooden leg.

Dido was on the point of saying "No thanks,
mister," in the firmest possible way, when he halted
her with upraised hand.

"You are about to refuse my offer. You are afraid
of me."

"No I ain't!" she retorted crossly (though she was,
a little). "It's jist that one dassn't trust a soul in this
rabshackle town."

"Spoken like a wise child! But you may trust me."

"How can I be sure, mister? I been gulled afore."

He sighed.

"You may trust me because it is not in my power to
harm. I can *prevent* harm, sometimes; sometimes not
even that."

Dido studied him a while longer. That's what *you*
say, she thought.

He disconcerted her by reading her thought.

"It is what I say. And it is the truth. I tell nothing
but truth."

"Humph!"

Dido was still not at all sure that she trusted him. But there was something about him that pricked her curiosity greatly. He looked as if he knew such a lot! She had a notion that, if he chose, he would be able to answer any question she cared to put to him.

At last she said, "How do I know as you ain't pals with that pair as nabbled me?"

"Oh, how, *how*?" he exclaimed impatiently. "How do you know that two and two make four, or that your name is Dido and your sister's Penelope? I know because I know, but I could explain for years, and *you* would still be in the dark."

Dido was so amazed at this answer that, after a moment, quite meekly, she said, "Reckon I'll go with you, then, mister, and thank you kindly."

Tad and Solly, reassured, returned to their work on the rudder, nodding in a friendly way to Dido as she walked off with the stranger.

She said, "How did you know about my name and my sister's, mister?"

"You may call me Bran," he answered. "And I told you—I can't give you any explanation that you would understand. You must simply accept that I do know."

Dido digested this in silence for a minute or two. At first she felt rather mortified. He must think her a ninny! And yet he seemed friendly enough. Then something came into her mind, and she exclaimed, "Your name's Bran?"

"That is what I am called by some."

"Was that *you*, then, singing, a while ago? When I was shut in that place? About your heart being pink?"

He smiled and stroked the great white cockatoo, which all this time had been sitting as quiet as a stuffed bird on his shoulder.

"Sometimes my heart is white! Eh, Chanticleer?"
The bird croaked gently and puffed up its feathers.

"He sure is a big 'un," said Dido respectfully. Then she repeated, "Was that you singing?"

"I was singing, yes. I am a jongleur."

"What's that?"

"A minstrel. I sing songs for a living. And tell stories."

Dido was interested. "That's a rare way to make a living."

She thought again, and went on, "If that's all you do, though, why was that pair of old witches so frit of you? And if you know sich a blessed lot—if you knew I was shut in there—why the blazes didn't you help me?"

"What need?" Bran said. "I knew that you would get out by yourself."

"Mighty fine talk!"

"True talk."

"Why was they scared?" she persisted.

"They have good reason to fear me," Bran said. "And you too, now."

"Why me?"

"For various reasons. But one reason why they fear both of us is that we have escaped from them, and are now on our guard."

Dido reflected that this was true. "Did *you* escape from them too, mister?"

He smiled. "I was their prisoner for more years than there are hairs on your head."

"Go on! You can't gammon me like that!"

But, still smiling, he stroked the great bird, which suddenly spread out his wings in a wide stretch, then folded them again.

"I have been in the dark," said Bran, "listening to the drops that fell from the roof, till those drops had bored a hole deeper than thrice the height of Mount Catelonde. It was during that time that I made up my songs and my stories."

"Could you tell me a story now, mister?" said Dido hopefully, as they started up the steep hill that led to The White Hart. She was walking rather slowly. Her bones ached, her bruises throbbed, she felt queasy from the effects of the poisonous pincushion, and hollow from hunger. But she added fairly, "I can't pay you for it, though—I guess you knows that! On account you seem to know everything else about me."

"I will tell you a story for love, then," Bran said, smiling. "It is about a stick. A young boy was the youngest of twelve brothers, and so his father thought little of him."

Dido was interested at once, being the youngest in her own family.

"When the older sons were grown," Bran went on, "their father gave them each a horse, sword, and suit of armor, and sent them out into the world. But to the youngest he gave nothing, saying, 'You are too undersized and puny. It would be a waste to give you armor.' "

"What a blame shame!" said Dido indignantly.

"The youngest son, however, went into the wood, and cut himself a stick, from which he made a hobbyhorse. And when he rode on it, saying, 'Fly quick, my stick!' the stick flew up into the air, and carried him wherever he wanted to go."

"Coo!" said Dido.

"Riding on his magic stick, he was able to rescue his elder brothers, who were in great danger just then, and he also killed a dragon and saved a princess, and performed other feats. And was rewarded with fame and riches.

"But the day came when he started riding on the stick merely to astonish people and get their applause; he did it in the marketplace for money, like a circus rider."

"Dunno as I blame him," said Dido.

"No? But after he had done this for some time, the stick lost its power. And by degrees he lost all his wealth. Finally he was reduced to stealing and other bad ways, was imprisoned, and in the end sentenced to death."

Dido heaved a sigh, but said nothing.

"His brothers would not help him. His eldest brother was now king of the country; and at the last, since the condemned man was, after all, his brother, he sent a message that, on the night before his execution, the prisoner might have anything that he wished."

"*I'd* have wished to be let out!"

"Anything but that."

"So what did he wish?"

"He asked that someone should go to the wood and cut him a stick."

"Did they?"

"A stick was brought to his cell. And the prisoner— who now, through wild living and vice and despair, looked like an old, old bent man—mounted, trembling, on the stick and said, 'Fly quick, my stick, carry me away.'"

"And did it?" said Dido eagerly.

"Here we are at The White Hart," said Bran. "Good night, Dido Twite."

"But—mister! Hey! The end of the story! Did it carry him?"

She heard a laugh in his voice as he said, "We shall meet again." Then he disappeared into the darkness.

Dido went gingerly into The White Hart. For all she knew, the two dressmakers would be somewhere about, waiting to waylay her again. But luckily the first person she saw was Captain Hughes, pacing about the hall with an expression of wrath and perturbation on his brow. When he saw Dido he pounced on her and almost shook her.

"*Miss Twite!* Where the deuce have you *been*? We have had the whole place turned upside down searching for you. How dare you go out when I forbade you to?"

"Here, hold hard, Cap!" said Dido aggrievedly, rubbing her bruised arms where he had gripped them. "Don't *you* go a-banging me, now! It were that dicey pair as called 'emselves dressmakers—they took and abducted me."

"Balderdash! Do not seek to pull the wool over *my* eyes, miss! Fabricate me no Banbury stories!"

"Wool? It were a blasted *pincushion*—not any fabricoction," Dido was beginning indignantly, when Mr. Holystone came down the stairs. His face broke into a beaming smile of relief at the sight of Dido, and he exclaimed, "*There* you are! We have been so concerned about you."

"I was nabbled," Dido repeated, and, encouraged by Mr. Holystone's sympathy and evident belief, she poured out the story of what Mrs. Morgan and Mrs. Vavasour had done to her. Taking the two men up to her room, she pointed to the chest which contained the secret entrance.

"It does not open," said the captain, trying it. "It is nailed shut. This must be pure invention!"

Mr. Holystone, however, pulled out his clasp knife and prized open the lid. The stair inside was revealed. On it lay a tuft of Dido's brown hair, a scatter of pins, and the buckle from her left brogan.

"Good God!" Captain Hughes was aghast. "Then the child's tale is true! This is atrocious! An outrage! Where was this warehouse, child? On the dockside? I shall have the constables summoned—those two women apprehended! Where is the innkeeper?"

He strode toward the door, turning round to bark, "Do you keep watch over the child, Holystone! Don't let her out of your sight for a single instant!"

"I say, Mr. Holy," said Dido, as the captain clattered off down the stairs, shouting for the landlord, officers of the watch, Bow Street runners, and justices of the peace, "I say, I ain't half hungry."

"You poor child, you must indeed be famished. Come down to the inn parlor and I will bespeak a meal."

In the parlor, a pleasant, shadowy, paneled room, they found a fire burning, for the temperature of New Cumbria, hot during the day, dropped abruptly once the sun had set. Mr. Holystone summoned a waiter and ordered food for Dido. While it was being prepared, she told him her story in greater detail. He shook his head.

"I doubt if those two women will be caught. They have probably discovered by now that you managed to escape, and will have made themselves scarce. They may be miles off."

Dido was inclined to agree.

A bowl of oyster stew arrived, with some thin cassava biscuits. While she was hungrily eating this, Mr. Holystone told her of the captain's meeting with Mr. Pryce, the mayor, or *jefe,* of the town.

"What the mayor told him was one reason for his being so distressed over your absence. It seems that the rocs, or aurocs, the great birds that live in the mountains, fly down over the town at early dusk, and carry off many children, especially girls. There is great danger for young persons who go out alone."

"That's why old Brandyblossom is leaving town, then," observed Dido, carefully wiping her stew bowl with a piece of cassava. "So the little angel won't be swiped by an auroc. But how does those two old hags come into the business, I wonder? If I'd been found missing, Cap'n Hughes would've thought an auroc got me. But *them* two ain't aurocs—unless they're in the catering way, a-selling tasty tidbits to the aurocs."

A sizzling shark steak was brought in, garnished with peppers and slices of lime.

About to commence eating, Dido paused at the sound of a heartrending, famished mew, which seemed to come from under the oak settle on which she was sitting. She looked down. A thin, golden cat had emerged from under the seat and was stretched up beseechingly, with both slender paws on her knee.

"Why—it's *Dora*! How in tarnation did *she* get here? Reckon she followed you, Mr. Holy?"

Dido put down a good-sized morsel of shark; the ravenous cat caught it with both paws before it reached the ground, and set upon it avidly.

"No, that is not Dora," said Mr. Holystone, carefully inspecting the animal. He rubbed with a gentle thumb between the copper ears and tufted eyebrows. "My cat has a little silky curl, just here, in the middle of her forehead—and this one has none."

"This one's thinner than Dora, too," agreed Dido, feeling the bony ribs and dropping another piece of shark. "But ain't that rum—to find one so simular! Are we close to your land, then, Mr. Holy? Or is cats like that common all over Roman America?"

"We are not *so* far from Hy Brasil," he said, sighing. "But cats such as this are not so frequently met with— they generally belong to rich people—the nobility. How now, what have we here?"

Around the cat's neck his stroking fingers had discovered a thin, plaited collar, with a leather disc and a tiny packet attached to it. The disc said *Titten Tatten*. Mr. Holystone, feeling the collar, uttered a soft exclamation.

"This collar is made from human hair," he said.

"Holy snails! Someone ain't half got long hair. Must take a *deal* o' combing out," Dido said, running her fingers through her own short locks. "Does the packet give the owner's name?"

She set down her plate, with the rest of the shark steak. The cat was too interested in this bounty to object to the removal of its collar, and Mr. Holystone unfolded the little packet with careful fingers, while Dido went on to a final course of pineapple and pawpaw.

"My, ain't that tasty! What's the paper say, Mr. Holy?"

He was frowning over the little square. It was a tiny printed page:

Bee. The animal that makes honey, remarkable for its industry and art.

Beldam. An old woman, generally a term of contempt, marking the last degree of old age with all its faults and miseries.

Cat. A domestick animal that catches mice, commonly reckoned by naturalists the lowest order of the leonine species.

"That's rummy," said Dido, looking over his shoulder. "What'd a person stick that in a collar for? Bee? Beldam? Cat? What d'you make of it, Mr. Holy? It looks like a page from a dictionary."

"It is a dictionary. If I mistake not, it is Dr. Samuel Johnson's *Dictionary of the English Language.*"

"Why would someone stick it in a cat's collar?"

Dido took the paper from him and stared closely at the printed lines.

"Looky here," she said after a while. "Somebody made marks here and there—see—like it might be with a thumbnail, under some o' the letters. Think that means summat? Look, here, in *animal*—there, in *remarkable*—a, r, r—"

"—a, b, e—I believe you have hit on something!" Mr. Holystone wrote down the letters on the tablet he kept for noting good recipes.

"*Arrabeelamye.* What the blazes is that?"

"Arrabe. Elamye. They are two of the Children of Silence."

"Children of Silence?"

"The mountains that lie between New Cumbria and Lyonesse. Ambage and Arrabe, Ertayne and Elamye,

Arryke, Damask, Damyake, Pounce, Pampoyle, Garesse, Galey, Calabe, and Catelonde."

"What a *deal* you know, Mr. Holy! But what's this last one? *Elen*? Is that a mountain, too?"

"No, it is not a mountain," said Mr. Holystone, looking very troubled indeed. "Elen is a girl's name."

4

They boarded the riverboat at a black and silent hour of night, when all the citizens of Tenby were abed and asleep. The night air was sharply cold, and Dido grumbled to Mr. Holystone as the small party walked through the silent streets.

"Why in the name of Morpus does we have to start off *now*?"

"It is on account of the bore."

"Bore? It's a right *plague!*"

"No, child." She could hear the smile in his voice. "A bore is a tidal sweep of water which will, I am informed, carry us upstream as far as Bewdley."

They crossed a bridge to the island in the middle of the Severn River, and walked to a cobbled quay where a strange-looking craft lay waiting. It had a cowlike rounded bow, three open decks, and a huge paddle wheel at the stern.

"Mussy," said Dido. "Will *that* thing take us up the river? It looks like a floating chicken coop."

Captain Hughes also eyed the riverboat with some disfavor; but its wooden structure was gray with age and green with waterweed, which seemed to prove that it must have battled its way up and down the Severn River a great many times without mishap. The passengers climbed down a ladder from the jetty and were shown to their quarters. Captain Hughes had a small cabin to himself on the upper foredeck. The others went down to the middle deck, which was open right through the middle of the boat from stem to stern, with a large dining table in the center, and a row of small boxlike cabins on either side. The lowest deck was for cargo, and Dido, looking down a flight of wooden steps, observed that it was packed with freight: bales, barrels, tied-up cows, and crates of poultry. The space by the rail was kept clear, and on each side twelve great wooden handles protruded through slots in the deck.

"What's those for?" Dido asked Mr. Holystone.

"I infer that is how the boat is propelled. Rowers pulling those levers cause the paddle wheel to revolve."

Indeed, the passengers being now all embarked, and the mooring cast off, twenty-four Cumbrian oarsmen, wearing nothing but black cotton trousers, took their places at the levers and, after a shouted command from a coxswain, hauled repeatedly on the handles and let go, until, with a mournful creaking and groaning, the boat was set in motion and worked out into midstream.

"It's a mite slow, ain't it?" said Dido doubtfully.

It was not slow for long. After about ten minutes, when the dim lights of Tenby had fallen away astern, Dido began to hear, above the creak of the levers and the groan of the paddle wheel, a kind of huge sigh that began far away and came closer and closer, becoming so loud at last that it drowned all other noises. At this moment a vast wave overtook the paddleboat and rolled it along the river as a leaf is bowled along by an eddy. The rowers continued to work at their levers; Dido would have liked to ask why, but could not possibly have made herself heard. But after a while she guessed that the motion of the paddle wheel helped to steer the boat and keep it on course in the middle of the stream.

The members of the *Thrush*'s crew settled themselves in the after part of the boat, stretched out comfortably on canvas cots. Dido found herself a cot and placed it up in the bows, where, when day broke, she would get the best view, and also be as far as possible from Silver Taffy.

She found it difficult, however, to get back to sleep. She had slept for a few hours at The White Hart (with Mr. Holystone mounting guard over her slumbers) and now felt fresh, alert, and rested, ready to begin the next day. But the next day was slow in coming; there was no sign of dawn. Up above, huge southern stars blazed in a dark blue sky; on either side, high ramparts of tangly black forest moved endlessly past. Sometimes a pair of eyes could be seen flashing in the darkness; sometimes a menacingly large winged shape coasted overhead. For a long time these were the only signs of life in the forest of Broceliande.

The deafening thunder of the tidal bore gradually decreased until it became a low, rushing gurgle, like the sound of a distant waterfall. After an hour or so, Dido began to catch sounds in the forest: the shrill cries of night birds, the wail of a peafowl, the hiccuping cry of a screech owl; the mewling cry of a great cat, the bellow of an alligator, the bark of apes, the grunting of wild pigs.

Sure is a lot going on in those woods, thought Dido. I ain't sorry we're doing this bit by boat. Guess I wouldn't care to live in Bath Regis if the only way to the sea is through this forest. There's too many critters in there a-waiting to bite and sting and scrunch.

There were humans, too, equally fierce, as she presently discovered. After a while the moon came climbing up over the forest trees, and then, once or twice, by its light, she saw shaggy, wild-looking men, who came down to the water's edge with drawn bows and discharged long jagged arrows after the boat; fortunately the arrows, in each case, fell short, and the bowmen, dancing and gesticulating with rage, were soon left behind.

The next thing that Dido saw was so strange, terrifying, and dreamlike that, for a while afterward, she wondered if perhaps she *had* dreamed it.

The boat had by now arrived in a region where the forest was not so thick; wide open glades, clearings, and savannahs alternated with great spreading creeper-hung trees, whose black shadows were encircled by areas of silvery moonlit jungle grass. Sometimes the ship was in shadow, sometimes in moonlight as it swept upstream, and Dido, yawning on her canvas cot, was beginning to be lulled by the change from light to dark and from dark to light; she had been on the point of stretching out and falling asleep when her attention was caught by the sight of mounted horsemen galloping toward the right-hand bank. As they neared the river's edge, it could be seen that the riders were cloaked and hooded, all in black, and that there were hounds, galloping silently along with them. The hounds were very large, pale-colored, white perhaps, all except their ears, which seemed to be brown or black.

"Fancy—a hunt!" thought Dido drowsily. "Rummy time o' night to go tally-hoing. Wonder what they're after? There'd be plenty to choose from in that wood."

The riverboat, on the crest of the bore, overtook the riders, passed them, and drew ahead, round a bend of the stream; in a few minutes they came within sight of the hunters' quarry. Dido saw with horrid shock that this was a human being—whether male or female she could not be sure—somebody apparently carrying some heavy object, running and stumbling among the bushes close to the river's edge, blundering with the frantic speed of terror through the low-growing scrub, slipping, staggering, recovering, and floundering on again.

"The riders are going faster than that," Dido realized with horror. "Whoever it is ain't a-going to get away. Not unless they can swim out to us. . . ." And she jumped up, and had started up the companionway toward Captain Hughes on the top deck, when the leading hounds came up with their prey. There was a lot of noise from the bank—a shrill, triumphant baying, a shriek of despair—then came a splash, as the fugitive apparently took to the water. A couple more splashes followed—several of the hounds must have plunged in likewise—but the main pack bounded along the river bank, yelling, baying, and whining with excitement and frustration.

The hunters, now evidently abandoning hope of securing their quarry, called in the hounds with shouts and short, shrill blasts on a horn, then drew away from the water's edge; but meanwhile all this commotion had alerted the members of the *Thrush*'s crew, and Dido, hesitating on the companionway, heard Lieutenant Windward call, "Hey! The poor devil's in the water! Stand by to throw him a line!"

The boat's coxswain evidently objected, for Windward exclaimed, "Stuff and nonsense, man! I saw him myself! It must be done! Throw a line, I say!"

Then there were various cries and splashes.

Greatly relieved that Lieutenant Windward had the matter in hand, Dido returned to her cot; half of her wanted to go and see what was happening, but the other half still felt shocked to death by such a sight. Hunting *people*? Who could do such a thing? She would just as soon not know any more about it. Suddenly she felt very sleepy indeed, and, without intending it, she fell into a profound slumber.

When she next woke, it was full day. The middle deck of the riverboat remained just tolerable, since it was in shade, and the air could pass through from prow to stern; but Captain Hughes soon found it necessary to quit his superior quarters on the top deck, which received the full heat of the sun blazing straight overhead. He came down the companionway in a disgruntled frame of mind, and Mr. Holystone placed a cane rocking chair for him on the forward end of the deck, where he sat, occupying himself with designs for flying craft. Several times he threw chilly glances at Dido on her canvas cot nearby, as if intimating that she ought to have the politeness to withdraw and leave him in privacy, but Dido did not choose to take notice of these hints; I got here first, she thought. Let him keep hisself busy drawing pictures of skiffs with wings and let me alone!

It was Dido who first broke the silence, however.

"Cap'n Hughes," she said after a while.

"Well?" His tone was extremely rebuffing, but she went on.

"Did you hear that ruckus in the night?"

"What do you mean?"

"Why, the hunt. There was coves on horses, a-chasing some poor so-and-so who jumped in the river. What d'you reckon was going on? Who *were* they?"

"It is no affair of ours!" he said sternly.

"But I thought Lieutenant Windward had someone pulled on board? Didn't they say—"

"Miss Twite: I have said this before and I will say it again; I must beg that while we are in New Cumbria you do not meddle in matters that do not concern you."

"But—"

"Hush, child! Run along now; I hear Mr. Holy-stone calling you to breakfast."

Out of patience with the captain, Dido unwillingly rose up and took herself off to the long central table, where a couple of Cumbrian crewmen were serving breakfast to the passengers. The meal consisted of greasy fried eggs, lukewarm tea, and fried plantain, which, as Mr. Multiple observed, was like warm oily oak chips. Mr. Holystone, having taken the captain his breakfast on a tray, sat down with the others. He looked unlike himself, Dido noticed: pale, hollow-eyed, and slow in his movements. Probably he saw the hunt, too, Dido guessed, and she immediately asked him about it.

"Who *were* they? And what happened to the one they were after? Did you save him, Mr. Windward?"

Both men appeared reluctant to answer. But Silver

Taffy had no such scruples, and struck in jeeringly from farther up the table.

"Miss Long Nose wants to know, eh? It'd serve your quisitiveness right if the same thing was to happen to *you!*" He laughed in a very disagreeable manner. "Swimming in the Severn River ain't too healthy for the complexion—as you'll see if you go look in that cabin!" He nodded sideways toward one of the little boxlike cubicles which nobody had wished to occupy because they were too stuffy.

"Now, Taffy!" broke in Noah Gusset. "Let the young 'un be! You didn't oughta tell her that."

"*No*, child! Do *not* look in the cabin!" exclaimed Windward and Mr. Holystone at the same moment. But Dido, abandoning her unwanted breakfast, had crossed the deck and looked through the half-open door. At the sight of what lay inside she gasped, half in fright, half in almost disbelieving astonishment. For the inmate of the cabin, reclining on its canvas cot, was a shining white skeleton, with its grinning face turned to the door, as if expecting someone to bring it breakfast on a tray. Only one hand was still intact—the left, on the third finger of which gleamed a gold ring.

Determined not to let Silver Taffy see her shock and distaste, Dido stepped away from the door. She felt rather cold and queasy; the dancing reflections thrown up by the water on the bamboo ceiling swam and jiggled in front of her eyes. Mr. Holystone had moved toward her anxiously. He looked pale and troubled. She asked him in a low voice, "Taffy ain't gammoning me, is he? How can—how can *that* there be the one they was after? How *can* it?"

"I am afraid Taffy is speaking the truth," Mr. Holystone answered gravely. "The small fish that swim in these waters—they are called piscadores—have such a rapacious appetite that three or four minutes in the water is enough to reduce any red-blooded creature to what you see there. The hounds that jumped in suffered the same fate."

"Murder," muttered Dido. She thought of the poor fugitive jumping into the water, knowing full well what would be the result. What had he—or she—been carrying? What fate could have been worse, to make death in the river better than capture?

"This is a right dreadsome country," she said, and shivered.

"Best not go paddling in the river, Madam Nose in Air!" shouted Silver Taffy, and stumped away to the stern, spitting over the side.

Dido did not trouble Captain Hughes with any further questions. She spent the rest of the day playing cat's cradle with Mr. Holystone, who was also unusually silent, and seemed languid and drowsy. Once or twice he pressed his temples with all his fingertips, as if he had a headache, glancing about him in a bewildered manner.

"What's up, Mr. Holy? Ain't you feeling quite the thing? It is perishing hot in this nook-shotten forest. Like sailing along inside of a baker's oven."

"I do not think it is the heat. I am used to heat. Where I come from, in Hy Brasil . . ." His voice trailed off absently. He said, as if to himself, "*Is* that where I come from?" And then to Dido, simply, "I keep forgetting who I am."

Oh, mussy, thought Dido. Supposing he's sunstrook? What'll we do then? He's the only one with any sense in this lot.

"You better put a wet cloth on your noddle and lay down for a bit, Mr. Holy," she suggested anxiously.

But then he smiled, and seemed more like himself, and even taught her a couple of unfamiliar varieties of cat's cradle. And she taught him one invented by herself and christened the Battersea Basket.

During that day the pace of the riverboat gradually slowed down, as the momentum of the bore decreased, and the rowers had to work harder at their levers. Now flies and mosquitoes came on board—all kinds of terrible little buzzing, biting creatures hummed and clustered and plagued the passengers, stinging and piercing every inch of exposed skin, creeping cunningly under the folds of clothes to jab in unexpected and tender spots. Fortunately Mr. Holystone's dark green cactus lotion for repelling cockroaches also proved a useful defense against jungle insects, but there was only just enough to go round. Poor Noah Gusset, a big, pink-faced, towheaded boy, was bitten so badly that he could hardly see out of his eyes. Dido, small and wiry, did not suffer so much, but by the day's end she was heartily weary of the river.

Once, as the boat passed through a narrow, tunnel-like reach, with the distant mountains lost to view behind dank, massed trees, a sudden commotion in the boughs overhead resulted in a slithering thump and a cry of warning from one of the Cumbrian deckhands: a thirty-foot snake had fallen in a tumble of coils down the companionway with a half-swallowed iguana protruding from its jaws. While one of the crew seized the iguana, three others grappled with the snake and tossed it overboard. There was an immediate and frothing convulsion of water where it had fallen; it struck out like an arrow for shore, but Dido saw, almost with disbelief, that before swimming more than a few yards it was picked clean to the bone by the rapacious little river fish; a white snake skeleton sank slowly through the brown water.

"Ain't that *something*!" she said in wonder to Mr. Multiple. "No worry getting rid o' garbage hereabouts."

But Mr. Multiple, usually so cheerful, had gone white to the roots of his carrot-colored hair. "I—I can't abide snakes," he gasped. "Excuse me, Miss Dido—" and running to the stern of the ship, the poor boy was violently sick over the rail. To draw attention from his sufferings, Mr. Holystone said to Dido, "It is a custom among the tribes of these forests, I have heard, that when someone dies, the dead person's body is lowered into the river and left for three days. Then the skeleton is drawn up again and placed in a sacred cave, set aside for the dead, up in the mountains."

When they sat down for the noon meal, Dido was disgusted to find that the iguana which had been rescued from the snake's jaws was served up, roasted and sliced. She could not bring herself to try it, but nibbled a little mango and papaya. However, the rest of the crew—even Mr. Multiple, now quite recovered—ate up the iguana and pronounced it first-rate, or at any rate better than fried plantain chips.

During the afternoon they entered a region infested with alligators, or caimáns, as the Cumbrians termed them: ugly brown wrinkled brutes lying, sometimes scores together, on sandbanks, or floating with only their snouts and bulging eyes above water. They made a grunting bubbling noise, and sometimes bellowed loudly and dolefully. Dido thought they were quite the most unpleasant beasts she had even seen.

Once or twice, as the craft wallowed its way upstream, a heavily barbed arrow whistled through the air and stuck, quivering, in the soft gray wood of the deck. One of these landed uncomfortably close to the arm of Noah Gusset, who was trailing a fishing line over the side.

"Lucky that missed you," said his comrade, the taciturn Plum, "or you'da been rolling round like a catherine wheel in a brace of shakes. The Biruvians that live in the woods tip the barbs with what they call angel juice; a drop of that'd turn you to an angel for sure."

"If any of us gets back from this trip, it'll be a wonder," grumbled Noah Gusset.

At last they left the forest behind. The huge trees, thick creepers, and dangling mosses were replaced first by groves of bamboo and rush, then by wide grassy plains, then by pine-clad foothills. Beyond these, reared against the sunset like ghost castles, were the true mountains, the Children of Silence, Ambage and Arrabe, Ertayne and Elamye, Arryke, Damask, Damyake, Pounce, Pampoyle, Garesse, Galey, Calabe, and Catelonde. And somewhere among them, Dido thought, a girl called Elen. Their sides were so steep that they looked like the fingers of two great hands held up in the air as if to say, "Stop! There is no way past us."

Just as the sun set between the cratered peaks of Ertayne and Elamye, the riverboat came to a stop at a tiny town in the jaws of a deep and narrow gorge.

This was Bewdley, where they must leave the river and take to the rack railway.

Nobody was sorry to go ashore. They were to spend the night in Bewdley, which seemed a pleasant little place, very ancient, its narrow, timbered houses thatched with palm leaves or roofed with great slabs of mountain stone. There were wide cobbled quays on either side of the rushing Severn, and thick black pine forest came down the steep valley-sides to the very garden walls. Market stalls along the riverside, lit by flaring torches, displayed reed mats, fruit, earthenware pots, and straw hats. The air blazed with fireflies and buzzed with the sound of six-foot bamboo horns, which half the population seemed to be blowing.

"They are called bocinas," Mr. Holystone told Dido. "The people blow them at sunset to keep evil spirits away. Otherwise they believe the spirits might climb in your ears during the night."

"Well, surely they've chased the spirits away by *now*? They've nigh blasted my ears off my head," said Dido ungratefully.

As the party from the *Thrush* straggled along the quay toward the inn, Dido noticed a very short woman pluck at the arm of Silver Taffy, who was walking by himself. The woman was almost completely shrouded in a black shawl; her face could not be seen. Taffy started at her touch, then turned and followed her up a side alley.

The other travelers went on to The Black Tree Tavern, where they were to pass the night. This was not such a large establishment as The White Hart. It seemed comfortable enough, but Captain Hughes was affronted to discover that there was no private parlor where he could dine by himself; he must eat in his bedroom, or with the rest of the crew.

"Vexatious!" he said shortly to the landlord. "I have not been used to sit down to sup with my own steward!"

Dido heard this with some indignation. Mr. Holystone, she privately considered, was far more gentlemanly than Captain Hughes, and it would do the latter no harm at all to have his toploftiness reduced.

The captain was due to be further vexed. Just before dinner Silver Taffy came to him and, in a deferential manner but with a very determined look in his eye, requested a week's shore leave.

"What, you rascal!" exclaimed the captain. "At your own request I include you in the shore party, and this is how you repay my kindness? We are under strength as it is—I cannot spare you! A week's furlough? It is out of the question."

Respectfully, Silver Taffy reminded the captain that, in a gale off Cape Orange, he had saved the second lieutenant at risk of his own life, and had been promised leave as a reward.

It was Captain Hughes's pride that he never went back on his word.

"Oh, very well!" he said testily. "But a whole week! That is the outside of enough. You may have three days—no more. And you must rejoin the party in Bath Regis."

A gleam of satisfaction came into Taffy's eye.

"Very good, Cap'n," he said, and speedily left the inn.

"Very good riddance, I call it," Dido muttered to

Mr. Holystone. "I daresay that was his auntie—the short old girl he was talking to as we came along."

Mr. Holystone, however, had not seen her. He seemed excessively tired this evening, slow in his movements and troubled in his thoughts.

After supper—which was a silent and somewhat constrained meal, with nobody in good spirits—Mr. Holystone requested a private word with the captain.

"God bless my soul, *now* what?" irritably exclaimed the latter. "Private? There is nowhere to be private in this wretched little hostelry. Oh, well, you had best come up to my bedroom. You too, Miss Twite; I daresay whatever Holystone has to say is fit for your ears, and if it ain't, it can't be helped; I am not leaving you to be abducted a second time."

Rather put out at being considered such an encumbrance, Dido followed them to the small room under the eaves, which was the best accommodation that could be provided for the captain.

"Well, Holystone, what is it? Make haste, man; I have my log still to write, and my aeronautical calculations."

"Sir," said Mr. Holystone desperately, "I believe I ought not to accompany you on this expedition."

"*What?*" The captain stared at him with bulging eyes. "Oh, stap me—this is too much!"

"I believe I should return to the ship, sir. My presence with you may be endangering all your lives."

"Return to the ship? And leave me without a steward? What is all this about? I won't have it!" said the captain, now thoroughly roused. "It's bad enough that one of my most able-bodied men should virtually abscond—and now you wish to slope off too! Well, it's not to be thought of! So you may put that in your pipe and smoke it!"

"Sir, allow me to explain," said Mr. Holystone, who looked miserably ill and shaky, but was endeavoring to maintain his calm. He's sick, Dido thought anxiously; he oughta be in bed. Maybe that's what he's a-going to say.

"Explain till you are blue in the face," snapped Captain Hughes. "It won't make a particle of difference."

"Sir, as you are no doubt well aware, the three kingdoms of New Cumbria, Lyonesse, and Hy Brasil meet, like three segments of cake, at one point only—the southernmost tip of Lake Arianrod, or Dozmary, which lies among the high mountains to the west of this region."

"A geography lesson, now!" grumbled the captain. "I thank you; you need not teach *me* my hornbook, man; I daresay I am as well acquainted with the topography of this locality as you!"

"I doubt that, sir," civilly replied Mr. Holystone, "since I, as a child, was first discovered lying among the rushes at the southern end of Lake Arianrod."

"Oh you were, were you? Well, what is that to the purpose?"

"The whole extent of this lake," flatly pursued Mr. Holystone, "is contained in New Cumbria, but Hy Brasil and Lyonesse each claim one yard of shore, where the river Camel, which forms a boundary between the latter countries, flows out of the lake—or did before it was dammed."

"So?"

"I was found on the yard of shore pertaining to Hy Brasil. I was discovered at midnight by one of the king's advisers, a wise man who was making astrological observations and collecting medicinal mosses at the time. This man read my horoscope, since it was plain I was but a few hours old. From that and from a birthmark which I have on my forearm he ascertained that I come of very ancient blood. Accordingly the king of Hy Brasil, Huayna Ccapac, took me and had me brought up in the palace with his son Huascar. I was given the name of Atahallpa."

"Humph, were you though?" remarked the captain, not best pleased, evidently, to discover that his personal steward came of ancient blood and had been brought up with royalty. "So why ain't you there still, hey?"

Mr. Holystone labored on with his tale, speaking more and more slowly.

"My adopted father—who always treated me with the utmost kindness—had me tutored with his son until I was fourteen. But then—" the level voice faltered for a moment; then he recovered and went on firmly—"but then my royal foster father judged it best to send me to a university in Europe. So I traveled to Salamanca with my tutor, and remained there for many years."

"Humph," muttered the captain again. "Should think all that eddication'd fit you to be something more than a steward. Did you never go back to Hy Brasil?"

"Many times I wished to," said Mr. Holystone simply. "I wished to see my kind old foster father and my cousins."

"Cousins? Thought you said you were a foundling?"

"Foster cousins," Mr. Holystone amended. "King Mabon, the ruler of Lyonesse, was a cousin of Huayna

Ccapac. His children, Artegall, Martegall, and Elen, were my playmates and companions when I was small. But no—I never went back. At the death of Huayna Ccapac, twelve years ago, his son, Huascar Ccaedmon, ascended the throne. He is no friend to me; never has been. My tutor wrote to warn me that if I tried to return, Ccaedmon would have me put to death."

"Bloodthirsty lot these Incas, whatdoyoucallems," commented the captain. "What about the ones in Lyonesse, King Mabon and his brood?"

"I have heard, at infrequent intervals, from my foster uncle, King Mabon. There is little love lost between him and Ccaedmon, who is a harsh ruler and a touchy neighbor. At present a doubtful peace obtains between Lyonesse and Hy Brasil; twice, however, Ccaedmon has broken the peace and seized strips of land on the Lyonesse boundary. But Mabon's relations with New Cumbria are even more delicate, and so he hesitates to retaliate."

"Aha!" exclaimed Captain Hughes, who, in spite of himself, was becoming interested. "Has Ccaedmon also committed acts of aggression against New Cumbria? Is that what Queen Whatshername's complaint is about, think you? Devil take it, man, why would you not let me have all this information while we were still aboard the *Thrush*? It is worth twice what that dolt Brandywinde had to tell me."

"My position is so awkward," said Mr. Holystone sadly. "King Mabon sent me a message three years ago, suggesting that I lead a revolt against Ccaedmon. But who am I, after all? My parentage is unknown. In spite of Mabon's friendship I told him that I had no right to lead a rising against the ruler of Hy Brasil."

"What about the queen of New Cumbria?"

"Cumbria is a closed country," said Mr. Holystone, shaking his head. "It is a secret land. The port of Tenby is its only entrance. Nobody goes in or out. The queen holds no communication with her neighbors. Citizens of Lyonesse or Hy Brasil may not cross her frontiers. It has always been so."

"*We* got in."

"That is because the queen has sent for you."

"Well," said Captain Hughes, "all this is deucedly interesting—though why you were not prepared to divulge it two weeks ago, bless me if I can see. But what has it to do with your not wishing to accompany us to Bath? That's what has me in a puzzle."

Holystone looked at him hopelessly, as if he had come to the end of his strength. The captain reflected and said, "No, I believe I do understand. It is because you might be considered a pretender to the throne of Hy Brasil—is that it, hey? You think it might put me in an awkward spot if you were recognized so near the country you came from?"

"Just so, sir."

"Does you credit, I daresay. Should have thought of it sooner, though. Suppose you were tempted by the chance to revisit these parts, hmm? But then—it ain't all that likely you *will* be recognized, is it? If you haven't been back since you were fourteen?"

Maybe he's ashamed, thought Dido. After all, he was a kind of a prince then—only fancy, our Mr. Holystone! Well, I allus reckoned there were more to him than met the eye—and he wouldn't want his old chums to see him now he's only a steward.

Mr. Holystone looked very unhappy, but made no direct answer to the captain. "Pray give consideration to my request, sir," was all that he said.

"Well—I will think about it, and let you know my decision in the morning. Meanwhile, kindly see that child goes to bed—and that a watch is kept over her during the night."

"Yes, sir."

Dido's bedroom was even smaller than the captain's—a tiny slip of a room. On the bed was curled something that Dido, for one nervous moment, took, in the dim candlelight, for a large spider. She was still unsettled by the events of the river trip. But then, with much relief, she saw that the sleeping creature was a small cat, curled up in a tight ball.

"Hey, puss!" Dido said softly. "Come to keep me company, have you?"

She stroked the cat and found, as on the one at Tenby, a collar with a disc, this time bearing the name Tom Tildrum, and a packet consisting of a small scrap of folded paper.

"Hilloo, Mr. Holy!" she called in a whisper. He had made himself up a pallet outside the door, and came directly.

"Look what's here, Mr. Holy! Another of 'em."

They both studied the words on the small printed page, which said:

> Chirurgeon. One that cures ailments, not by internal medicines, but outward applications. It is now generally pronounced, and by many written, surgeon.

Under this was written, in small, desperate dark-brown letters (could they be blood?):

Help! I am a prisoner in a cave on Arrabe. I do not have air for many more days.

"Why's she so skint on air?" demanded Dido. "That's one thing nobody bothers to sell, acos no one'd buy it—there's always plenty."

"Not in the mountains," said Mr. Holystone hoarsely. He had gone deathly pale; his high forehead gleamed with sweat. He muttered, "Up on the slopes of Catelonde one must carry enough air to breathe. There are flowers—night-blooming lilies—shepherds always carry them. . . ."

"Oh, Mr. Holy! What can we *do* for this poor girl?"

But Mr. Holystone was past replying. He had slid to the floor in deep unconsciousness.

5

The rack railway train that was to carry the party from Bewdley up to a height of twelve thousand feet above sea level was such a strange-looking little conveyance that when they first set eyes on it Dido exclaimed, "Love a duck! That thing couldn't pull pussy across the parlor!"

Captain Hughes, equally glum and dubious, observed that it resembled a row of dominoes in process of falling down. The rolling stock of the little train did indeed have a curiously tilted appearance, since most of its journey would be spent going up the side of a slope like a church steeple; consequently, while on flat ground the whole thing leaned forward as if engaged in studying its own toenails. The tiny wood-burning engine carried a top-heavy smokestack with a fuel box and water tank behind. There were three wagons: a baggage-and-mail car, loaded with straw bales, goats, poultry, salt, and dried fish; a boxcar crammed to its thatched roof with standing passengers, all wrapped snugly in the local garb of ponchos and long cloaks, which they called ruanas; and a first-class car which, for the benefit of the foreigners, was supplied with a few narrow wooden benches.

The train ran on three rails, the center one having large cog teeth, which engaged with similar teeth on a set of wheels under the cars, so that, however steep the slope, the train could never slip backward. Gay red roses and green leaves had been painted along the sides of the wagons a long time ago. The paint, like everything else about the train, was old, dirty, and worn.

After considerable delay the engine started with a great snorting and straining and blowing of steam and a shriek so prolonged that it seemed to be protesting against its task.

Almost as soon as it had clanked away from Bewdley, the track stopped being level and began to climb. They rounded a corner of the Severn gorge, crept up a steep hillside, and were immediately presented with a view so magnificent that it made Dido gasp. A mile west of Bewdley the valley of the Severn was barred by a great semicircle of cliffs over which the river came racing in a huge horseshoe of boiling white water, full three quarters of a mile from side to side; white vapor rose from it like smoke, and the roar was loud enough to drown even the screeching and chugging of their engine.

"That's what I kept a-hearing last night. I thought it was lions roaring and tigers caterwauling," Dido said to Mr. Holystone, who whispered that the cascade was known as the Falls of Hypha, and formed the lowest in a series of seven, all equally majestic. "The others are Stheino, Euryte, Medusa, Minerva, Nemetone, and Rhiannon—the seven witches who guard the secret land of Upper Cumbria."

"Ain't there *no* way to Upper Cumbria but by this railway?" asked Dido.

"Not from the sea. Before the rail track was cut, men thought the precipices too high to scale."

"Then," said Dido skeptically, "how did the first lot ever get there? The ones who came over after the Battle of Dyrham?"

"They had landed farther down the coast and traveled north through the mountains and the valley of Lake Arianrod."

"Come in by the back way, I see."

"That way, too, leads in through a very narrow pass; it wants but one great rock to fall, which hangs poised on the lip of Mount Catelonde, and the way would be blocked, and Upper Cumbria would be sealed off."

"Only if the railway stopped running," Dido pointed out. "What a lot you know about it all, Mr. Holy!"

"I have always—always been interested in ancient history. . . ." His weak voice died away in a great yawn, and his head nodded forward. He roused up again, however, to say to Captain Hughes, "Sir, do not forget—that when we reach Bath Regis—which is thirteen thousand feet above sea level—all the party must be careful to avoid undue exertion at first—the air is so thin that—the least effort causes palpitations of the heart. You will—ache all over—headaches and nosebleeds are not uncommon—"

He toppled over on his side; he had been sitting on the wagon floor, propped against the wall. Dido, kneeling by him worriedly, saw that he was in a kind of half-sleep, half-swoon. His fainting fit last night had occasioned a great deal of concern. He had recovered only after a great many restoratives had been administered, and Captain Hughes had said firmly there could be no question of his returning to the coast by himself, or of his remaining in the small and primitive inn at Bewdley. He must accompany the party to Bath, where there were sure to be doctors and he could be properly cared for. Poor Mr. Holystone had been too weak to protest, although he seemed wretched in his spirits, as if the whole atmosphere of Cumbria oppressed him and made him ill. In the morning he had to be carried on board the train.

"Best leave him to sleep," said Captain Hughes. "Poor devil, maybe it is merely the altitude that is affecting him, and he will recover in due course."

Dido felt sure that it was more than that. She had not informed Captain Hughes about the messages in the cats' collars—she could just imagine the scorn with which he would dismiss such idle nonsense—but she herself felt certain that they had something to do with Mr. Holystone's infirmity.

As the train zigzagged its way upward, she occupied herself by looking out of the dirty window at the scenery, which was certainly very astonishing. Day wore slowly on as they climbed higher and higher, curving over mountainsides and through narrow passes, creeping along narrow rocky valleys, and yet again up and up, following the course of the river Severn, now transformed to a boulder-strewn torrent. They passed many more waterfalls, some plunging from thousand-foot crags into vapor-filled gorges, others pouncing down hillsides step by step.

At last Dido became bored with her own company—

for Noah Gusset was curled up asleep, Mr. Multiple and the lieutenant were playing chess, and Plum, a silent man at all times, was knitting himself a sock, while Captain Hughes, having written up his log, was deep, as usual, in aerostatics.

Seizing the chance when the train stopped at a wayside halt to take on more wood and water and allow a customs official to inspect the foreigners' credentials, Dido slipped out of the first-class car onto the rock platform beside the track.

"Hey, young 'un! Where are you off to?" demanded Lieutenant Windward, sticking his fair head out.

"I'm a-going in the boxcar for a bit," said Dido. "I'll be all rug; don't you fret your fur."

She was startled at the bitter cold of the mountain air, high up here between Ambage and Arryke; she made haste to scramble into the second-class car, where the atmosphere was as warm as a nesting box. There were no seats at all in here, and the passengers—who were mostly sunburned peasants, bringing their goods to the city—all squatted on the floor. They wore sandals, ponchos, goatskin trousers, and a dozen hats apiece, and the floor was littered with melon seeds, pineapple tassels, and plantain rinds. However, the human climate was a great deal more cordial than in the first-class accommodation; Dido was greeted cheerfully enough, and offered cherries from a basket, a bite of a delicious fruit called chirimoya, and a mugful of chicha, a drink not unlike cider. She learned, partly by sign language, since the peasants mostly spoke Latin, that they came not from Tenby, but from small clearings in the forest, and that they were coming to sell their hats in Bath. She herself was bombarded with questions.

"Why is the gringo captain coming to Bath? Why is he permitted to do so? Why does he leave his ship?"

"He is coming to visit your queen," Dido said.

"Wants to see Her Mercy, do he? Why, in the name of Grandmother Sul?"

"No," said Dido, "*she* wants to see *him*. She wants him to do summat for her."

This was received with puzzlement and wonder.

"What could the gringo captain do for Her Mercy that her couldn't do for herself? A powerful wise woman she be!"

"Pick up the Cheesewring with her bare hands and sling it into the middle of Dozmary Pool, her could!" Dido gathered that these were local names for Mount Catelonde and Lake Arianrod. "Make old Damyake Hill blow sparks into King Mabon's beard. She's a powerful one, she be. Could turn Severn Water back'ards through Pulteney Bridge. Ar, she'm a rare 'un, old Queen Ginnyvere."

"Why doesn't she have a king?" Dido asked. "In England we have both."

They were all amazed at her ignorance.

"Course there be a king! Didn't you know that? Lives in his own place, top o' Beechen Hill—in the Wen Pendragon. But he don't come out. Wounded, he were, in the wars."

"What wars?"

"Long-ago wars. Old, old wars. He won't get no better till the red rain do fall. Then the great gates'll open, and he'll go home again."

"What red rain?"

Nobody was certain about that. "He'll get better in his own time, maidy. Simmingly."

"Maybe that's what the queen wants," said Dido.

"Maybe she wants Cap'n Hughes to recommend a doctor from England."

This precipitated a great discussion among the peasants, some saying that the queen could do anything, and consequently needed no help from outsiders, others pointing out that she must have had *some* reason for summoning the gringo captain.

In the middle of this, Dido was greatly startled to see the tall, thin, black-clad figure of Bran the storyteller unfold himself from a corner where he had been dozing unnoticed and move into the middle of the car. He had his white bird on his shoulder, and greeted Dido with a friendly nod.

"Oh!" cried Dido, delighted, "now you can finish the story about the man and the stick."

But the word *story* instantly aroused a commotion among the other passengers.

"A story—a story! Your Excellency—Your Venerable —Your Squireship—Your Knowingness—do'ee now, kindly, tell us a story!"

"Very well," said the man called Bran. "If you will all be so good as to keep quiet, so that I can make myself heard." Instantly a dead silence prevailed, apart from the spitting of melon seeds.

Bran thought for a moment, cleared his throat, and began.

"Once a man called Juan applied for a post as nightwatchman at a warehouse. He had been promised the job. But when he got there, the overseer said to him, 'That job has been given to someone else.' 'To whom?' furiously demanded Juan. 'To that man who just left.' Looking out of the door, Juan was amazed to see that the other man exactly resembled himself. 'Stop, you impostor!' shouted Juan, chasing him along the street. 'You have stolen my job.' But the other man turned a corner, and Juan could not find him.

"Then Juan fell in love with a beautiful girl. But when he asked her to marry him, she said, 'I am already promised to that man on the other side of the marketplace.' And he looked across, and there was his double again. 'Now I shall catch you, you wretch!' he bawled, and he rushed across the square. But when he reached the other side, his rival had gone. And many times this happened; if it was the last loaf on a baker's counter, or the last place on the ferry, it was always the double who got there first.

"Then, one day, as Juan was going down the hill toward the river, he saw his double not far ahead. *Now I shall catch him,* thought Juan, and he began to run. But as the other man walked out on the bridge, a great flood came roaring down the riverbed and washed the bridge away. And Juan wept and raged and would not be comforted. 'For,' he said, 'now I have lost my enemy forever.' "

"Is that the end?" asked Dido.

"That you must decide for yourself," said Bran.

Dido reflected.

"Well, I think he was a looby, to carry on so," she said. "If *I'd* been him, I'd never—"

But Bran was briskly going round among the peasants, collecting small copper coins in a wooden cup. Then he sang a song, accompanying himself on his harp:

> *"I can hardly bear it*
> *Waiting for tomorrow to come*
> *Joy I want to share it*
> *Waiting for tomorrow to come*

> *Love I must declare it*
> *Waiting for tomorrow to come*
> *For that's the day*
> *When she, when she, when she, when she,*
>   *when she*
> *Will come*
> *My way.*
>
> *Time seems to creep*
> *Waiting for tomorrow to come*
> *Clock has gone to sleep,*
> *Waiting for tomorrow to come*
> *Patiently I keep . . ."*

His voice was drowned by a tremendous shuddering, creaking, and clanking as the train drew to a standstill.

"Are we taking on more wood and water?" asked Dido, as Bran stopped singing.

"No," he said. "We have reached our destination. We are in Bath."

The peasants began leaping out of the boxcar. In two minutes they were all gone. Dido skipped out after them, and found herself on an icy, windswept stone pavement, inadequately sheltered by a thatched canopy. The air was bitter.

"Make haste, if you please, Miss Twite!" came the captain's voice. "No time to loiter about—and much too cold. We must get poor Holystone into shelter. Come along!"

"But Bran," said Dido, looking round. "Won't you please tell me—"

Bran's tall figure, however, had vanished among the peasants in their flowing ruanas and high-piled stacks of panama hats. Reluctantly Dido followed the captain's impatiently beckoning arm and walked, shivering, through a kind of open-fronted station hall to a paved courtyard beyond. Here there were hackney carriages waiting, and a number of sedan chairs with their poles resting on the ground, and the blue-coated chairmen standing by them.

"Sydney Hotel!" Captain Hughes ordered one of the hackney drivers in a loud, authoritative voice. "Gusset —Multiple—take Mr. Holystone up carefully and lay him on the carriage seat."

Mr. Holystone was still asleep, it seemed.

"Sydney Hotel?" one of the chairmen said to Dido. "Hop in, missie, and we'll have you there in the flick of a pig's tail."

Dido would have liked to ride in a chair—they had gone out of fashion in London and she had never seen one—but Captain Hughes called irritably, "Into the *carriage*, Miss Twite—look sharp now! We don't want to keep poor Holystone hanging about in this bitter cold!"

"Sorry, mister," Dido apologized to the hopeful chairman, and she clambered into the carriage. Glancing through the window next moment, she nearly dropped her cloak bag—for an instant she could have sworn that the rear chairman was Silver Taffy. But then he moved into the shadows and disappeared. It can't have been him anyway, Dido thought; what would he be doing here? We left him behind at Bewdley.

Dusk was falling as they clattered out of the station yard, over bumpy cobbles. Dido looked down to see if they were silver, but the light was too poor to be sure. It was freezing cold inside the carriage; and the steam from the horses' nostrils looked like dragons' breath. Dido shivered on the slippery leather seat and huddled against the comfortable warmth of Mr. Midshipman Multiple. He, Noah, Dido, and Plum rode in this carriage; Captain Hughes, Mr. Holystone, and Lieutenant Windward were in the other, which had already started.

Despite the cold, Dido would not have minded a long drive if it had been possible to see anything of the town, but there were hardly any streetlights; the only illumination came from dim gleams, here and there, behind lace-curtained windows. Bath Regis, for a capital city, seemed very quiet and glum.

Luckily it proved no more than a ten-minute trot from the station to the Sydney Hotel, over a covered bridge with closed market stalls on either side, and along an extremely wide street; then the travelers had reached their destination and were being solicitously helped to alight by half a dozen porters and footmen.

By the time Dido entered the vestibule, she heard Captain Hughes giving orders that a dressmaker be fetched immediately to fit his young companion with a court dress.

Oh no, thought Dido in despair, not again!

"Madame Ettarde is Her Majesty's court dressmaker and mantua maker, sir," the landlord was respectfully informing the captain. "Her establishment is in Orange Grove, no more than a step from here. But it will be all shut up at this time of night. My counsel to you, sir, if the matter is urgent, would be for the young lady to call round there first thing in the morning, with her abigail, and see what Madame has on the premises; that way, no time will be wasted."

Captain Hughes thought well of this advice. "If Holystone is feeling more the thing, he can take you there tomorrow as soon as this Ettarde female opens shop," he told Dido briskly. "I wish to spend no more time than need be in Bath, which seems a devilish dismal place, and is cold as a coffin. If Madam can rig you out in time, perhaps we can got to see Her Majesty tomorrow afternoon."

Ettarde, thought Dido. Where have I heard that name before?

She packed the name away in the corner of her mind which held unanswered questions. Such as the name Elen—where had that been mentioned, apart from on the cats' collars? And who had worn a gold ring? And what did Bran's stories mean?

"Meanwhile," went on the captain, "we had best dine, and then you, child, may retire to your chamber. I have instructed Mr. Multiple to keep watch outside your door, as Holystone is ailing; we want no repetition of what occurred in Tenby."

Dinner, in the large, bare, and ice-cold dining room, was a horrible meal of hot water with bits of egg and potato floating about in it, succeeded by what Lieutenant Windward unhesitatingly identified as boiled llama and beans, followed by hard green bananas. Dido, who, like the rest, found herself breathless, aching, and limp, affected, as Mr. Holystone had prophesied, by height sickness, was glad to go off to bed, exchanging a rueful grin with Midshipman Multiple, who took up his station outside her door on a cane cot. A doctor had been summoned for Mr. Holystone, who had been carried to his chamber long before, but no doctor would come out at night in Bath, it seemed.

Dido tumbled into her damp and freezing bed— which consisted of a heap of quilts on a wooden frame —and was soon asleep.

She woke before dawn, hearing the cry of the watch: "Six o'clock and a fine, frosty morning!" and was thereafter kept awake by other street cries—milk girls, porter boys, straw-hat vendors, needle and powder sellers—and by the mewing of cats and the clatter of ironbound wheels over cobbles.

Recalled to wide wakefulness and curiosity, Dido scrambled out of bed (she observed now that the bed-clothes were simply a pile of hides with the shaggy wool attached), pulled on such clothes as she had taken off the night before, and went to the window. Drawing back lace curtains adorned with blobs of red and blue wool, she discovered a stone balcony outside, so she opened the window and stepped out into the blistering cold. Sucking in her breath with shock, she retreated, wrapped herself in one of the shaggy hides, and returned to study the scene before her.

The city of Bath Regis lay in a kind of natural hollow. The biggest and most impressive buildings were grouped at the bottom, and streets of smaller dwelling-houses, elegantly laid out in circles, squares, and crescents, rose in tiers up the sides of the hilly basin. Cactuses, among the buildings, and spiky trees (which Dido later learned were called sigse thorn and capuli cherry) here and there indicated the location of a park or public garden. The houses were square, handsome, and clean, built of cream-colored stone; they looked brand-new, though most of them were many hundreds of years old, being preserved in excellent condition by the dry mountain air. The Sydney Hotel stood at the end of a large oval circus, and faced down a wide street.

At the far end of this street was the covered bridge which the travelers had crossed last night. Already morning traffic was plying busily up and down—carriages, carts, and a kind of streetcar which consisted simply of a roofed platform on wheels, drawn by mules. Burros were plentiful; also to be seen were numbers of the large fawn-colored llamas, ambling along at their leisurely gait, and gazing about them with absentminded expressions; these did not pull carts, but carried bundles on their backs, and were led by drovers, sometimes in processions of twenty or more. Leaning farther over her stone parapet, Dido discovered with amazement that the story had been true—the cobbles *were* made of silver, or some similar metal; though littered over with a layer of dry, pale dust, they gleamed where a hoof or wheel had scraped off the dirt.

"This must be a rich town!" thought Dido. "After all, I'm glad I came. Wonder which of them buildings is the palace?"

Away to her left rose a high wooded hill, on top of which she noticed a tall slender tower—but that seemed too small for a palace. Dido craned about inquisitively, wishing that she could see farther—a thin mountain mist concealed the more distant buildings.

And then, suddenly, as the sun climbed higher, the mist was drawn into the upper air and disappeared. Dido fairly gasped at the prospect which then lay revealed. Now she could see that Bath nestled in the scooped-out summit of a low hill in the middle of a high, flat plateau encircled by a ring of thirteen volcanoes—Ambage and Arrabe, Ertayne and Elamye, Arryke, Damask, Damyake, Pounce, Pampoyle, Garesse, Galey, Calabe, and Catelonde. All around the city their great symmetrical cones reared up like ninepins: some quite near at hand, some farther off, some snow-covered, or laced over by glaciers, some reddish, some llama-colored, some blue with distance, some flashing in the sun, some rising out of dazzling ice fields, some shrouded by forests on their lower slopes. From half a dozen ascended gray-white or black columns of smoke, showing that these great chimneys of the inner world still contained fires in their hearts and might erupt. One, Catelonde, had an enormous rock, big as a cathedral, balanced on its summit.

"Wow!" muttered Dido. "I wouldn't fancy being here if they all sneezed together. Guess it wouldn't be quite so chilly in Bath Regis then!"

However, the larger of the smoking peaks appeared to be some thirty or forty miles away; it was to be hoped that there was no great danger from them.

Becoming too cold to remain on the balcony, Dido made her way down to the breakfast parlor. Here she found Noah Gusset, Mr. Windward, and Mr. Multiple, partaking of gravelly barley bread and cups of hot chocolate that seemed to consist principally of brown sugar and boiling water.

"How's Mr. Holy?" was Dido's first question.

"He's still sleeping," the lieutenant told her. "Captain Hughes is waiting for the physician. The sleep is so heavy that it hardly seems natural. Meanwhile I have instructions to escort you to the dressmaker, Miss Dido."

Dido pulled a face at the prospect, but still she was longing to go out, and bolted down her unappetizing breakfast with dispatch. In ten minutes they were out in the street, accompanied by Mr. Multiple.

There were no shops in Pulteney Street, the wide thoroughfare which led to the hotel. But on the covered bridge over the rushing Severn they found many

little booths; Dido was interested to see that these
advertised their wares by means of flags: red for meat,
white for milk, green for vegetables, fruit, or flowers,
yellow for bread. The stall holders were in the process
of unlocking their premises, using enormous heavy
keys, shaped like swans or lions or fishes. Many of the
people walking about seemed to have wooden legs.
Why? Dido wondered. Had they been bitten by aurocs?
Rich people, who rode in sedan chairs, wore elaborately piled and powdered hair. The market women
had black mantos, or shawls, wrapped tightly round
the upper part of their bodies, above long black skirts,
and often a kind of blanket, folded in three, on their
heads. The men wore ruanas, black jackets and trousers, wooden clogs on their feet, and straw hats. As in
Bewdley and Tenby, there were no children to be
seen, and Dido was a target for many stares of astonishment, and some hostility.

Mr. Windward pulled his watch from his pocket and
consulted it; then he tapped it, with some annoyance.
"It's stopped; it never did that before. Still, we must
be in good time if the lady opens up shop at nine. It
was half past eight when we left the inn."

Orange Grove, a small street of superior dwellings,
lay to their left, not far beyond the bridge.

"Bless my soul!" exclaimed Lieutenant Windward.
"Half these houses are Roman villas."

"Well, a lot o' Romans did come and settle here;
Mr. Holy told me so," Dido reminded him. "Look,
here's a sign that says Mme Ettarde, Modiste."

Madame Ettarde's establishment had been adapted
from a Roman villa, and was built around a court
where a fountain splashed and pinched-looking orange
trees grew in tubs.

Dido could tell, as soon as they stepped inside, that Madame Ettarde had been tipped off to expect them.

"Is this the lucky young lady who is to see the queen?" cooed a welcoming voice. "Step in here, miss, if you please!"

During the night the recollection had returned to Dido of where she had previously heard the name Ettarde. It had been mentioned by Mrs. Morgan and Mrs. Vavasour. This was not likely to recommend it; nor did the appearance of its owner. Lady Ettarde was a dwarf, hardly more than three feet high. Her shoulders were crooked, giving her a lopsided walk. She had a pale, sharp-featured face and greenish eyes, rather close set, which studied Dido appraisingly. Her hair, dressed high and lavishly ornamented with pearls, was a much more brilliant red than nature could have managed on its own. She was richly dressed in dark-olive silk taffeta pinstriped in yellow.

She was also—Dido felt almost certain—the short woman who, wrapped in a black shawl, had limped along the quay and spoken to Silver Taffy at Bewdley.

"What a fortunate coincidence," purred Lady Ettarde, beckoning a couple of assistants, one tall, one short. They wore black silk dresses, muslin mobcaps, and black half-masks. "We have here, my dear, a dress originally ordered for a young lady who had been planning to make her come-out at court this spring—when, only last month, she unexpectedly disappeared. Young ladies *do* have a way of suddenly popping off in these parts! But I believe her gown will fit you to a tee, miss—with just a tuck or so, and a take-in. See, now, if that isn't just the article—complete to a shade

—gown, silver scarf, sandals, gloves, petticoat, feathers —everything needful for you to make your curtsey to the queen!"

A very pretty silver-embroidered white mull dress was displayed by the silent assistants.

"That looks well enough," said Lieutenant Windward, who appeared somewhat weighted down by this unusual responsibility. "But I reckon she'd best try it on?"

"The fitting room is behind that curtain," said Lady Ettarde, smiling.

The assistants took a step toward Dido.

But nothing was going to get Dido behind that curtain.

"Oh no!" she declared. "I ain't a-going in there. I'll just slip the dress on over my shimmy," she added carelessly, removing her pea jacket.

"In front of a gentleman? Impossible, dear!" said Lady Ettarde, shocked, and her assistants murmured, "The idea!"

"You jist turn and face the other way, Mr. Windward," Dido told him. "Don't you leave the shop—not nohow!"

Mr. Windward did feel de trop, but recognized the appeal in Dido's voice; besides, he had had very firm instructions from Captain Hughes. Accordingly he sat himself down on a spindly gold love seat facing the window.

"Young ladies will take these nervous fancies," murmured Lady Ettarde pityingly.

But Dido, ignoring the scornful smiles of Lady Ettarde and her workwomen, pulled the mull dress over her head, as she did so remarking conversationally to Mr. Windward, "There was a fellow called Bran who come up on the train yesterday; he was telling a real rum story about a man who kept seeing his double."

A long cheval glass stood by Dido; sharply watching Lady Ettarde in this while buttoning her dress, Dido observed the dressmaker turn white as the dress itself. One of the assistants dropped a box of pins, while the bigger one let out a little whimper.

"B-B-B-Bran?"

"Quiet, you nuddikin!" snapped Lady Ettarde. Then, resuming her polished manner, she remarked to the lieutenant, "This Bran, as they call him, is quite a quiz, indeed! He is the queen's jongleur, you know, so he may do as he chooses. He wanders about collecting tales and songs; it is said that sometimes, even, he works in the silver mines. Imagine it!" She gave a light, contemptuous laugh.

"They say he can hear anything that's said, anywhere," whispered one of the women.

"Pick up those pins, fool, and hold your tongue!" said Lady Ettarde, and she made one or two slight alterations in the dress, pinning back a fold at the side, adjusting the shoulders, taking up the hem. Dido, wonderingly studying the image in the glass, could hardly believe that the shimmering stranger was herself.

"Feathers?" suggested one of the masked women, offering a bunch of white-and-silver plumes.

But Dido's hair was so short that the feathers could not be attached to her head.

"I don't like 'em above half, anyhows," she said, handing them back. "They make me look like a circus pony."

"They are quite the wear at court," Madame Ettarde informed her coldly.

"Can't help that," Dido replied, as coldly.

A little silver-and-crystal tiara, with a spun-glass spray, was found instead, and Madame Ettarde undertook to deliver the whole costume by an hour after noon. Lieutenant Windward then paid the staggering price, and he and Dido took their leave.

Mr. Multiple was waiting for them outside.

"Croopus," said Dido, "it ain't half *costing* the cap, jist to have me pass the time o' day with that queen. Wonder why he's so fixed on the notion?"

Lieutenant Windward, too, thought it queer, but he had been trained not to question his commanding officer's decisions, and so made no comment.

"Look," he said, "I believe that must be the royal palace over there. See the guards? But what a very singular building!" He peered at it through narrowed blue eyes and said incredulously, "It appears to be *revolving*."

"Guess you're right," said Dido after a minute's study. "Well, if that don't beat all! Wouldn't you think Her Royalty would get a bit giddy inside there?"

Bath Palace was indeed an unusual dwelling. Large, circular, and five or six stories high, it rose beside the rushing Severn, part of which had been diverted in order to surround the palace with water. A narrow bridge led to the entrance, which was guarded by gray-uniformed soldiers with pikes. They wore silver-visored helmets with gray plumes, which made them look, Dido thought, like ghosts. But the great oddity was certainly the palace itself.

"Is it made of silver, d'you reckon, Mr. Windward?"

"Some kind of metal," he confirmed. "But it can hardly be silver, surely?"

"It don't half dazzle," Dido said.

It dazzled indeed. Scattered up and down its shining height they saw the city of Bath reflected in a series of somewhat distorted images. The windows (there were not many) interrupted these reflections like black pockmarks. There was an immense main door—of bronze, Lieutenant Windward thought—and, set into this, a much smaller wicket, composed of two interlocking metal surfaces put at right angles to each other. These continually revolved, so that people could pass through if they were fairly nippy about it. And the whole building itself kept turning round very slowly, almost imperceptibly unless you took your eyes away and looked again.

"Wonder who thought that up?" said Dido, much impressed. "D'you reckon that's the way we'll go in, Mr. Windward—through those spinning doors?"

"I imagine so. There appears to be no other entrance."

"Well, I wouldn't want to live there," Dido decided. "If you ask *me*, it looks like an outsize milk churn."

"Shall we go to inspect some of the other sights in the town?" suggested Lieutenant Windward. "Captain Hughes has dispatched a note to the vicar general, asking what time it would be convenient for him to wait on Her Majesty. But he said we need not be back until noon. It must be quite early still." He pulled out his watch, tapped it impatiently, and said to Mr. Multiple, "Do you have your timepiece on you?"

"Mine's stopped too," said Mr. Multiple, inspecting it. "That's rum. Can I have forgotten to wind it? No matter; we shall be sure to hear a clock strike. Look—

while you were at the dressmaker's I bought this guide-book. Shall we visit the market, or the assembly rooms, or the museum?''

"All of 'em!" said Dido. "Let's be off!"

Mr. Multiple had already studied the map of the town, and he was able to lead them directly to the main market. This, not far away, was a glassed-over series of arcades where dozens of stalls sold fruit, toys, salt, barley, tobacco, vegetables, gaily decorated leather pouches, harnesses and saddles, meat, fifes and guitars, fur caps with decorated ear flaps, straw hats, woven woolen materials, and small animals made from clay and straw.

"I'll buy some of those for my sister's children," said Mr. Windward, halting by a display of the latter. "Which do you think they'd like, Miss Dido?"

Dido, inspecting the animals, began to be conscious of the stall holder's angry stare.

"Hah! Very fine for the gringo child to choose her-self a toy!" the woman said harshly. "Play! Play while you may, foreign brat! *Vae pueris!* My daughter was taken by the aurocs, and so was my sister's child. Think yourself lucky you don't stay here long, milkface!"

A warning glance from Lieutenant Windward pre-vented Dido making any retort; he quickly bought a couple of clay llamas and hurried his companions away. Looking back, Dido saw the woman spit after them furiously, then fling her shawl overhead and sit rocking herself to and fro.

"Poor thing," Dido muttered. "You can't blame her for being a bit aggly. It's a rum do about them aurocs, though, ain't it, Mr. Windward? We keep hearing about 'em—it's a wonder we ain't seen more of 'em, seeing they swipe so many young 'uns." She glanced up apprehensively but nothing was to be seen overhead save a couple of condors wheeling about.

They inspected the museum, an ancient Roman building not far from the palace. Over its door was a woman's head carved in stone, with a very beautiful face and snakes for hair. The lieutenant said she was a Gorgon.

"What's that, Mr. Windward?"

"A kind of witch. She could turn people to stone."

"Wonder she gets any sleep at night with them all hissing round the pillow," said Dido.

The museum contained the Thirteen Treasures of Britain, which the settlers of New Cumbria had brought with them at the time of the exodus from that land—the Basket, Sword, Drinking Horn, Chariot, Halter, Knife, Cauldron, Whetstone, Garment, Pan, Platter, Chess-Board, and Mantle—but it was plain that the museum staff were not too active in caring for their treasures. The sword was missing from its scabbard, the basket was worm-eaten, the garment and mantle were alive with moths, and the other exhibits were in equally poor condition.

"What a lot of fusty old stuff," said Dido. When Mr. Multiple drew her attention to an arrow on the wall and a sign that said, "To the Zoological Garden containing the Four Ancient Creatures, Ousel of Cilgwri, etc. Admission One Bezant," she said, "Don't let's see any more old things. Let's go somewhere else."

They were much more impressed by the Roman baths. These were still in regular use, and indeed both Lieutenant Windward and Mr. Multiple declared their intention of returning for a dip later in the day, since the Hotel Sydney's plumbing left almost everything to be desired. The visitors saw a series of immense chambers, five baths of varying heat, two swimming pools of warm pale-green water with wreaths of steam rising, sweat rooms, cool rooms, and robing rooms, all roofed with pale vaulted stone. The keeper of the baths informed them that the water was heated by the nearest volcano, Mount Damyake—so, indeed, was the whole town, by means of a series of underground ducts.

"Damn Ache don't do a very good job then," grumbled Dido. "Back there in the sweat room was the first time I been warm today."

"Mount Damyake is thought to be cooling down," explained the keeper. "In a hundred years, who knows? The city of Bath may be too cold for its inhabitants to remain here. Some of the people think that the queen (heaven smile on Her Royal Mercy) uses too much of Damyake's heat for her own personal convenience."

"Why, what does she use it for?" asked Mr. Multiple.

But the keeper, evidently feeling that he had been indiscreet, would say no more.

The travelers went on to inspect the pump room, where they drank a glass of very nasty mineral water, which Dido said tasted like unwashed ducks' feet, and Mr. Multiple kindly bought her a large Bath bun. Then, since they could not discover the correct time (there appeared to be no clocks in the city of Bath), they returned across the Rialto Bridge and so back along Pulteney Road to the hotel, observing for the first time the handsome public gardens in the oval circus behind the Sydney, which contained two sham castles, two Chinese cast-iron bridges, some thatched umbrellas (in case it was ever warm enough to sit out of doors), and a rotunda, besides a great many cactus plants.

At the hotel, Captain Hughes was walking up and down impatiently by the big hourglass in the vestibule. (Strangely enough, all members of the party who possessed timepieces had discovered that these had simultaneously come to a stop at the moment when they were brought into the city of Bath. Captain Hughes, rather perplexed, had attributed this phenomenon to the altitude.)

"Matters are in excellent train," he told them. "I have had a most affable message from Queen Ginevra, instructing me to wait on her at two."

"What about the togs?" Dido said. "My clobber, I mean."

"Miss Twite, *please,*" said the captain. "Do not refer to your wearing apparel in that fashion. The garments have been sent home, and the chambermaid will assist you in robing yourself. A nuncheon has been sent to your chamber; you had best repair there directly and set about making yourself presentable. Do not omit to wash your face!"

"What did the doc say about Mr. Holystone?"

The captain's brow clouded. "He is not certain; he believes it possible that the man is merely suffering from altitude sickness and hopes that a day or two should show some improvement in his condition. I must say," Captain Hughes said aggrievedly, "it is deuced inconvenient having him laid up just now. Mr. Multiple, pray mount guard over Miss Twite's door while she is being appareled. We want no untoward incidents."

Dido went glumly to her room, where a surly black-haired girl was waiting to help. She had also brought up a nuncheon tray on which was a beefsteak as large as a paving stone, enough pepper-and-potato stew to feed a choir, and a dozen peaches.

"Blimey! I can't eat all that," said Dido, who was full of Bath bun. "I'd get the hiccups while I was making my curtsey to Her Royalty. I'll eat the peaches —would you like the rest?"

Waiting for no second invitation, the chambermaid swallowed the soup in three gulps and the steak in six enormous bites. Thawing, then, somewhat, in her manner, she helped Dido don petticoat, dress, slippers, and stockings.

"I don't half look a sight," Dido said, viewing herself uncertainly in the mildewed glass as the chambermaid brushed her hair.

"You go see Su Merced—Queen Ginevra?" inquired the girl timidly, pronouncing it *Huineffra*.

"Yes—worse luck! It wouldn't be so bad if I didn't have to curtsey." Dido attempted a bob, but since she was wholly unaccustomed to long skirts, the attempt was a complete failure; she fell over sideways, and her tiara rolled under the bed. Curiously enough, the chambermaid did not find this in the least amusing. She was gazing at Dido in something like horror. She made the sign that Silver Taffy had on the *Thrush*— a figure eight like a pair of spectacles in the air, done with fingers and thumbs.

"Go see queen," said the girl hoarsely, "she look at you through her glasses, you get caught by aurocs soon after. In two, five days."

"How do you know?" Dido tried to sound calm about it, but she had a nasty crawling sensation down her backbone.

"Everyone know. *Nemine dissentientae*. Everyone say."

"Everyone say." Despite her fear, Dido could not help feeling impatient, too—the girl's excited whisper and staring eyes made what she said seem less, not more, believable. "Who says?"

"Many, many people."

"Have *you* ever *seen* an auroc?"

"Jeeminy! No me!" For the first time, the chambermaid looked cheerful. "When I am five my mater and pater send me work in silver mines. No aurocs there! I stay work underground till I am fifteen. Work in silver mines is not nice"—she exhibited her hands and arms, blackened and scarred from heavy work—"but is better than aurocs."

"Young 'uns of *five* work in the mines?"

The girl nodded.

"Many, many! Safe there—if no get squashed by truck."

"How many get squashed by truck?"

The girl shrugged. "Some. *Suum cuique periculum*. Danger anywhere."

Here the conversation was interrupted by a melancholy mew. It seemed to come from under the bed.

"That's funny," said Dido. "Everywhere I go, I keep hearing cats. Thought I heard one all night."

She knelt down to retrieve her fallen tiara, and found herself looking into a pair of desperate golden eyes.

"Well, I'll be bothered! It's another like Dora, Where the blue blazes do they all come from? Well,

step along out, then; no sense lurking in under there!"
said Dido, and she put down the plate with the gristly
end of the beefsteak.

In four famished bites the cat had demolished the
unappetizing fragment, then eagerly licked out the
peppery stew bowl.

"Ay-ay-ay!" whispered the chambermaid, watching
this with startled eyes. "Old Grandmother Sul herself
be watching over you, gringo *puella!*"

"Who? Who is Grandmother Sul?"

The girl, without answering, bent over the cat,
which was still engaged in pushing the soup bowl over
the cactus matting, and deftly twitched out a long,
silvery whisker from each cheek.

"What d'you do *that* to the poor thing for?"

But the chambermaid, knotting and twisting the
whiskers together, plaited them into a loop and slipped
it over Dido's index finger. "There! You keep on under
glove, not nohow take off, maybe you safe. Maybe not!
Cum grano salis . . ." And, making the figure-eight
sign again, she snatched up the dishes and ran from
the room.

"Humph! What'll we do with you, puss, eh? Poor
thing, you're still half starved. Ribs like railings. Well,
what do you know—you got a collar too? And *another*
page from that pesky dictionary? New Cumbria," muttered Dido, detaching the little packet, "ain't *half* full
of eddicated cats!"

This cat's page, after informing Dido that a cough
was "a convulsion of the lungs, vellicated by some
serosity," had another message in dark brown ink.

For mercy's sake help me. Only air for 3 days.
Elen.

Dido studied this appeal with compressed lips and knitted brow, then, as a double thump sounded on the door, tucked it into one of her white elbow-length gloves.

"Miss Twite? Are you ready?" came Multiple's voice. "The captain is calling for you!"

"I'm a-coming, I'm a-coming," said Dido hastily. "Tell His Whiskers to keep calm."

And, hitching up her draperies of silver-spangled mull, she opened the door.

"Reckon you'll have to help me downstairs, though, Mr. Mully, or I'm liable to go tail over tip."

"Very proper," approved Captain Hughes at the foot of the stairs, observing Dido's cautious descent, assisted by the midshipman. "Now you look just as you ought! Mind those skirts! I have a carriage waiting."

He wrapped a shawl of white vicuna wool round Dido and put her in the carriage, where Mr. Windward was already seated, looking stiff and uncomfortable. Both the captain and his first lieutenant were rigged up very fine in full-dress uniform, with knee breeches, gold-laced jackets, epaulets, cocked hats, feathers, and swords, which clanked a great deal and tended to trip the wearers.

"Glad _I_ ain't coming," murmured Mr. Multiple with a grin, passing Dido her fan.

"Keep an eye on Mr. Holy! And feed the cat in my room!" she called, just before the footman slammed the door.

6

The short distance between the Sydney Hotel and the revolving palace on its island was swiftly accomplished, and the carriage drew up before a flight of black marble steps, flanked, on either side, by three gray-clad, silver-plumed sentries. The coachman opened the door, Dido was lifted out, and the small party from H.M.S. *Thrush* ascended the steps.

"Oops!" said Dido. "There ain't no front door."

"I reckon we have to wait here till it comes round," said Lieutenant Windward.

"Vexatious!" muttered the captain. "It is hardly dignified to be obliged to stand on the doorstep like petitioners!"

The rotating silver building had its back to them, and they were forced to wait five or six minutes until the entrance slowly crept round to where they were standing. Meanwhile Dido glumly studied her reflection in the glistening walls and hoped that the palace was not full of aurocs; in her long skirts, she thought, it would be very hard to give them the slip.

"Does the building come to a stop so that we may enter?" Captain Hughes asked one of the sentries. The man shook his head and laid a finger on his lips. Irritably the captain put his question to another sentry, who made the same gesture.

"I fancy they are all deaf and dumb," murmured the lieutenant in an undertone. He shivered a little. All of Bath was cold, but a particularly icy wind seemed to whistle round the palace. Then he added, "Here comes the entrance, sir—and I don't believe it *is* going to stop. We had best lose no time, or we shall have another ten minutes to wait while the plaguey thing takes another turn."

"Dem'd ridiculous arrangement!" grumbled Captain Hughes. However, pressing his lips together, he strode into one quadrant of the revolving door as it came opposite him, calling over his shoulder as he did so, "Step lively, Miss Twite! Do as I do!"

Dido skipped after him into the next quadrant, hitching up her skirts and losing a portion of her egret's-plume fan, which caught in the door and snapped off. Better that than my finger, she thought. This twirling door don't half buzz round quick! It's like the giddy-go-round at the Battersea Fun Fair.

Lieutenant Windward just had time to follow Dido before the whole entrance moved out of reach.

"It is really a capital notion," he remarked as he emerged on the inside. "It means the queen never has more than about three visitors at one time. I wonder what motive power causes it to revolve?"

"Maybe heat from Mount Damyake," suggested Dido. "Like the old cove at the baths was telling us.

Praps that's what drives the whole twiddledum palace round; and that's why folk reckon the queen's using up too much steam."

The lieutenant looked at her with surprise, and a touch of respect.

"Well thought, young 'un! I believe you may have hit the nail on the head."

Captain Hughes was handing his credentials—a scroll tied with red ribbon—to a bearded, white-robed official, who beckoned the visitors forward.

They were directed to wait in a gloomy, windowless reception room lit by blue gas flares and furnished with hard chairs and a couple of ottomans covered in gray velvet. The room was stuffy and smelled rather disagreeably—of salt fish, Dido thought. Hanging on the walls, arranged in circles, squares, and figure-eight patterns, were a number of objects the size and shape of coconuts; Dido, wandering over to inspect these (she did not like to sit down for fear of creasing her skirts), discovered that they were model heads, gray-brown and shiny, with the hair, on those that had any, braided into little tails, the whites of the eyes painted pink, silver rings set in ears and noses, and the lips sewn together by a kind of blanket stitch. Dido did not care for them at all; the pink-colored eyes made them look very watchful. After studying them for a few minutes she murmured to Lieutenant Windward: "I reckon they're *real* heads! Mr. Holy said summat about coves in the forest as shrinks people's heads."

Lieutenant Windward said distastefully, "I have certainly *heard* of such practices, but is it likely the queen would display the objects in her palace? A most uncivilized adornment!"

"Mr. Holystone said the lips are sewn up to prevent

the ghosts getting out and haunting anybody," Dido told him.

Lieutenant Windward threw up his eyes at such superstitious folly.

Captain Hughes had time to become exceedingly impatient before they were summoned to the queen's presence; he strode up and down the small room a great many times, irritably kicking his sword aside. At last a gray-clad majordomo came to lead them to the throne room. They had to ascend a high, wide stair, and walk along a very extensive, curving gallery, which appeared to follow the outer circumference of the circular palace. At last they reached the entrance to a dimly lit, pillared hall, quite fifty yards long.

In the middle of this chamber they were intercepted by a group of white-bearded, white-robed dignitaries, who bowed politely and introduced themselves.

"Manuel Fluellen, at your service, Her Majesty's vicar general."

"Daffyd Gomez, Her Majesty's grand inquisitor."

"José Glendower, advocate of Her Majesty's tribunal."

"Juan Jones, Her Majesty's physician and chirurgeon."

These men wore chaplets of silver oak leaves, and carried white wands of office tipped with mistletoe.

"Happy to meet you, gentlemen," grunted Captain Hughes. "I trust that Her Majesty is in good health and still prepared to enlighten me as to her wishes?"

"She is so, yes indeed," said Jones, the physician. "But I should impress on you, sir, that Her Mercy, being now decidedly elderly, should on no account be thwarted, overset, crossed, distressed, or in any way unduly excited."

Captain Hughes grunted again. "Ha! Hm! You need not agitate yourself on that head, sir—I know how to deal with elderly females, *and* persons of high degree."

"There is a further point, sir." Now it was the turn of the grand inquisitor, whose beard was even longer and whiter than that of the physician. He drew Captain Hughes to one side and talked at some length and earnestly, in a low tone, his mouth very close to the captain's ear. Upon the face of the latter, as he listened, Dido began to observe an obstinate and wary expression, as if Captain Hughes intended to let nobody persuade him to do anything against his own judgment; and after a few minutes he said shortly, "Sir, I am here as the emissary of King James's government, and must act as I believe His Majesty's government would require me to. But do not be anxious"—as the other man began to protest or remonstrate "—I will not put Her Majesty into a fidget. I can be diplomatic when it is necessary, I assure you!"

"It is not precisely *that*, sir," the grand inquisitor said smoothly, as the captain began to turn away from him. "It is just that, sometimes, Her Mercy's wishes do not accord with the best interests of the—"

"Be easy, man! I will undertake no foolish capers, I promise you!"

But the grand inquisitor was evidently by no means easy.

Dido could see that. His face, as he moved after the captain, wore a dark expression of disappointment and calculation that boded little good to the success of the British mission.

Best watch out for *him*, Dido thought. They all looks to me as if they'd come from a thieves' kitchen. I'd not buy a pennorth of brass nails from any of them;

but that inquisitor's the loosest screw in the bunch, or my name ain't Dido Twite.

Captain Hughes, now detaching himself from the court officials, strode hastily on ahead of them toward the end of the hall, so that Dido and the lieutenant had to hurry to keep up with him. Dido, glancing from side to side, observed that gray gauze draperies dangled in the gaps between the pillars all the way down the long room; the chamber appeared to be empty, but any number of persons could be hiding behind the curtains.

At the far end of the throne room was a daybed set on a dais approached by three steps.

The daybed was hung about with more of the gray gauzy draperies, and on it, leaning against a great many cushions, lolled a lady whose plump and billowy shape was to some extent concealed by her loose, filmy white garments.

The four officials bowed almost to the ground.

"Your Mercy—may I present Captain Hughes of the Britannic Navy," said the vicar general.

The queen impatiently gestured Messrs. Glendower, Gomez, Fluellen, and Jones to retire out of earshot, which they did, looking disgruntled about it. Then she said, "My dear Captain Hughes! So *very* kind of you to come all this way. I am delighted to meet you. Pray consider yourself quite at home in my capital."

Her voice was high, light, and fatigued.

"Ma'am," said Captain Hughes gruffly. He climbed the three steps, went down on one knee, and kissed the hand she extended. Then, rising, he added, "I have the honor to present Lieutenant Windward, of His Majesty King James's sloop *Thrush;* and—harrumph —this is Miss Dido Twite from—er—Battersea."

Dido curtseyed. It was not one of her more success-
ful efforts, but Queen Ginevra appeared to find no
fault with it. She turned her protuberant light-gray
eyes on Dido. The fixity of her stare made Dido wish
to wriggle, but she could feel Captain Hughes's sharp
and critical eye on her, too, and tried to keep still.

"A child from England!" breathed the queen. "What
a *remarkable* coincidence!" She did not explain her
words, but continued to study Dido until even Captain
Hughes became a trifle fidgety.

"Er—ahem!" he said. "Understand there is some way
in which I can be of service to Your Majesty. Only too
glad to oblige in whatever it is—do my possible, that
is to say."

"Ah . . . yes," answered Queen Ginevra, on a faint
sigh, as if she had dragged her thoughts back from
some immense distance, from something that was very
pleasantly occupying her attention. "Yes, you can help
me, Captain. Listen, and I will explain."

She did not invite the captain to be seated; indeed,
there was nowhere to sit, so he and Lieutenant Windward continued standing in front of the dais. Dido,
unbidden, squatted down on one of the steps, and
earned a scowl and a head shake from the captain;
but he did not dare interrupt what the queen was
saying.

"You must be aware—my dear Captain—of the history of New Cumbria's settlement—that the founding
fathers sailed here after the unfortunate outcome of
the Battle of Dyrham in 577 A.D.?"

Captain Hughes nodded, and the queen went on:
"In the course of that battle, as you will recall, my
husband King Arthur received a number of wounds,
one very dangerous, and was ferried away over the

water of Arianrod to be healed of his hurts on the
island of Avalon by his aunts, the Cornwall sisters."

At the queen's words Captain Hughes turned first
extremely pale, then bright red. He cast one nerve-
racked sideways glance at Lieutenant Windward, who
was standing, equally red faced, staring rigidly ahead.

"Your h-h-*husband*, ma'am? King *Arthur*? I'm afraid
I don't quite—"

"My husband, King Arthur," she repeated. Her high,
fatigued voice held a hint of irritation. "To be healed
of his wounds in the isle of Avalon."

"But—but good gad, ma'am, that would make
you—"

"Thirteen hundred years old," the queen said coldly.
"You do not think I would be such an undutiful wife
as to die before my husband returned to me?"

Captain Hughes did not look as if he had any
thoughts on the subject at all. He stared at the queen
with glazed eyes.

Dido stared, too. Never before had she seen a lady
thirteen hundred years old. Queen Ginevra certainly
was very fat. She must have been getting fatter and
fatter all those hundreds of years, Dido reflected. Don't
look as if she walked about much. Or went out in the
fresh air.

The queen's skin was pale and soft, like white bread
dough. She lolled back wearily against her pillows.

Lucky she ain't bald, Dido thought.

An abundance of limp, rather greasy yellowish-white
hair was swept back from the queen's brow and con-
fined by a diamond-studded snood. Like Queen Victoria, she had very little chin, but her eyes, large as
poached eggs, made up for that—they were extremely
sharp and gave the impression that they observed all

that went on, not only in front of the queen but also to the side and behind her. They observed, but they held no expression; they were like birds' eyes. The short fingers of her small, fat hands were loaded with rings.

"The Battle of Dyrham was fought in the winter," Queen Ginevra went on. "After my husband had been conveyed away by his aunts, the lake, Arianrod, very fortunately froze. So we were able to bring it with us to New Cumbria."

"Bring it with you, ma'am? The *lake*?"

"In the form of ice blocks—as ballast," she answered rather impatiently. "Had it been liquid, of course the task would have been by no means so easy."

"By no means," Captain Hughes echoed faintly.

"Of course you will appreciate the necessity of bringing the lake."

"Necessity, ma'am?"

"Do not be continually repeating my words like a gaby, Captain, I beg! Of course it was necessary that the lake should be here, because when my husband returns, it will be by boat *across that lake*—into which, as you will recall, the sword Caliburn had to be dropped in order to summon his aunts."

Captain Hughes remained silent. A light sweat had broken out on his brow.

"When we reached New Cumbria," Queen Ginevra went on, "a convenient location was found for the resiting of Lake Arianrod in a dried-up depression— doubtless volcanic in origin—between Mount Dam- yake and Mount Catelonde; and it has remained there ever since. Some of the peasants call it Dozmary; but of course Arianrod is its real name."

"Just so," said the captain.

"Now to my purpose," went on the queen. She looked sharply at Captain Hughes. "Captain—Lake Arianrod has been stolen!"

"Gracious me, ma'am," said the captain, after a slight pause.

"It shall be your task to get it back for me."

"Er," said the captain, after another slight pause, "I shouldn't wish to cast doubt, Your Majesty, but— but you are quite *sure* it has been stolen, and not—not merely trickled away—or evaporated—or sunk into the ground?"

"It has been stolen, Captain," repeated the queen coldly. "I am aware of the motive—and I am cognizant of the culprit."

"But how could somebody steal a *lake*?"

"Without the slightest difficulty. The lake frequently freezes, since it is at an altitude of fourteen thousand feet. It was purloined, and removed across my boundary, on llama back, in the form of ice blocks, just as we imported it from Camelot County in the first place."

"You did say, you did mean, ma'am," said the captain a little wildly, "I just wish to be sure I did not misunderstand—you *did* mean that your husband was the King Arthur who established the Round Table?"

Ignoring that, the queen said, "You had best peruse this impudent document!" From among the folds of her draperies, she produced a scroll, embossed with a crowned dragon, and handed it to Captain Hughes.

"You may read it aloud, for the benefit of your companions," she ordered.

Accordingly he read:

"Dear Cousin, Pendragon, and Ruler of New Cumbria. Since you have unlawfully and barbarously vio-

lated the treaty of alliance that binds our two countries
in that you have seized my child, heir, and most
precious treasure, be it known to you that I have seen
fit to retaliate by removing one and one half million
tons of inland water from the boundaries of our two
realms, which water I shall be prepared to return to
you immediately upon restoration to me of the said
princess, in good health and unharmed. Mabon, Rex."

"What is this about?" inquired Captain Hughes,
when he had digested the contents of the epistle.
"Mabon? I understand him to be the ruler of the
kingdom of Lyonesse, which lies to the southeast of
Your Majesty's dominions? But what is this heir, this
princess of whom he speaks?"

"Oh, it is all such nonsense! The most ridiculous,
laughable mistake!" exclaimed Queen Ginevra pettishly. "The idiot has taken it into his head to accuse
me of abducting his daughter. Why should I do such
a thing? And in consequence, he had the effrontery—
the outrageousness—to remove my sacred lake."

"There is no truth in his accusation?"

Queen Ginevra drew herself up. "Do you doubt me,
Captain?"

"Of course not, ma'am. Of course not. Who is this
princess?"

"Oh, the child's name is Helen, or Elaine—some
such thing."

Dido started. Instinctively she clenched her white-
gloved hand.

"The girl went to boarding school in England,"
Queen Ginevra continued. "As you may not have
heard, there is a popular, superstitious belief that the
climate of these latitudes is unsuitable for young
female persons. I believe the young lady attended a

seminary in Old Bath. Upon her return home, what happens? Undoubtedly her ship was captured by pirates—the South Seas hereabouts teem with them.

"And yet Mabon immediately accuses *me*! Without the least grounds for doing so! And has the impudence to steal my lake. Imagine it! Suppose this should be the time—and it might well be so, for the soothsayers have given this year as a particularly fortunate, auspicious period—when my dearest husband, my dear *Quondam Rex*, should be due to return? What would happen if the lake were not in its place? The thought is not to be borne!"

A very strange mixture of expressions blended and battled in the queen's countenance: resentment, wistfulness, anger, coyness, grief, pride, self-satisfaction. Dido did not care for any of them. She supposed she ought to feel sorry for a deserted wife who had been sorrowing so many hundreds of years for her lost husband—but how *could* you feel sorry for anybody quite so fat?

Besides, she oughter got used to doing without him by now, Dido thought.

"What did you wish *me* to do in the matter, ma'am?" Captain Hughes sounded exceedingly glum.

"Well," Queen Ginevra replied, in a tone that was unexpectedly cheerful and chatty, "I *had* originally intended you to go and reason with King Mabon, Captain Hughes, and, if necessary, threaten armed intervention by British forces; my own army is, unfortunately, sadly depleted. But since you have brought your charming young friend to see me, I have been visited by a much better notion." She fixed her pale eyes on Dido.

"You shall go to King Mabon, Captain; I will give

you a safe-conduct across the frontier through the Pass of Nimue. Young Miss Twite there shall accompany you, and you will inform King Mabon, who will know no better, that you are returning his daughter to him!"

"*What?*" gasped the captain, who could hardly believe his ears. "What, ma'am? You cannot be serious! You *cannot* intend the substitution of that young person there for—for the missing princess?"

"Why not, pray?" said the queen coldly. "The princess has been away at boarding school for ten years. *He* will never know the difference. Why, you could easily pretend to be his daughter, could you not, child? Of course," she added, with what was evidently meant to be a winning smile, "I should greatly prefer that you remain with me, as my dear little guest—but you would do this small service for me, would you not? You need not remain with King Mabon for long, you know—merely until he has restored my property. Then you can run away and return to me here, and we shall have such splendid times together!"

Dido gaped at the queen. So many snags in the plan presented themselves to her that she did not know which to mention first. Meanwhile the captain was spluttering like a firecracker.

"But—but—but, ma'am! That would be rank deceit —fraud—imposture—knavery! It is not to be thought of!"

"No?" Queen Ginevra turned her protruding eyes on him. The look in them was now far from friendly.

"I could by *no* means countenance such sharp practice in the name of King James's government, or my masters at the admiralty."

The queen sharply clapped her hands. Immediately a dozen gray-clad guards appeared from behind the curtains at the side of the hall. Queen Ginevra gestured toward Captain Hughes.

"Take him to the Wen Pendragon prison," she said. "He may cool his heels there, until, perhaps, he has second thoughts."

Captain Hughes was dragged away, struggling, cursing, and protesting loudly. "I object! This is an outrage! An act of war! Disgraceful detention of a diplomatic official! One of King James's subjects! Monstrous! Intolerable!" His voice died away in the distance.

Ignoring him, the queen looked thoughtfully at Dido.

"As for you, child . . ." Ginevra reflected for a little, as if undecided. Then she said, "You may have two days to decide. If you are prepared to go on this mission to King Mabon for me—I daresay that young man would escort you?"

Dido and Lieutenant Windward eyed one another uncertainly; after a moment Dido slightly jerked her head, and he answered, "Y-yes, ma'am," in a faltering voice.

"Very well! If you undertake the mission for me— if King Mabon returns my lake—your captain shall be released. Now you may leave me. In forty-eight hours— or sooner, of course—I shall expect your decision."

Dido found voice enough to croak, "Might we go look at this here lake, missus—Your High and Mighty? Where it was, I mean? Jist to make sure it has really gone, like?"

"You doubt me?" asked the queen formidably.

"No—no, ma'am! But—you never know—somebody mighta put it back by this time."

"Most unlikely! But, in any case, if you travel to the

court of Mabon in Lyonesse, you must cross the frontier at the head of Lake Arianrod, so you will see it
then. You will need a safe-conduct to show to the
guardian of the Temple of Sul, which commands
the Pass of Nimue. If you agree to go, I will see that the
grand inquisitor supplies you with the necessary pass."

"Thank you, ma'am."

Mr. Jones, the queen's physician, now approached
and, deferentially but firmly, wrapped a black bandage
round the queen's plump arm, pressed a pigskin bulb,
and studied the motions of a small dial.

"You should rest, Your Mercy," he said. "The audi-
ence with the gringo captain has tired you more than
you are aware."

"Oh, very well, very well," snapped the queen, who
did not appear particularly tired, so far as Dido could
judge. However, she accepted a dishful of pills—red,
yellow, green, black, and pink—which the doctor
handed her, swallowed them with a little milk, and
said to Dido, "You may depart, child. On your decision
rests whether you see your captain again."

The atmosphere in Bath Palace was stifling, warm as
a conservatory. Despite this, Dido felt icy cold as she
walked away from the dais; Queen Ginevra's glance
seemed to pierce like an oyster knife between her
shoulder blades. It was a comfort to have Lieutenant
Windward's firm clasp on her arm. He was walking at
a measured pace, trying to avoid undignified signs of
nervous hurry. Dido had leisure to observe that the
side hangings were in fact spiderwebs—huge, sagging
curtains of them, swinging from roof to floor. They
sparkled, here and there, with precious stones, diamonds perhaps. And the spiders, occasionally to be

seen lurking in thickety knots of web, were as large and hairy as coconuts.

In the curving gallery outside they found Daffyd Gomez, the grand inquisitor, waiting to intercept them.

"Here comes more trouble," breathed Dido, as the venerable white-bearded figure extended a skinny hand.

"Er—young man! Miss!" The inquisitor's voice was conspiratorial; he gave them a sly smile.

"Sir?" Lieutenant Windward's tone was sharp with worry. He was a capable, conscientious young man, a good second-in-command, but not used to dealing with such a crisis as this.

"I know—I know—you are in a pucker about your captain! Small blame to you. Her Mercy is so impulsive. That was what I tried to warn him, but he would not be advised. Now, doubtless, he is sorry. But listen to me: Do not *you* be so hotheaded. Take my advice. *Pretend* to agree to the queen's mission—then come to me. Will ye do that?"

"Not really go to King Mabon, you mean?" Windward said cautiously.

The grand inquisitor shook his head.

"Mabon has not taken the lake—gracious me, no! Y Diawl, he would not do such a thing. It will have sunk away from natural causes. She will only make us into a laughingstock with such a message. Their queen is cracked in the head, Mabon will be saying. A great pity that would be."

"But—" Dido began. It seemed plain the grand inquisitor had no idea of her part in the plan: the queen's intended deception of King Mabon. Gomez looked at her severely.

"Hold your tongue, child! Little girls should be seen and not heard."

"But what about Captain Hughes?" Windward asked doubtfully.

"Leave that to me. I can talk the old lady round, by and by. Second thoughts she will be having, after a day or two. Just now, best to leave her alone. *Quieta non movere.*"

"I see," Windward said. He did not sound convinced. "Well—thank you, sir. We will be sure to remember your advice."

Gomez gave them another cunning look, then glided away round the curve and out of sight.

It was a relief to descend the stair, to go out through the revolving door into the bitter cold of the palace yard—a sharp but welcome contrast to the steamy heat inside.

Neither of the pair spoke until they were safely in the carriage, when Lieutenant Windward exclaimed, "What the *devil* do we do now?"

"Think hard," said Dido. "Talk it over with the others—somewhere we can't be listened to. I don't trust anybody in this murky town. Oh," she sighed, "it *would* be handy if Mr. Holy were a bit better and could talk sense when we gets back."

"That queen is a regular shocker!" muttered Windward, who could not get over the horror of seeing his commanding officer dragged away so helplessly at the whim of a fat old woman. After a moment he added, "It's rum, though—she seemed to take quite a shine to *you.*"

7

A council of war was held in Dido's bedroom at the Sydney Hotel. The participating members were Lieutenant Windward, Mr. Multiple, Dido, Plum, and Noah Gusset. Mr. Holystone had fallen into a high fever; the doctor was perplexed by his condition, which did not respond to treatment.

"All we can do is wait," he said, not too happily or confidently. "I am afraid the air of Bath does not agree with your friend."

"You mean to tell me this old girl believes she's King Arthur's *widow*?" Mr. Multiple incredulously demanded of the two who had visited the palace. "Round Table King Arthur? That one?"

"That's what she said. Didn't she, Miss Twite? Seemed to believe it, too. She's clean gone in her wits, of course; rats in the garret. But the thing is, what are we going to do? She's got Cap'n Hughes in the lock-up; for all we know, she's liable to chop his head off, or have it shrunk, like those ones in the waiting room, if we don't keep her sweet."

"Yes," said Multiple very doubtfully, "but even if Miss Twite goes to this King Mabon, and lets on to be his daughter, how do we know *that*'ll help the cap'n? It sounds to me like a tottyheaded scheme. First, Miss Twite doesn't *look* like any princess—axing your pardon, Miss Twite."

"Oh, call me Dido, can't you," said Dido impatiently. "O' course I don't look like a princess."

"So it's odds but King Mabon'd twig our wheedle right from the start. And then *we'll* be rolled up too. Probably thrown into jail in Lyonesse. And he won't give back the old lady's lake."

"Supposing he *did* steal it," said the lieutenant skeptically.

Dido thought of the mysterious procession she had seen through the captain's telescope—all those loaded llamas slowly making their way over the mountain-tops with their heavy burdens. But wait, she said to herself, I saw that *after* Cap'n Hughes had the message about the theft. Still, maybe llamas travel very slowly—specially with a heavy load, and maybe going only at night. Maybe it would take them two, three weeks to go from New Cumbria to Lyonesse?

"I reckon the lake *was* stolen," she said slowly.

"If it was stole, then King Mabon oughta return it," said Noah Gusset with stolid justice.

Plum, surprising everybody, said, "Mayhap she *do* be King Arthur's widow!"

They all stared at him, and he turned brick-red, but went on, "When I were a boy, in Usk, my gramma'd be telling us about King Arthur. Come back one day, she said he would, no matter how long. Sleeping in the mountain, him, till his time be come, with his knights around him. An' when his time be come, he'll pull his sword outa the rock again, an' put on his golden crown."

"Oh, flummery!" said Lieutenant Windward irritably. "Anyway—even if that were so—how could his widow survive him for *thirteen hundred years*?"

"The old medico Cap'n Hughes fetched in for Mr. Holystone said the climate up here was supposed to be devilish healthy," said Mr. Multiple.

"Not for poor Holystone it ain't!"

"Nor for all the young gels as gets took by the aurocs," said Dido. Then she stopped short. A perfectly horrible idea had come into her head. It was so strange, and so frightening, that she did not like to utter it aloud. Instead she said slowly. "I've had a kind of a notion. I believe I know where King Mabon's daughter might be."

They all stared at her in amazement.

"You *do*?" said Mr. Multiple. "How can that be?"

"I better not say here." Dido glanced round the room. "I don't trust this place above half." She looked under the bed. "What happened to the cat?" she asked Mr. Multiple.

"It dashed out when I opened the door."

"I reckon we'd better play along with the old lady a bit," Dido went on in a very low tone. "Say we'll go visit this King Mabon. That can't do no harm. Then we'll get a pass from the grand whatshisname, saying we're allowed to climb Mount Dammyache and Mount Catelonde and the other one."

Mount Arrabe, she thought.

. . .

Captain Hughes was thrust into a smallish stone-walled room, and the door slammed to behind him. He heard the rattle of bolts. For a moment or two he stood blinking (his head had been thrust into a black bag during his removal from Bath Palace); when he recovered his sight, he recognized a familiar figure in the small, plump man sitting dolefully on the floor by the window, with his buttons undone, his hair disheveled, and his cravat hanging in a loose tangle. He did not look up at the captain's unceremonious entry, but continued staring miserably at his own outspread fingers.

"Mr. Brandywinde! Upon my soul! I had thought you were upon the high seas! Do you mean to tell me that that hag of a queen imprisoned you too?"

"I don't mean to tell you anything," retorted Mr. Brandywinde moodily. "What's the use of talking? Oh, my hands, my poor hands!"

And he hunched his shoulders, turning his back rudely on the captain, who felt justifiably irritated. He had enough troubles of his own without being snubbed by this wretched little twopenny-halfpenny fellow.

Ignoring Mr. Brandywinde's sulks, Captain Hughes inspected the room, walked across to the window, and glanced out indifferently at the magnificent prospect of Bath encircled in its ring of volcanoes (the window was very high; they were at the top of the Wen Pendragon tower, which, in its turn, was at the top of Beechen Cliff). Then, discovering a second door, which stood ajar, the captain went through it into a second room, where he found a large loom, already strung with the warp for a carpet or a piece of tapestry. A door beyond the loom led on, and he discovered a circular suite of rooms, all interconnected and furnished with various materials for indoor occupation: a piano, a kiln and quantity of clay, paints, canvas, wool and needles, mathematical instruments, sewing equipment, canes, rushes, pipes, flutes; there was even a harp. What the captain did *not* find was any other exit apart from the bolted door through which he had been thrust by his captors.

"What the deuce is this place—a college?" he demanded, returning through a door opposite that from which he had started. "Or does Queen Ginevra propose to keep her prisoners at work weaving carpets?"

The British agent looked up at him with dismal bloodshot eyes.

"Oh, no," said Brandywinde. "She don't give a rap what happens to *us*. Unless we're some use to her. No, this ain't a college. It's a prison. But it's also King Arthur's castle. Where he's supposed to be residing till he's healed of his wound."

Forgetting his sulks, he imparted this information in a tone of condescension.

"Oh, what fustian!" exclaimed the captain irritably. "He is not really dwelling here, I collect?"

"O' course he ain't! But a good few o' the townspeople believe he is, an' that suits the queen's book an' keeps them contented. Every month or so she buys another set o' flutes or some wool and a crochet hook 'just to keep His Majesty diverted during his illness.' That's what all that clobber is in the other rooms."

"The jailors know it's not so."

"Ay, but they're all dumb."

"Why does she keep up the pretense?" asked the captain, shivering despite himself. "Does she really believe it herself?"

"Not that he is here. . . . Oh, who knows *what* she believes?" said Mr. Brandywinde morosely. "But whether she believes it herself or not, the rumor that he's in here is enough to keep King Mabon, or Ccaedmon of Hy Brasil, from invading and snapping up New Cumbria for themselves. A sick king is better than none."

"Oh. Ha. Hum. I see. Why the deuce didn't you tell me all this on the *Thrush*?" demanded the captain.

"Eh? Oh—well . . . I never thought you'd get as far as Bath Regis," Mr. Brandywinde said evasively. "And —and—about to set sail myself . . . preoccupied with plans for departure . . ."

"So why did you not embark? Why are you here in prison? And where are your wife and child?"

At these questions, to Captain Hughes's horror, his companion began to whimper distressingly. Tears coursed down his cheeks; he rocked himself to and fro.

"Oh, I am a wicked, wicked wretch!" he lamented in a thin, reedy voice. "I did wrong—dreadfully wrong— and now I'm being punished for it. And what's worst of all, I didn't even *benefit* from my wrongdoing. On the contrary! Oh, my hands! My poor hands!"

"Why, what the devil *did* you do?" inquired the captain without much sympathy.

"I sold that child of yours—Twitkin, Tweetkin, whatever the name is—to Lady Ettarde, for our passage money. Five hundred gold bezants."

"*Sold Miss Twite to Lady Ettarde?!*" exclaimed the captain in wrath and astonishment. "As a slave, do you mean? How can you have sold her? She was not yours to sell!"

"Oh, I shouldn't have done it, I know!" blubbered Brandywinde. "And anyway it didn't do me a particle of good—because those two cursed witches, Morgan and Vavasour, swore they never got their hands on the brat—the little monster escaped—they wouldn't give me the ready after all, the cheating harridans! So the boat sailed without us, and my wife and child are lost forever, and worst of all—"

"What became of your wife and child?"

But at this question Mr. Brandywinde went wholly to pieces, rocking, gulping, and gibbering. The only words Captain Hughes could distinguish among those he gasped out were, "Hunted to death—to death!"

A grisly thought flashed into the captain's mind.

"*Hunted*? Good God, you can't mean that hunt in the forest . . . ?"

"If she can't get 'em by other means, she'll send her hell hounds after them!"

Captain Hughes shuddered. He said, uncertainly, "Do, pray, man, pull yourself together." He had not the heart to ask any more questions; the subject was too dreadful. And no more sense could be got from Mr. Brandywinde for the time; the little agent wept and trembled and shivered, moaned that he wished he were dead, and then in the next breath voiced a longing to get his hands round the throat of Lady Ettarde and strangle her. "Only how could I?" he wailed. "My hands don't work anymore!"

"How do you mean?" demanded the captain, exasperated after an hour or so of these continual lamentations. "Your hands do not appear to be injured or crippled? I can see nothing amiss with them."

"But there is! She overlooked them. She was angry—said she would teach me to cheat her—not that I had any intention of cheating her—indeed, *indeed* I didn't!

She blew on my fingers, she said, 'From now on they will be as soft as paintbrushes; that will teach you not to bamboozle me'—and they are, they are—look at them! I cannot even tie my cravat."

"Oh, fiddlestick, man. This must be moonshine! A mere disorder of the senses. Let me see you tie your neckcloth."

But if it was a delusion, it was a very deep-seated one. Mr. Brandywinde fumbled limply and hopelessly with the linen neckpiece, as if his fingers had lost the power of obeying his will; and later, when one of the guards opened the door and thrust a basin of thin soup into the room, Captain Hughes was obliged, with disgusted reluctance, to feed his fellow captive like a baby, while Mr. Brandywinde whimpered and sobbed and snuffled, repeating that he was a wicked, wicked wretch and he wished that he were dead.

Early next morning Mr. Windward was informed that a letter had come from Her Mercy for Miss Dido Twite.

"Fancy her remembering my name!" said Dido, impressed, and she opened the note. It was an engraved card, bidding her present herself at the palace between the hours of four and five that afternoon.

"Humph!" said Windward suspiciously. "I hope there isn't anything skimble-skamble about this. What do you think Dido had best do?" he said to the others. They were all assembled, shivering, in the cactus gardens behind the Sydney Hotel.

"Tell you one thing—if I go, I ain't a-going to put on that fancy court rig again," said Dido. "I was perishing well frozen in it yesterday, except jist in the palace, an' it's turned a lot colder today, and I felt a fool in it. I'll jist wear my breeks and duffel jacket."

"Multiple and I had best come with you."

Somehow, without further discussion, it had been accepted by all of them that Dido had better keep the appointment. Lieutenant Windward went on, "Plum and Gusset can stay to keep an eye on poor Holystone."

"Let's take a dekko at that big map of Cumbria that hangs in the hotel lobby," said Dido. "Try and see how long it'll take us to get to King Mabon's place, if we go."

"What about the grand inquisitor, though?" said Mr. Multiple. "You say he didn't want us to go to Mabon."

"I don't trust him," said Lieutenant Windward. "He looked about as straightforward as an adder. I reckon he has his own ax to grind."

"So we diddle him too? Pretend we're just *pretending* to visit Mabon?"

"Just so's we don't get into a mux ourselves, about what we're a-going to do," said Dido.

"*I* think maybe we *should* visit Mabon," said Mr. Multiple. "Maybe he's a right 'un. There must be some good coves somewhere in these frampold parts. All we know about Mabon is, he took the lake because he had his daughter stole. You can't blame him for that."

The trio that set out for the palace that afternoon (they went by streetcar, in order to save money) were in very poor spirits. Dido was worried about Mr. Holystone, whose fever had somewhat abated, but who remained alarmingly pale and comatose. The other two were troubled about the fate of the captain. And who was to say that this unpredictable queen might not today take offense and throw the rest of them into jail?

Moreover, the air, as evening approached in this upland region, became icily, bitterly cold, and thinner than ever, so that they were continually obliged to gasp for breath as they crossed the palace yard; Mr. Multiple could not stop coughing, and Dido had a stitch in her side. They stopped in the middle of the big cobbled square while she clutched her chest with both hands, panting like a flounder. A black-cloaked, wooden-legged man, observing their predicament, advised Mr. Multiple to buy some rumirumi lilies. "*Cavendo tutus,*" he remarked.

"What the blazes are rumirumis?" coughed Multiple, drawing a long, difficult breath.

Without replying, the lame man (who wore such a high-piled stack of hats pulled low over his brow that his face was invisible) went to one of a row of flower stalls along the side of the square and purchased a handful of large, dark-pink trumpet-shaped blossoms with deeper splotches of color in the calyx and fibrous, spiny leaves. "You sniff those," he said, returning to the three travelers, "you soon better, *sic itur ad cura.*"

His remedy, indeed, proved remarkably efficacious. After sniffing at the big, velvety, potently scented trumpets for a few minutes, all three gringos found themselves able to breathe more easily.

"Must have oxygen in 'em," remarked the lieutenant. "Mighty useful kind of plant. Best take some with us up the mountains. Thank you indeed, sir," he said to the Cumbrian, who had started to limp away. "Pray allow me to reimburse you."

"It is nothing—*nihil, nihil,*" the man called back. "*Mens sana in corpore sano!*" His voice sounded familiar to Dido, who suddenly exclaimed, "I do believe it was that Bran again! Did you notice a white bird peering out o' one of his hats?"

But Bran, if it was he, had already vanished down a side street.

The glassy palace shone green and iridescent in the cold evening light. The sun was about to set behind the black cone of Mount Damyake, and the palace, slowly revolving on its islet, caught the last flash of the descending orb.

Lieutenant Windward, who had been studying Mr. Multiple's guidebook, informed them, "The palace is properly known as Caer Sisi."

"That just means Spinning Castle," said Mr. Multiple, who had studied the book, too.

They had to wait for a complete revolution of the palace to get in, and were half frozen by the time the bronze door with its whirling panels came round to face them.

"Quick!" said Windward, and they all hurled themselves through.

But once they were inside, Dido's escorts were not allowed to proceed any farther. They were firmly shown into the waiting room with the shrunken heads, and only Dido was permitted to climb the stair and continue into the great throne room where Queen Ginevra reclined on her daybed.

"Dearest child!" Her Majesty greeted Dido with a wide but languid smile. Like many of her subjects, Queen Ginevra had a set of silver teeth. "*So* kind of you to come so quickly in answer to my summons," she added, swallowing a handful of pills.

"I only come when you said," Dido replied matter-of-factly.

"*Touchingly* considerate. You guessed I might be feeling lonely. Ah, no one can guess, though, the depth of my loneliness. Yet people are so kind to me! They all indulge me—my dear, dear subjects!" The queen threw up her eyes in roguish amazement. Dido stood looking at her silently.

"Do take a seat, my dear. Ah . . . the steps . . . a trifle hard. . . . Let's see . . . perhaps a cushion . . ."

Groping feebly among her draperies, Queen Ginevra at length found a small gray bolster. Using as little energy as possible, she nudged it over the edge of the couch, so that it rolled down the steps and landed at Dido's feet. It appeared to be made of cobwebs. Rather gingerly, Dido sat on it.

"Now we can have a lovely gossip," said the queen. "I want to hear all about you."

What she really meant was that she wanted to talk about herself; she embarked on a long and rambling history of her childhood. "My father was a darling man—utterly devoted to me; but what chance did he have? None. Mother saw to it that he spent all his time at the Saxon wars, and he died when I was only seven. And she—I'm sorry to have to say it, but she had a really hateful nature. She could be a perfect fiend! I've always been sorry that Quondam—that's my pet name for Arthur, you know—and I didn't have any children. I longed for a child, to make up to her for all *I* had to suffer. . . .

"However, when my darling *rex futurus* comes back again, then perhaps . . ."

Her voice trailed away dreamily. Dido, staring at the queen, thought she seemed much too old to have children; although her skin was strangely smooth, as if constantly anointed with nourishing creams, there were deep, deep wrinkles round her eyes, and her puffy hands were spotted like two pale toads. There was something even odder about her today than on the previous visit—hazy, disjointed; Dido wondered if she was a trifle bosky.

"Do you think the king will come soon?" Dido inquired politely.

"I'm sure he will, dear; as soon as you get back my stolen lake for me, sweet child! And then we shall all be so happy! I hope you will stay with us and be our dear little guest. But in the meantime I want you to be a real friend to me; I can see how very perceptive you are, my love, and that is so rare! I *have* had various little friends among the Cumbrian children, but their intelligence is not of a high order."

"There don't seem to be many kids at all in this country," said Dido, wondering if this was why Queen Ginevra's army was depleted, and if the queen would say anything about aurocs, and if it would be wise to mention the safe-conduct across the frontier.

"Unfortunately . . . no . . . that is so. But when my dear Quondam returns, *all* will be different. Meanwhile, we have to count our little blessings as best we can," said Queen Ginevra, receiving a silver bowl of gruel from Dr. Jones, who handed it to her with a deep, ceremonious bow, casting a sharp glance at Dido as he did so. "My evening collation," the queen explained graciously to Dido. "It is such a treat to chat to a young friend while I partake of it; nothing is quite so tedious as to eat a nuncheon alone."

She dipped a spoon into the gruel, which was of a very thick consistency, and perfectly white.

"Bone porridge, dear," she informed Dido. "Prescribed by my doctor. When you have a life as full of trials and sorrows as mine, your meals must be light, but *very* sustaining."

The porridge (though it looked exceedingly nasty) reminded Dido that she was hungry, too.

"Your Royalty," she said, having glanced round to make sure that Dr. Jones was out of earshot (but who knew how many listeners were hiding behind the curtains?), "I reckon I will go on that errand to King Mabon—that is, if you still wants me to? So—if you'd jist give me that travel permit you said as how—"

The queen looked for a moment almost disappointed. What might have been a flash of irritation passed over her face.

"Permit?" she replied vaguely. "Permit, child?"

"To climb Mount Damyake and see where the lake was pinched from. And then," said Dido doggedly, "go on to King Mabon, like you said."

"You are sure you want to do that? It is so enjoyable," said the queen, "to have you here and get to know you. One so seldom gets to know anyone really well. A person that she knows well," she added obscurely, "can do one so much more good than a stranger."

This queen, thought Dido, is as nutty as old Great-Aunt Bella. Only thing to do is to humor her. Like Aunt Bella used to shout, "The end is coming!" on Battersea Bridge, and the only way to get her home was to agree.

"I can come back and see you again," she said. "After King Mabon's sent back your lake."

"Ah," said the queen. "True. But I wonder," she murmured to herself, "I wonder if I am being practical? Will Mabon return the lake? Or should I keep the bird in hand—two birds in hand—should I forget

about Arianrod? But then, my dear Quondam—sweet
Quondam—how could I be sure of his return?

"When you have waited a *very* long time for someone," she said, fixing Dido with a glassy eye, "your
mind becomes tired—perplexed—you hardly know
what to do for the best."

Dido, remembering nutty old Aunt Bella, became a
little sorry for the queen.

"Don't you worry, ma'am," she said kindly. "I daresay he'll turn up all right and tight."

Suddenly the queen's face became suffused with
dusky color, turned to a mask of rage.

"*You* expect he will turn up!" she hissed. "Who are
you to predict when the Pendragon will see fit to return? Here! Take this!" And she contemptuously
tossed down her silver porringer, which, more or less
by chance, Dido caught. When she looked up again,
she saw that the queen had put on a pair of gold-
rimmed spectacles, through which, to judge by the
angle of her face, she was staring at Dido. Dido could
not be sure, because the lenses were like two small
mirrors; they threw back reflections of the gray-
curtained room, but the queen's eyes could not be seen
behind them. One-way glass, Dido thought; what a
naffy notion!

"Now I will show you what *you* are worth," said the
queen bitingly. "Look at yourself in the side of that
dish."

The silver bowl was highly polished; yet, rather to
her surprise, Dido could not find her own reflection
in its curved side, either upside down or the right way
up.

"Not there?" Ginevra's voice was mocking now.
"Nor in my glasses?" She leaned toward Dido, who

peered warily at the two shining discs. "Not there either? How about in this?" She passed Dido a small hand mirror, its silver back and frame encrusted with diamonds. That, too, showed the long shadowy room with its cobweb hangings, but no Dido.

"Rum lot o' looking glasses you got round here," said Dido firmly, to cover a most uncomfortable feeling inside her.

"Blockhead! The glass is not at fault. I have destroyed your image, don't you see? And I can do the same with you yourself. It only—"

Perhaps fortunately, a voice was heard at this moment, calling,

"Make way there, make way, for the queen's mistress of the robes!"

Queen Ginevra calmed down. Her freckled hands, which had been shaking, relaxed; two red spots disappeared from her cheeks; she began to smile again and tucked her chin, what there was of it, among her draperies.

"Dear me! Talking politics!" she said. "That will never do." Looking over Dido's shoulder, she remarked, "Dearest Ettarde! Just when I need you, as ever. Advise me."

Turning round, Dido saw, without joy, that the dressmaker was approaching, accompanied, at a respectful distance, by her two assistants. All three were dressed very elegantly, in spangled lace gowns over silk petticoats, with feathers in their high coiffures, and silver-embroidered velvet cloaks. The two assistants still wore their black loo-masks. All three curtseyed deeply. Lady Ettarde, tiny and hunchbacked, looked grotesque, like some overdressed doll. She clambered up the steps of the dais.

"Your Royal Mercy," she said. "How can I help you?"

"Counsel me about this child," said the queen. "Should I send her off to Mabon and get the lake back? Or—or keep her here?"

Lady Ettarde turned and stared at Dido disparagingly, from brogans to threadbare jacket. Dido, trying to look nonchalant, stuck her hands (one of them holding the little mirror) into her pockets. It was some comfort, at this moment, to remember that she still had the cat's whiskers knotted round her index finger.

"You said as how if I went to King Mabon you'd let out Cap'n Hughes," she began.

The ladies ignored this.

"Madam," said the dressmaker, "you would be well advised not to keep her here. The child is a troublemaker. She has a bad horoscope. Send her where she can be of use. What need to keep a sparrow when you have a bird of paradise?"

"Blister me!" muttered Dido. Nobody heeded her.

"Besides, dear lady! Think! Only this year—according to the astrologers' predictions, this very year—if all go well—your noble Quondam lord will be restored to you."

"They predicted other years as well. If I could be sure . . ." murmured the queen.

"Then—Your Royal Highness will have no further need of—birds. *His* presence will restore you—like the sun's rays on a growing plant."

"Perhaps you are right." But still the queen looked at Dido; as if she found it hard to let her go. It was a covetous, greedy stare; it made Dido quite fidgety.

"If I could jist have that permit, Your Royalship," she said politely, "I'd be on my way."

"Permit? What permit?" demanded Ettarde sharply. "You would not send the child by the pass—"

But now there came another interruption: shouts of "Make way, make way there, for the queen's soothsayer!"

To Dido's amazement, who should come walking forward but Bran.

He had changed from the shabby clothes in which Dido had last seen him to a stiff taffeta gabardine gown, striped in red and black, richly lined with fur. His long white hair flowed smoothly back over the collar; on his high, thoughtful brow he wore a square black cap. The white bird sat motionless on his shoulder. Both of them looked extremely dignified.

But, as he approached the queen, Bran surprisingly burst into song, and caroled, in a manner that seemed highly inappropriate and carefree:

> *"Eating a nuncheon*
> *All by myself*
> *Isn't much fun;*
> *But when it's with you*
> *Any old stew,*
> *Any ragout*
> *Would do!*
> *When it's with you, it's a whiz*
> *Who cares a fig what it is?*
>
> *Going upstairs*
> *All on my own*
> *Isn't much fun;*
> *But when it's with you*
> *Any venue*
> *Would do!*

Just name a rendezvous . . .
When it's with you, it's a treat
Who gives a hoot where we meet?"

The queen, Dido observed, looked quite startled, even alarmed, at these words; in fact her expression, as Bran approached, seemed a mixture of pleasure and apprehension, as if he were a much-respected teacher who was almost certain to find fault with her, but who was able to tell her secrets that she could find out nowhere else.

Lady Ettarde, on the other hand, seemed wholly put out at Bran's arrival; her brow grew dark and she muttered something furious under her breath. As for the two assistants, they let out faint whimpers of distress and slipped away into the shadows.

The queen greeted Bran in a rallying tone as he bowed slightly.

"Well, my soothsayer? Why have you been absent from our presence for so long? Where did you go, and what have you been doing?"

"Oh," he answered rather vaguely, "I have been wandering here and there about Your Grace's dominions, to and fro, up and down. Today I was in the silver mines; I brought this for you," and from a pouch slung at his girdle he produced a great chunk of rough sapphire, as large as a brick. Even Lady Ettarde let out a squeak of admiration.

"You could make yourself an hourglass from it, or some such thing," Bran said carelessly.

The lump was so heavy that the queen could only just hold it in her weak, puffy hands. After turning it about to catch the blue gleams of light, she let it roll to the ground. "Why should I want an hourglass?" she demanded pettishly. "The hours go slowly enough as it is. Tell me a story, Bran, to while away the time."

"I should have thought your time passed pleasantly enough," observed Bran. "You have company."

His eyes rested on Dido, but she was surprised to see that he gave no hint of recognition. On the point of greeting him, she changed her mind.

"Company? Oh yes," said the queen coolly. "But your stories are better than all. Because one day you will tell me that the king has returned, and it will be true."

"Meanwhile I will tell you a story that I heard in the silver mines."

The queen settled herself comfortably to listen. Lady Ettarde, like a monkey, hopped up on to the couch, and began carefully brushing Ginevra's hair with a silver brush.

"There was once a poet who worked in the silver mines," said Bran. "He kept a cockatoo, which he daily left in his house while he was working in the pit." Bran stroked the white bird that sat so still on his shoulder.

"But one night the poet dreamed that the bird had picked up his heart—which he took out every night before he went to sleep, and hung on a stand by his bed—the bird had taken his heart in its claws, and flown up the chimney, carrying his heart with it. Next morning, when the poet woke up, sure enough, the bird *was* up the chimney, and he had to go to work in the mine leaving it there. He told his dream to the companion who worked in the same gallery with him. But that afternoon the gallery roof caved in, and the poet was killed. His mate escaped. But now, the miners say, nobody will live in the poet's empty cottage, because his dream is still up the chimney."

"His dream, or the bird with his heart?" asked the queen.

"His dream, his bird, his heart; they are all the same."

"What does the story mean, soothsayer?"

"It is a true story; so you may choose your own meaning for it, ma'am. Now, are you going to give that child her permit to climb Mount Damyake and go to Lyonesse?" Bran asked without any change of tone. Dido was very much startled.

"Oh—do you really think I should? Very well—very well; in a minute or two; there's no hurry," said the queen petulantly, jerking her head, so that Lady Ettarde gave a smothered exclamation and nearly dropped the hairbrush.

"Bran—dear Bran," the queen went on, "can't you give me any news? Any hope? No matter how faint? How far distant?"

"All I can tell you, lady, is that it will be this year. When I know more—more shall be told you. If there weren't such a lot of cobwebs and shrunken heads in this palace," Bran said—his tone was not critical, merely matter-of-fact—"I might be able to see further."

The queen appeared to ignore this remark. After a moment or two she said, "Well . . . another story, then!"

Bran sighed a little, as if he found the request tiresome, but he thought for a minute and then said rapidly, "A man called Ianto was walking across the town to his place of work when, looking down, he saw a gold and diamond necklace lying on the cobbles.

That cannot be real gold, he thought. It must be worthless, or someone else would have picked it up already. And so he left it lying and went on. But when he was halfway across the town, waiting to cross a busy street, he looked down and saw the same necklace, or one just like it, lying in the roadway. The civil guard are laying police traps for me, he thought. If I pick it up, one of them is sure to jump out of a doorway and accuse me of intending to steal it. So he left the necklace lying where it was, and crossed the street. But when he came to his place of work, there, in front of the entrance, he saw what appeared to be the self-same necklace, lying in the dust. Well, thought Ianto, now I know it must be meant for me. It is my destiny to have this necklace. So he picked it up. And it turned into a snake and bit him."

"Well, really!" exclaimed the queen indignantly. "What kind of a story is *that*? What are we to make of such a tale? Did the man die?"

"He was a doctor," Bran said, "and his place of work was a hospital, so he was able to treat himself with snake antidote. He was ill, but he did not die. And from his adventure he learned that if life has a necklace for you, or a snake, you may as well take it the first time, for it is sure to come back sooner or later."

So saying, Bran presented the queen with a gold and diamond necklace which he drew from his pouch. She accepted it, half laughing, half nervous.

"Will it turn into a snake and bite me?"

"No, ma'am. It is only dust—yellow dust and sparkling dust. A snake would be worth much more."

"Why?" demanded the queen, as Lady Ettarde clasped the chain round her throat.

"A snake is alive. Each live creature is unique. Take

its life, and something is gone forever. But stones have no life, no identity. You cannot kill a stone."

An odd silence followed Bran's words. After quite a long pause the queen said irritably, "But if he had picked up the necklace the *first* time, his life might not have been saved. . . . What was it that you wanted me to do? Oh, I recall—a permit for the girl. Where are my tablets? Asclabor!"

A chamberlain came forward, bowed, and offered her writing materials. She scribbled on a scrap of parchment; the attendant dropped hot wax on it; then the queen pressed her signet ring on the wax.

"There you are, child! I am sure I do not know what all this fuss is about. Run along—be off—make yourself scarce. Gracious knows why you have been bothering me for so long."

Dido took the signed and sealed parchment. She would have liked to make some retort, but prudence withheld her. She curtseyed and turned to go, noticing that Lady Ettarde's assistants, halfway along the hall, were moving unobtrusively toward the entrance.

"I will escort the child to her companions," said Bran.

"No! Stay and tell me more tales!" said the queen.

"In a moment, Highness; I will tell you the story of the sailor who dropped his anchor down a well. In one moment I will return."

With two rapid limping steps Bran overtook Dido, and walked beside her down the length of the hall and round the curving gallery. Dido noticed that all the officials they met bowed to Bran very respectfully. None of them approached him.

"I liked that story about the bird, mister," said Dido. "Did it happen to you?"

"Why should you think so?"

He began levering himself down the stairs by the marble handrail.

"Because—I dunno! I just thought it might! Hey, there's Lieutenant Windward and Mr. Mully. I thought they mighta got tired o' waiting and gone home." Dido flourished the ribboned permit joyfully at her companions and called, "I got it, all right and tight!"

"Took long enough!" remarked the lieutenant. "Did she—?" He was evidently about to say, "Did she give much trouble?" but checked himself, seeing Dido's escort.

"This here's Mr. Bran, the queen's soothsayer," said Dido.

"I say, sir, do you think there's any chance that Her Majesty will change her mind and let Cap'n Hughes out of jail?" Lieutenant Windward asked. But the soothsayer shook his head.

"She will not let him out. But he will not be in prison for very long." Then he glanced at the revolving door, which was stationary. Apparently it began to move only when it was in the correct position for people to use it. "You have another five minutes to wait," Bran said.

"When do the big doors open?" asked Dido. "The ones that the whirling door's set into?"

"Not until the return of the king. On that day, and that day only, they will be opened."

"I say, sir, isn't that a load of moonshine?" suggested Lieutenant Windward diffidently. "I mean, about the king's return?"

"Moonshine? No indeed. All the omens predict that his return is close at hand."

Mr. Multiple, overjoyed to find someone both

knowledgeable and prepared to answer questions, burst out with one that had been bothering him. "I beg your pardon, sir, but—those heads! The ones on the waiting room wall, you know—are they *real?*"

"Certainly they are real." Bran turned to glance through the waiting room door at the rows of shiny, shrunken objects. "There are tribes in the forest of Broceliande who make them. It is an ancient skill. They extract the skull, insert a hot stone, then sew up the lips and the slit through which the skull was removed. The head is then hung upside down for a year, to appease the owner's spirit."

"Wouldn't appease *me*," said Dido.

"Foreign travelers buy many of them; they are one of Cumbria's principal exports."

"I call that a bit much," grunted Lieutenant Windward. "I mean—for the queen to have them in her palace . . ."

"She wishes to encourage native crafts," said Bran. His face was quite devoid of expression. "Now the door will start to revolve," he added. "You can tell, because it begins to make that humming sound." In a lower tone, covered by the hum of the door, he went on, "Make all possible haste to leave Bath. And take your sick companion with you. Bath is excessively dangerous for any person suffering from a disorder of the consciousness. Or for children."

"How did you know about Mr. Holy?" Dido asked.

But he had already turned and was beginning to ascend the great staircase.

The revolving door began to spin, and they hurried through it.

"I wish he could come with us," said Dido, when they were outside.

"Him? Climb mountains with a wooden leg? Are you dicked in the nob?" said Mr. Multiple.

"I say, don't the mountains look queersome, though," said Dido. For the ring of great peaks, some of them spouting lurid smoke threaded with sparks, now stood silhouetted against the pale sunset sky, like a stony crown encircling the twilit town.

"We will start at dawn tomorrow," decided Lieutenant Windward. "I'll ask the hotel to provide us with a guide, and provisions for the journey. Now we had best go back and study the map."

8

The hotel provided them with a dozen burros, for riders and baggage, and so they proceeded at donkey pace. Two of the burros had a litter slung between them, into which the unconscious Mr. Holystone was fastened. The procession was led by a guide, Marcus Dylan, who, with provisions for the journey, had also been supplied by the hotel.

"What did you do about paying?" Dido asked Lieutenant Windward, edging her burro alongside his. Captain Hughes had had much of the expedition's supply of ready cash about his person when he was imprisoned, and so they were short of funds.

"Oh, the management at the Sydney would give us anything when they saw the queen's permit! I told them that we would return in six or seven days, and that the captain would pay the whole shot at the end of our visit. I do not propose to fork out any of my own bezants while he is a prisoner. We may need what little money we have on our way to Lyonesse."

"I dunno what we'd spend it on," said Dido. "I don't see too many hot-pie sellers or cockle stands round here."

They were crossing the stony upland plain which surrounded Bath Regis. Much of the ground was rocky and uncultivated, studded, here and there, by sigse thorn and a species of cactus resembling a giant spiny hand. Not another human being was in sight.

"It sure is a drearsome part." Dido shivered. Yet, despite the cold, her spirits had lifted on leaving the town of Bath. So had those of her companions. Even the waxen face of Mr. Holystone had taken on a faint tinge of color. Having left it, they realized for the first time to the full what a terribly oppressive atmosphere permeated Queen Ginevra's capital.

"We have several hundred miles to go before reaching Lyonesse," pointed out the lieutenant. "There must be towns or villages along the way."

"Hope so," grunted Multiple. "Or it's going to be sharp sleeping at night."

The predawn air was razor-cold. As they left the plain and began to crawl at what seemed snail's pace up the vast slopes of Mount Damyake, the increasing altitude rendered breathing harder and harder. Lieutenant Windward had, however, prudently seen that the party was equipped with a large bundle of the rumirumi lilies, wrapped in damp moss, for the use of the travelers when distressed by lack of oxygen. The donkeys, fortunately, seemed unaffected by the thinness of the air. Dido was very glad of her mount; she was not certain that she would have been able to walk far on her own. Moreover, it was comfortably warm, like riding on a barrel of hot tar covered by a hearth rug.

Presently, however, the sun shot up, and at once began to send down rays of such torrid heat that they made haste to don the straw hats with which Windward, on the advice of the guide, had also provided them.

"Awkward sort o' climate," remarked Dido. "Freezing one minute, roasting the next. Hey, Noah—don't you want to lay a hat over poor Mr. Holy's face? No sense in getting him sunstrook on top of all else."

During the days of Mr. Holystone's illness no one had shaved him, and his beard, of a brownish-gold color, had grown several inches; so had his hair, which previously he had worn very short. He's a right good-looking fellow with a beard, Dido thought, as Noah carefully balanced a sombrero over the invalid's face.

As the sun climbed higher, it illuminated the gigantic symmetrical cones, the fantastic snow-covered peaks, and pinnacles like spectral cities of ice, that surrounded them on every side. Bath Regis was now a mere dot in the distance.

When they reached the top of a lofty ridge Dido, looking back, let out a cry of wonder.

"What's to do?" inquired Mr. Multiple, kicking his burro till it came level with hers.

"Look at all that flat land we been riding across, Mr. Mully. See them lines on the rock?"

"I could hardly miss them," he said. "I reckon they are geological strata. They are far too huge for people to have had anything to do with them. Why, some of them must be more than fifty miles long!"

From side to side of the upland plain long lines were to be seen, as if some god or giant had leaned down from the heavens and with an idle fingernail scraped a series of huge drawings over the countryside. More and more of the pattern became visible as the party mounted higher.

And when they halted for the noon meal, Dido said, "Well, I wasn't certain before, but now I am! Look, Mr. Windward—ain't those marks down there the exact same as Mr. Holystone's birthmark?"

"Holystone's birthmark? Can't say as I even knew he had one," Mr. Windward said rather skeptically. Dido, however, rolled back the blanket to show the sick man's forearm, and Mr. Windward was obliged to agree that there was a remarkable likeness.

"I often noticed that mark when he was a-peeling spuds," said Dido.

"It *must* be nothing more than a coincidence," observed Windward. "For why should a man have a mark on his arm that's the same as one nobody can see unless they're on top of a fourteen-thousand-foot mountain?"

"*I* dunno," said Dido. "But I reckon it's lucky for us as we brought Mr. Holy along. Looks like he belongs to these parts all right."

Lieutenant Windward absently pulled his chronometer from his pocket to check it against the position of the sun in the sky, and uttered an exclamation.

"What's up?" said Multiple.

"It's started going again!" He set it to the correct time.

"So's mine," said Multiple, pulling out his turnip watch. "Well, if that don't beat cockfighting!"

They soon started off again. Dylan, the guide—a wizened, talkative little man—was emphatic that they must reach the valley of Lake Arianrod before dusk, and not risk being overtaken by night on the bare mountainside, or they would freeze to death, not to mention having their blood drained by vampires or being pecked to pieces by giant owls.

"Aurocs bad along here, *etiam atque etiam;* yet remains a long way to go, sirs," he kept saying anxiously.

Dido felt she would be quite pleased to see an auroc; she had heard them mentioned so frequently, without ever actually encountering one, that she had begun to doubt their existence and wonder if they were not bearing the blame for somebody else's activities.

"Which is Mount Arrabe?" she asked Dylan.

He pointed ahead and to the left.

"We now go round, *circumvenimus,* back of Mount Damyake. *Lacus sacratissimus*—Arianrodwater—is lying between Damyake, Arrabe, Calabe, and Catelonde mountains; Arrabe not first mountain you see, but second; having two big teeth like cayman. Very bad mountain, Arrabe!"

"Why bad?" Dido wanted to know, studying Arrabe's towering twin peaks.

Dylan made the double-circle sign. "Belong to King Arawn, king of the Black World! Aurocs roost on top, pecking at stars. Old Caradog the guardian live there in the temple of Sul, in Sul's town. I not taking you past Arrabe. Ladies of night come there, too."

"Who," inquired Dido, "are the ladies of night?"

Dylan traced the two circles again, and squinted through them at Dido.

"Owl ladies. Better not speaking names." He made a gesture as of snipping with shears. "Queen owl ladies who make dress."

"Do you mean," said Dido, greatly puzzled, "the queen's mistress of the robes? And her people? Lady Ettar—"

"Hssssh!" Dylan nodded nervously, glancing around

as if on the lookout for eavesdroppers, then urged his donkey faster, to get away from Dido, who rode on very thoughtfully.

If this Elen, she thought, is a prisoner on Arrabe, I reckon I know who put her there. And I reckon I can guess why. But no use talking about it to Windward or Mr. Mully! They'd think I'd got windmills in my head. I'll jist have to keep a sharp eye out myself. Best do that anyhows, if there's really aurocs about.

The existence of aurocs was soon confirmed. A huge shadow drifted across the track, and all the burros shied and brayed nervously. As they descended the pass, more of the great triangular shadows crossed the mountainside.

"Blimey," said Dido to Mr. Multiple, "if we could put a couple of *those* on show at the Battersea Fun Fair, we'd all lay by enough mint sauce to buy Thread-needle Street. Ain't they the ugliest monsters you ever saw?"

The aurocs, becoming inquisitive, wheeled in closer and closer to the calvacade, with hardly a flip of their great fur-covered, leathery wings. Their claws could clearly be seen, and their cruel beaks, with protruding tusks on either side. Though Dido tried to joke about them, it was plain they were no laughing matter. They were evidently attracted by the sight of Mr. Holystone, motionless on his litter; they drifted lower and lower. Once or twice Lieutenant Windward discharged his musket at them, and then they would flap away to a distance, with raucous shrieks; but they invariably re-turned, and their numbers increased as the day drew on.

Mr. Multiple, an excellent marksman, managed to wing one with a pistol shot; it fluttered, wabbling away, squawking hideously, to a cactus-studded knoll a hundred yards from the track, and the travelers then witnessed a horrible spectacle, for the other aurocs all swooped down on their wounded comrade and in a very short time devoured it completely, leaving nothing but a few shreds of fur and splinters of bone on the sandy ground.

"Ugh, the cannibals!" shuddered Noah Gusset. "Still, at least it keeps their nasty minds off us!"

Unfortunately, by the time the aurocs had finished their repulsive feast, the travelers had reached a very dangerous section of the pass they were traversing. This was a valley region of strange heaving, pulsing bogs and quagmires, colored in bright prismatic hues, dark red, ochre yellow, and sulphurous, iridescent blue; great gouts of steam drifted up from the ground, and from time to time an explosive fountain of mud would suddenly spurt up into the air, each time from a different spot.

"It is a thermal region," said the knowledgeable Lieutenant Windward. "I have seen such places in Iceland, when I was second mate on the *Arctic Tern*. These are geysers, caused by the volcanoes round about."

"Careful! *Quam celerrime* here, sirs, but *extra* careful," warned Dylan. "Get stuck in mud here, you sink down, down, to King Arawn."

The burros were evidently well aware of the danger; they flapped their long ears, heehawed, and stepped nervously and delicately along the narrow, slippery path, which wound a circuitous way between heaving, steaming pools and spouting fountains. Every now and then the party were spattered by hot mud. A dismal stench hung around the place, "like unwashed Christmas socks full o' rotten potatoes," Dido said.

Strange vegetation grew in this valley, nurtured by its dark, unwholesome warmth; fleshy gray-green leaves clustered round the bubbling pools, and grotesque, sickly scented flowers hung from fat pale stalks on the rock faces.

"I'll be glad when we get out o' here," commented Mr. Multiple, thumping his burro to make it go faster.

But the aurocs, emboldened by the slow pace of the travelers, now circled in closer and closer; one of them wheeled so near to Plum's donkey that it panicked and shied away sideways, slipping off the track and tossing its rider into a great heaving pool of mud. Plum yelled frenziedly, trying to extricate himself from the gluey, dripping morass.

"Keep *still*, man!" shouted Lieutenant Windward. "We'll throw you a rope! Don't struggle—you will only sink yourself faster!"

But before Windward could drag a rope from his saddlebag, the hovering aurocs, assured of a helpless prey, had swooped down in a flurry of black, hairy wings, snapping beaks, and flailing talons. Two of them fought for the donkey, and the larger won; with a screech of triumph it snatched up the wretched animal by its saddle and flapped away, dwindling in no time to a speck in the distance. Meanwhile, two others had dragged poor Plum out of the mud pool and were battling over him while Windward and Multiple, cursing with frustration, waited for a chance to shoot without injuring their companion. No such chance was given; while the two aurocs were fighting, a third swooped in, snatched up the hapless man, suddenly soared up on a rising current of hot air, and disappeared behind a crag. Windward and Multiple both fired at it, but both missed.

"Devil take the brute!" cried Windward, reloading with shaking hands. "We must go after it. We must rescue Plum!" He kicked his burro to urge it to a gallop.

"No, sir—no gallop, no gallop!" shouted Dylan urgently. "*Festina lente!* You go in mud, we *all* go—aurocs eat the lot of us. No possible save that hombre. He done for. Aurocs eat quick."

Remembering the hideous speed with which the aurocs had devoured their own companion, Lieutenant Windward was reluctantly obliged to give way.

"He's right, sir, I'm afraid," said Multiple, and Noah Gusset muttered, "Ay, those greedy monsters can swallow a man before you can prime your pistol. Poor old Plum's mincemeat by now no doubt of that. Ah, he had a rare voice for a shanty, when he were in the mood, did old Plum, and could knit faster than anyone in the fo'c'sle."

Daunted and appalled by this horrid mishap, the remaining five travelers drew closer together, Mr. Multiple riding alongside the sick man with his pistol ready cocked. Fortunately, they soon left the thermal region, climbed up through a narrow, rocky defile, and presently came in sight of their first objective.

"Arianrod," said Dylan briefly, pointing ahead and downward.

For a moment the travelers were deluded into thinking that the lake was full of water.

"Can the queen have been mistaken?" exclaimed Mr. Multiple. "Or King Mabon have restored it already?"

"Perhaps a spring has replenished it," said Lieutenant Windward.

But then they realized that the vast, star-shaped

basin lying among the four mountains was filled only with white mist, which billowed and heaved like the waves of an insubstantial sea.

They spent the night on a rock ledge above the great hollow. Dylan kindled a fire to keep off jaguars and mountain lions, which it successfully did. The fire was of small use for cooking, since they were so high, up here, that water boiled at a very low temperature, but they toasted plantains on sticks and ate hunks of barley bread. Then, wrapped in ruanas and vicuna fleeces, they lay down to a cold and uneasy night's rest, with the burros tethered in a ring round them for added protection.

"What about aurocs?" Dido said to Mr. Multiple.

"Dylan says they all go to roost at night; they have weak vision. And they don't like dark or cloudy weather. At least we shan't have to worry about them till sunup."

But Dido could not easily dismiss the thought of the horrible creatures; they flapped and shrieked through her dreams. Mr. Holystone, too, seemed troubled by nightmares; he tossed and moaned, and cried out words in some foreign tongue. Dido remembered that he had said he was found as a baby on the shores of Lake Arianrod; she wondered if the knowledge that he was so close to his birthplace had somehow penetrated his slumbers.

Long before dawn Dylan was up and feeding the burros.

"I go now, sirs; I leaving you here," he announced briefly. "Arianrod you see below; you keeping south, sun behind you"—he gestured along the basin, between the steeply angled sides of Calabe and Catelonde

—"you soon coming to Pass of Nimue. Lyonesse on ahead. You finding stable of Caradog and guardian down below. Sul's temple up above on mountain. You showing permit to Caradog, he let you through pass."

Windward and Multiple tried to persuade Dylan to accompany them farther, but he shook his head emphatically.

"Arianrod nogood place, sirs. *Benigne.* I coming no farther, I going now, *celerimme.*"

"But what about the aurocs, man, on the way back? How the deuce will you ever get through safely on your own?"

"Keeping them off, no fear"—he gestured with his crossbow—"I riding best fast burro, so *valete,* goodbye, sirs."

Lieutenant Windward paid his fee, which he demanded in cash; Dylan kicked his mount into a rapid trot and departed, waving his sombrero, but without ever looking back. The rest of the party lost no time in setting off in the opposite direction.

A narrow track, dug out of the steeply sloping mountainside, led down in zigzags to the level of the lake basin, and then along beside what had presumably been the shore of the lake when it was full of water.

As they scrambled down the zigzags, the sun mounted behind Catelonde, which was plainly an active volcano; black clouds of smoke issued from its cup-shaped summit, throwing wild shadows over the white mist which still filled the lake bed. However, just as the party reached the narrow, level track that skirted the lake, all this mist rose up and hung in the sky overhead, so that the travelers were able to see the dry sandy and stony arena which was what King Mabon had left his neighbor Queen Ginevra when he removed her lake.

"Musta been a right job, taking it," said Dido. "Hey, Mr. Windward, why don't us ride along the bed of the lake, 'stead of this narrow track? Then we can all bunch together in case of aurocs."

Windward thought this a good suggestion, and the burros were urged down on to the lake bed. No aurocs, however, appeared today, presumably because of the heavy cloud overhead, which now obscured the sun. A great many dried fishbones were scattered on the sand; evidently, when the water had been removed a number of mountain predators had been furnished with an unexpected fish dinner.

"This looks like gold-bearing soil to me," said Mr. Multiple. "There's gold mines in Wales, where I used to stay with my uncle. The ground looked like this. I daresay we could all make our fortunes if we sieved up a bit of this sand."

"Best not touch it!" warned Windward. "Don't forget, Arianrod was a sacred lake. The queen would have our guts for garters, likely, if you began digging up the bed."

Mr. Multiple's face assumed an obstinate expression. He made no answer, but continued to keep a careful eye on the ground as he rode along. Presently he let out an exclamation.

"*Now* what?" demanded Windward. "For heaven's sake, man, keep up a better pace! We shan't reach the frontier by nightfall at this rate."

But Mr. Multiple, tumbling impetuously off his burro, had scooped something off the ground which he now triumphantly exhibited.

"What do you say to that, then? A diamond as big as a pullet's egg, or my name's not Frank Multiple!"

"Are you certain?" said the lieutenant skeptically. "It looks to me like any earthy pebble."

"That's no pebble, sir—it's a diamond. See here—" and he scraped with his thumbnail. "My granddad was a goldsmith; I could not mistake. *Hey*—there's dozens of 'em! Let us stop but half an hour, and we are all as rich as Crusoes!"

Windward was resolute, however, that they must press on, so Mr. Multiple discontentedly climbed back into the saddle, muttering privately to Noah Gusset that it was a hem shame! He stared hard at the ground as they rode along, every now and then leaping down to grab a stone, remounting, and kicking his donkey into a fast trot to overtake the others again.

Dido could not help being somewhat infected by his enthusiasm; she, too, began to study the ground as she rode, and so chanced to perceive what seemed to be a rusty metal cross, half buried in a shallow sandy depression. A wink of red at its extremity had caught her eye.

"Here—hold hard a minute, Mr. Windward," she said. "Maybe that thing's summat worth taking along —might be vallyble."

Sliding to the ground, she knelt and tugged at the cross-shaped object. To her surprise the buried end was far longer than it had appeared, and quite deeply embedded in the ground. She had a hard struggle to pull it out.

"Do, *pray* make haste, Miss Twite," said Windward impatiently. "We cannot be forever stopping for trifles!"

"This ain't no trifle—blimey, it's a *sword*!" cried

Dido in triumph. "And I reckon it's worth a packet, too—look at all them colored sparklers in the handle!"

"Yes, well, that's as may be, but the blade is all rusty—I *wish* you will not be lumbering us up with such useless articles! In any case, it indubitably belongs to the queen."

"Well, then, we'd better hand it to that there whats-hisname, the guardian, and he can send it back to her," said Dido reasonably. "It won't hurt poor old Mr. Holy to have it by him." She laid it in the litter and hopped back onto her burro.

No further incidents occurred to fidget Mr. Windward during the ride along the dried-up lake bed. Fortunately, the low cloud prevented any attacks by aurocs, but the atmosphere was very oppressive, sultry, and heavy. The burros slipped and stumbled on the shingly, powdery sand.

"I guess even the ground is hot hereabouts," said Dido, feeling it with her hand when they stopped for a drink; none of them felt hungry.

"It may well be," said Mr. Multiple. "After all, we're getting uncommonly close to that big volcano. Look, you can see lava running down it like toffee. Supposing that big rock toppled off when we were passing by?"

"I reckon it's been there for a good few thousand years," said Lieutenant Windward.

"This is a right spooky place. I ain't surprised Dylan didn't want to come here," Dido said.

Deep among the four surrounding mountains—twin-headed Arrabe, dome-shaped Damyake, cloud-girt Calabe, and smoke-belching Catelonde, with a huge stone balanced on its summit—the travelers felt as if they were at the bottom of a well, with black, steeply shelving slopes rising all around them. There were very few birds to be seen here, and no animals at all; the only sound that broke the silence was an occasional rumbling mutter from Mount Catelonde ahead of them. I'll be glad when we're past that one, thought Dido. She noticed that when Catelonde rumbled, Mr. Holystone stirred restlessly on his litter, as if he could hear the sound in his dreams.

In mid-afternoon, some three quarters of the way along the basin, they reached a point from which the far end was visible; they could see the narrow pass which led out and southward toward Lyonesse.

"You can see why the water didn't flow out when the queen first had the lake put here," said Mr. Multiple. "It's been dammed."

"Well, she wouldn't want it to trickle away, after having brought it so far."

"I suppose they brought it up in water-skins, on burros."

"Or llamas," said Dido.

Mount Catelonde gave a loud snort, and Mr. Holystone cried out sharply, stirring and rolling over on to his side. His hand, groping about, found the handle of the rusty sword that Dido had unearthed, and clasped it.

He murmured some brief remark and opened his eyes.

"Hey! *Mr. Windward!*" Dido called to the lieutenant, who was on ahead. "Mr. Holystone said summat—he's a-stirring—I believe he's a mite better! Maybe if we gave him a drink . . ."

Windward, sighing, turned his burro and came back.

"Did he really speak? It's not a Banbury story?"

But he, too, sounded hopeful. He, like everybody else, greatly respected Mr. Holystone's judgment. In the present circumstances, without the captain, and now their numbers reduced by the loss of Plum, the steward's restoration to health and consciousness would be a piece of great good fortune. "What did he say?"

"Sounded like 'halibut.' "

"Oh, fiddle-de-dee, Miss Twite!"

"No, it did! Truly! Listen!"

"Caliburn," muttered Mr. Holystone indistinctly, and then, louder and with more assurance, "Caliburn!"

Noah Gusset had already halted the pair of burros that carried the litter slung between them, and was taking out his leather water-bottle. Now Dido and Mr. Multiple assisted the sick man to sit up. He looked around him wonderingly, at the black, snow-streaked mountain slopes and the sandy lake bed, at their concerned faces watching him, and, lastly, at the sword in his hand. For the third time, in a tone of joy and recognition, he repeated the word. "Caliburn! My sword, come back to my hand!"

"Mr. Holystone!" cried Dido in rapture. "Are—are you feeling more the thing, now?"

His eyes rested on her with an expression of perplexity.

"I know the place," he said. "I know the sword. I know myself. But who are *you*? Who are these?" glancing again at Windward, Noah, and Multiple.

"Why—why, we're your *friends*, Mr. Holy! Don't you recognize us?" Dido was terribly startled and grieved.

"No, my child. But I can see that you are all good people. Your faces are—are trustworthy."

"*Trustworthy!*" said Lieutenant Windward rather shortly. "So I should hope! If you knew how far we had hauled you up these godforsaken mountains! Come now, do you not remember us? I am Lieutenant Windward, first lieutenant of His Majesty's sloop *Thrush*—this is Mr. Midshipman Multiple—this is Miss Twite—"

"Don't you remember all those times I helped you polish the cap'n's teaspoons, Mr. Holy?"

As it was quite plain that he did not, Noah Gusset sensibly suggested, "He be main weak and wambly yet. Why doesn't us give him a drop o' summat hot?"

Since it was impossible to boil water, they gave the recovering man a drink of aguardiente, and some of the cassava bread and baked turtles' eggs which none of them had fancied for their midday meal. The patient ate slowly, and could not take much, but the food visibly did him good. When he had finished, he stood up, unassisted, by slow and careful stages, stretched, and staggered, but kept his balance, leaning on the sword, which he had held tightly clasped in his hand since awakening.

Then, frowning in perplexity, he said, "You brought me here? On that litter? But then . . . where had I been before?"

He articulated his words very slowly, as if translating from another language in his mind.

"Brought you here? Why, from the *Thrush*, of course," Windward repeated. "You're the captain's steward. Don't you remember *anything*?"

Holystone shook his head.

"I remember battles. The alliance against us—King Mark, King Lot, King Anguish—and my nephew. Mordred. And then I was wounded—here—" he raised an uncertain hand to the back of his head. "I gave Caliburn to Bedivere to throw in the lake."

His hand lovingly caressed the hilt of the sword. He glanced down and said, "The blade is rusty. But a rub in the sand will soon mend that."

Lieutenant Windward exclaimed impatiently, "Come, come, my man, what the deuce ails you? This is moonshine! Battles—alliances! Ah, well, I reckon you are all tottyheaded yet. We had best be on our way. Make haste, the rest of you—pack up those things. There is no sense in lingering here. At any moment the clouds may lift and aurocs be upon us." And he added privately to Mr. Multiple, "Let us hope there will be some surgeon or physician at King Mabon's court who can set the poor fellow's wits to rights. Otherwise he won't be much use to us. Bustle about now, Miss Twite!"

Holystone, however, flatly refused to get back into the litter. He said that he was well enough to ride if they did not go too fast. While he and the lieutenant were arguing about this, Dido felt something rub against her leg.

"*Murder!*" she cried, her mind on aurocs; and then, looking down, she added in amazement, "Oh, no! If it ain't another o' them cats!"

Then, inspired by a hopeful notion, she grabbed the cat and, carrying it to Mr. Holystone, said, "See who's here, Mr. Holy! It's the spit image of Dora. Don't you remember Dora—your cat, El Dorado?"

"Dora?" he muttered doubtfully, rubbing his brow. "One of the cats of El Dorado?"

"That's the ticket, Mr. Holy. You'll remember soon enough! And this one's got a message, too, I'll be bound. Yes, it has! Another page from that dictionary."

Tim Toldrum, said the name on the leather disc. And the leaf of paper informed them:

To coax. To wheedle, to flatter, to humour. A low word.

Under the printed words the same desperate little hand had written in dark brown ink:

For pity's sake, help me! I am suffocating in the dark. Elen.

"Elen," said Mr. Holystone hoarsely. "Elen?"
A silence fell around him, as if he were standing on an island.
Lieutenant Windward cleared his throat and said, "Ahem! We really must—"
"Elen," said Holystone. "In the dark. Where? We must find her! How can we find her?"
The cat mewed insistently at his feet.
"Why," exclaimed Dido, "don't you see, it's dead simple! Moggy here will lead us to her—won't you, puss? 'I'm a prisoner on Arrabe,' the second note said. That's Arrabe—that big black hill up there on the left."
"We haven't time—" Lieutenant Windward began.
"Oh, come *on*, Mr. Windward! The poor girl's shut up, we *got* to rescue her, don't we? Look, the cat's started already."
The black flanks of Arrabe were broken, stony, and drear, as if they had been gashed and chipped and scraped raw by some great volcanic explosion. Here and there a bunch of rough ichu grass thrust out of a crack; there was no other vegetation. But the slope was not hard to climb. Leaving the burros hobbled on the lake bed, the party began scrambling up and

around and in among the ragged and tumbled boulders, following the cat, who trotted ahead purposefully, tail in air, every now and then stopping to glance round as if perplexed by the slowness of their progress. The wind, which had been rising all day, howled lugubriously, and a few pellets of hail dashed in their faces.

"Best get a move on there, puss," called Dido, who, being light and agile, was ahead of the rest. "We're all liable to be blown to blazes if we don't find this poor perisher soon."

Then she stopped short in dismay. For, after threading its way up a narrow gully, the cat jumped lightly up to the top of a massive boulder leaning against a rock face and then, next instant, slipped through a crevice behind the boulder and vanished.

"The blessed cat went in behind that there rock," Dido said to Mr. Holystone, who, surprisingly, in spite of his recent disability, was the first of her companions to come up with her. "*Now* what's to do?"

Although he was so changed and queer, she had at once fallen back into the habit of depending on his advice in difficulties.

He stood frowning, leaning on the sword, staring at the rock, as if trying to recall something.

Noah Gusset, arriving next, surveyed the rock, and said dubiously, "Reckon som'un's in behind there, Miss Dido? Us'll never shift that. 'Tis nigh as big as a house."

"The cat has led us on a fool's errand!" irritably exclaimed Lieutenant Windward, arriving at this moment.

"Wait, though!" said Mr. Multiple, who was close

behind him. "I've a notion." Bringing out a ship's whistle, which he carried on a string round his neck, he blew a long and piercing blast.

The sound was almost swamped by a great gust of wind that flung more hail in their faces. But not quite. And it had two unexpected results. From somewhere up above them on the rock face two huge mountain owls came flapping down; and from inside the rock a faint voice called, "Help!"

"There! What did I say!" shouted Dido triumphantly. "Somebody *is* shut up in back of that rock!— Hey! Murder! Lay off me, you nasty brutes!"

For the two owls, yellow eyes blazing, wings beating like flails, had swooped at the rescue party and were furiously attacking them.

"Devil take the fiends! Watch out for your eyes!" yelled Windward, who was already bleeding from a savage peck on the cheekbone. "Ugh! Get away, curse you—" slashing at one of the birds with his cutlass. They were as big as swans, and quite as fierce.

"Maybe that's their nest—in behind—" gasped Dido, clasping her arms over her face to protect it, as one of the owls alighted on her head, digging razor-sharp claws into her scalp. "*Croopus*! It's nigh pulling my head off!"

The next moment she almost had her breath knocked out as a body collided violently against hers; the cruel grip of the talons on her head suddenly slackened. She shook her head, abruptly freed from the owl's weight, and looked round her, rubbing drops of blood from her eyes.

"That has done for one of them!" said Mr. Holystone. He was surveying the blade of his sword, which now seemed darker than from mere rust.

The owl that had been on Dido's head flapped away down the gully, bleeding and shedding feathers; it perched on a rock, then slowly toppled off it, and was lost to view among the boulders on the ground. Its companion, screeching and hooting mournfully, circled around once or twice, then planed away into the distance and did not reappear.

Mr. Holystone hardly glanced at the vanquished owl; he had gone back to studying the surface of the rock that confronted him. Now, with a soft exclamation of satisfaction, he found what he was looking for: a small slit in the surface of the stone. A little lichen grew over it, which he rubbed away with his thumb.

"Looks like a keyhole," Dido said, and was immediately reminded of the great cumbrous keys in Bath, shaped like swans or dragons, with keyholes to match. "But where's the key?"

Mr. Holystone, without answering her question, inserted the tip of his sword into the rock and thrust inward strongly, so that the weapon, by slow degrees, vanished up to the hilt.

"All very well," muttered Windward, "but now what?"

"Help!" the faint voice called from inside the cave.

"We're here! We're a-trying to help you!" Dido called.

Mr. Holystone laid both hands on the hilt of the sword. His forehead bulged, his veins swelled; beads of sweat rolled down his cheeks into his beard. His wrists and forearms knotted with exertion. He began to twist the hilt.

"He'll break that sword, sure as a gun," grunted Windward. No one else said anything.

The hail was rattling down like grapeshot, but nobody heeded it; all their attention was focused on those two straining hands. Suddenly there came a sharp *crack!* like the sound of a sail flapping in a high wind; and a V-shaped crevice appeared in the center of the rock barrier, as its two halves gradually tilted sideways away from each other.

Mr. Holystone stepped back, slowly withdrawing the sword from the widening crack. He was gasping; his chest heaved with effort. But otherwise it was hard to believe that this was the man who, day after day, had lain unconscious without speech or movement. He glanced at his companions; his eyes lit on Dido.

"You are small; you can climb in through that gap," he said curtly. Without a word, Dido did as she was directed, ignoring Windward's peevish interjection of "Wait a moment, now—how do we know what's in there?"

Dido levered herself cautiously through the narrow aperture.

"Anybody at home?" she inquired.

It was pitch dark inside, but she was heartened and encouraged by the feeling of the cat vigorously rubbing against her leg. The air was terribly scanty, stale, and bad; she found it only just possible to breathe.

"Hey!" she gulped, putting her head back through the crack. "Fetch up some o' those rumirumi flowers, can you?"

"Ay, ay," answered Multiple, and she heard his feet thudding off down the gully. Then came a loud cry of amazement or fright.

Dido ignored that. Her eyes were becoming accustomed to the dim light, and she could see a small figure huddled in a corner of the cave.

"Hilloo?" she said softly. "Who's that? Can you speak? Are you Elen?"

"Yes . . . Elen . . ." came the faint answer. "Air . . . please, air!"

"Don't you fret. Air's just a-coming. Rest easy!"

Groping her way across the cave, Dido felt about and found a thin hand, which she clasped comfortingly; it seemed very small, not even as large as her own.

In five minutes or less, Mr. Multiple was back with an armful of rumirumi lilies which he thrust through the gap; outside, beyond the rock, Dido could hear him excitedly telling the others some piece of news which evoked gasps of amazement and disbelief from Windward and Noah. "Go look for yourselves!" said Mr. Multiple.

Dido meanwhile held the bundle of flowers close to the prisoner's face.

"There!" she whispered. "Breathe deep now. That'll set you right in a brace o' shakes!"

The prisoner breathed, gulped, and coughed. *Cough*, thought Dido; a convulsion of the lungs. She felt around on the floor of the cave and discovered a small, thick book, which felt as if it was bound in leather.

"Guess you won't need to tear out any more pages now, hey? Feeling stronger, are you? Think you can manage to climb out? Or shall I ask them outside to pass in a bit of bread and a hard-boiled egg?"

"No . . . no . . . I am better now, thank you. I think I can climb out."

"That's the dandy. Wait till I help you up. Slowly does it."

Assisted by Dido, the prisoner scrambled slowly

through the narrow crack. Willing hands were waiting
to receive her on the far side.

When Dido emerged herself, holding the book, she
discovered that the hail had changed to freezing, driv-
ing snow. Lieutenant Windward, Mr. Holystone, Noah,
and the rescued prisoner were already making their
difficult way down the gully. Mr. Multiple had waited
to help Dido.

"Well done, young 'un!" he congratulated her.
"Reckon she'd never a got out if it weren't for you!
But come on now—don't dally—it's cold enough to
freeze a brass baboon."

"You take this book and the flowers, then I'll carry
the cat"—for it had jumped back through the gap
with Dido. "What was all that yelling about?" she
asked, as they slipped and stumbled down the rocky
hillside in the blizzard.

"I'll show you. Just look here!" Mr. Multiple paused
by a big rock. Something purple and silver gleamed
beyond it. With total astonishment, Dido, coming up
beside him, saw the body of a woman sprawled among
the black boulders. Already snow was veining the folds
of her satin dress and whitening her disheveled hair.
She had been wearing a loo-mask, but the string had
broken, and it lay beside her face. Dido recognized her.

"It's Mrs. Vavasour, the dressmaker. How the *blazes*
did she get here? Is she dead?"

"As a doornail."

"But where did she come from?"

"You remember the big owl? The one that lit on
your head, and Holystone spiked it with his sword?
Well, that's her! I saw the owl fly to that rock, and
then it toppled off dead. And there she lies. *She* was
the owl!"

"Mussy save us," whispered Dido. She was really stunned by this discovery.

"I used to hear tell, when I was in the West Indies station," said Mr. Multiple, as they went on slithering down the hill, "of witches who could turn themselves into hares or foxes or birds; but I never believed it above half."

"There were two owls," shivered Dido. "I wonder where the other went?"

She thought of the two women who had abducted her; of the two who had accompanied Lady Ettarde. Were they the same? Where was Mrs. Morgan now?

"It better not come near me," said Mr. Multiple cheerfully, "or I'll give it neighbor's fare. I'll settle its hash like that one."

"Maybe you need Mr. Holystone's sword," said Dido.

By the time they reached the burros, the rest of the party was mounted and waiting for them impatiently. There was no time for talk or congratulation; the weather had become too wild.

"Come on!" called Mr. Windward. "I reckon the guardian's stable that Dylan told us of can't be too far off. If we don't get to it soon we'll all freeze in our tracks!"

The rescued prisoner had been laid in the litter, wrapped in sheepskins, and Mr. Holystone had mounted one of the baggage burros. They set off at a rapid speed. Snow slashed their faces like cutlass blades, and the donkeys slipped and staggered as the stones became coated with ice; it was horrible riding. Fortunately, in less than twenty minutes they reached the end of the lake; by then their faces, clothes, and all exposed surfaces were cased in a layer of ice. Not a moment too soon they came to a low building, solidly built of clay and thatched with ichu grass; the door, though closed, was not fastened, and they all bundled inside, pell-mell, riders and beasts together.

"Anybody about? May we come in?" shouted Windward, but there was no reply; the place was empty, save for a few mules and a couple of llamas, which stared placidly at the intruders.

Noah and Mr. Multiple instantly began to kindle a fire, having discovered a clay hearth and a pile of thorn and llama droppings apparently intended as fuel.

A wide clay shelf along the side of the building was evidently meant to serve as table, chairs, and bed for any travelers making use of the place. Lieutenant Windward heaped some ruanas on a section of this near the fire, and then assisted the rescued captive to lie down.

"How are you feeling now, miss?" he inquired very politely.

The fire blazed up. Dido could see now that the prisoner was a girl perhaps four years older than herself. Elen wore a very plain gray dress with a white tucker, and a brown pinafore over it, reaching to her ankles. She had blue stockings, buckled shoes, and a blue cap that fitted her head closely and had four square corners. She was desperately thin and frail. Despite that, she was the most beautiful person Dido had ever seen. Her face had a kind of transparent clearness—like the mountains at sunup, Dido thought, or one o' them waterfalls. Her eyes were large and gray, her nose straight, her mouth wide and smiling. Silky brown curtains of hair fell on either side of her forehead.

"I am alive!" she said, in answer to Windward's question. "Thanks to you all! And to Toldrum here."

The cat had jumped up beside her and she was fondling its head.

"How did you ever *get* behind that rock?" demanded the lieutenant.

"Are you King Mabon's daughter?" said Dido.

The girl smiled at her and held out a hand.

"Yes, I am Elen. And I have to thank you, especially, for climbing through that cranny, and thinking to get me the rumi flowers!"

You have to thank me for a deal more than that, Dido thought, taking the small, thin hand for the second time and smiling back at the princess of Lyonesse.

"How many o' them cats did you have to start?" she asked.

"Five. Poor faithful friends . . . I am afraid aurocs or wild beasts must have killed the others."

"Not all o' them," said Dido. "Three got through. But—like the loot here asked—who put you in there?"

"Queen Ginevra, of course," said Elen, as if surprised that anybody should ask such a simple question.

Dido noticed that Mr. Holystone—who, since entering the warm, dim stable, had seemed wrapped in dreamy reverie, gazing at the fire—started slightly at this name and looked round.

"The *queen* put you there?" Windward gaped at the princess. "But—why?"

"For a sacrifice to Sul. The Temple of Sul is up above here on the mountain."

"*Why?*" he said again, incredulously.

"For long life, naturally!" Elen raised her beautiful brows. "Many short lives make one long one. How can she live until her Quondam king comes back unless she takes a great many other lives—young lives, of girls?"

Windward stared at her, speechless, stiff with horror.

"That's why there weren't any girls in Tenby or Bath? It ain't the aurocs at all?" Dido nodded, her suspicions fully confirmed.

"I daresay the aurocs may have had one or two every year," said Elen. "But they mostly remain in the mountains. You have only to ask the guardian of this place; he will tell you how many years he has been throwing girls into Lake Arianrod. And his predecessors before him."

"I *never* heard *anything* so *disgraceful* in my *whole life*," said Lieutenant Windward hoarsely. "And she calls herself a civilized woman! But how did she manage to get hold of you, miss?"

"Well—when I was seven my father sent me to school in Queen's Square, in the other Bath—in England. Lyonesse ought to be safe enough; but, my father thought, best take no chances. So I went to school for nine years. And on the way back my ship was captured by pirates.

"Pirates? They were in Ginevra's pay; her watchdogs. Those three witches of hers throw their net far afield. And a king's daughter, by their reckoning, is worth far more than any ordinary girl. Her bones give six months of life; mine—who knows how long? Six years, perhaps . . ."

"Bones?" whispered Mr. Multiple, who, now that the fire was burning well, had been drawn by the sound of Elen's level voice.

"Thrown into the lake. Eaten by Sul's sacred fish. Then the bones are made into a paste, which, eaten daily by Ginevra, has preserved her life for many hundreds of years."

Dido thought of the fat queen, lolling on her couch,

languidly tasting thick white porridge from a silver dish. My reflection, she thought suddenly. I wonder if it ever came back—like those watches beginning to go again? But even if it didn't—better lose your reflection than be thrown into Arianrod for the fish to munch and then have your bones ground up into porridge.

"That was why your dad pinched the lake, then?" she said. "So you couldn't be thrown in? He guessed the queen musta got you?"

"Did he steal the lake?" A warm ripple of affection came into Elen's voice. "*Clever* father! He knew that would put a stone in her shoe!"

"So then she called in the British Navy," said Windward. "I begin to see. . . . But how could she hope to make King Mabon return the lake so long as she held you, Princess?"

"Because," said Dido, "she hoped as *I*'d let on to be the princess, and that King Mabon'd be fooled. That was why she didn't make *me* into porridge. Though I reckon she was fair itching to. But why were you left in that cave, ma'am? Princess?"

"Oh, pray call me Elen. All the girls at Miss Castlereagh's Academy did so. I was left in the cave because the sacrifice has to be made at a particular time of the month, when the new moon holds the old one in its arms. Lady Ettarde and those other women put me there. And the guardian used to come every day or so to feed me . . . when he remembered. He will not be best pleased when he finds that I have escaped. Ginevra will probably have *him* thrown in the lake. Oh, no, I forget—there is no lake. She must have been growing desperate."

Elen's eyes widened. The fire had now burned up

into a good blaze and, for the first time, she had
noticed Mr. Holystone, who stood gazing at the flames
with a puzzled frown creasing his brow, as if he were
groping in his mind for the verse of some ancient
rhyme which continually escaped him.

Elen said, "But why is my cousin Gwydion with you?
And why is he so silent?"

"*Gwydion?*" said Dido. Her eyes followed Elen's to
the silent figure by the fire.

"Gwydion," repeated Elen. "I recognized him at
once. Though he has grown a beard, which suits him
very well—and it is a long time since we used to play
as children. He used to carve me dolls from sigse
wood. He is the son—the adopted son—of my uncle
Huayna Ccapac. Atahallpa, they called him in Hy
Brasil, but father always called him Gwydion. How
are you, cousin?"

"No, madam," said a new voice, which made them
all, Holystone included, turn hastily toward the doorway. "He is not your cousin. He is of more ancient
lineage than you reckon."

Framed in the entrance stood a strange figure—what
seemed at first sight to be a walking snowball, but
proved, when he had shaken himself, to be a dwarfish
little man, hardly more than three feet high, with
white hair and deep, dark eyes and a long hooked
nose. He threw off the snow-caked toga which he had
wrapped round him, and stumped forward, giving his
unbidden guests some very unwelcoming looks, and
stopping in front of Mr. Holystone to launch at him
a stare of particular dislike while apparently making
an inventory of every detail of his appearance: from
the gold-brown beard, bronzed skin, and quiet gray

eyes to the birthmark on his right forearm and the hand which still clasped the hilt of the sword Caliburn. Splitting the rock had cleaned the rust from the sword blade; it now shone green and deadly, and more light than was reflected from the fire seemed to play up and down its length.

"I beg your pardon—are you the guardian—Caradog?" broke in Lieutenant Windward briskly, feeling that some explanation was owing to their reluctant host. "Ahem! Excuse me! I have a permit here, signed by Queen Ginevra, for travel through the Gate of Nimue and on to Lyonesse."

"Yes, yes, yes, I know all about that," testily answered the guardian. "I was expecting you last night; my sister had informed me of your intentions."

He spoke as if their journey seemed to him a tiresome fidget about a trifle, and went on, ignoring Windward and addressing Holystone. "But why trouble King Mabon about the lake, my lord, since you are already returned to us? What need to visit Lyonesse? Will you not rather return to your capital of Bath Regis?"

"*Gwydion*'s capital?!" exclaimed Elen. "Gracious me, whom do you take him for?"

"Why, who should he be but the Pendragon? He is Mercurius Artaius, true son of Uther. Let me be the first to salute you, lord, *Rex Quondam et vivens*, High King of New Cumbria, Lyonesse, and Hy Brasil," said Caradog, not sounding in the least pleased about it, but going rather creakily and grumpily down on one knee, nevertheless, to kiss Mr. Holystone's hand, which still rested on the hilt of the sword Caliburn. "*Ave rege! Vivat rex!*"

The party from the *Thrush* stared at one another, dumbstruck.

Elen exclaimed, "Gwydion? Can this be true? Or is the old man joking? Are you—can you really be the Pendragon?"

Holystone looked down at the sword in his hand. He said slowly, "Yes, it is true. I am beginning to remember it all—the battle by the winter sea, and how the queens came in a boat across the lake, and carried me away, and cast me into a sleep."

"In the Isle of Avilion," confirmed Caradog. He added rather sourly, "Your lady wife will be very happy to have you restored to her. She has waited and sorrowed for you these many hundreds of years."

"*Wife*?" exclaimed Dido in horror. "D'you mean that Mr. Holystone is married to that murdering old hag of a queen in Bath? Who's been killing off girls right, left, and rat's ramble, just so she could stay alive longer than ordinary folk?"

"*Finis coronat opus*," said Caradog.

"What's that mean, Mr. Guardian?"

"It means, the end justifies the means."

"No, it certainly *don't*! What do *you* think, Mr. Holy? King Whatsyourname? If you really are him? Do you think it's right for that fat queen to stay alive by having poor girls chucked into the lake? Why, she was fixing to chuck Elen here, if we hadn't turned up!"

Mr. Holystone appeared deeply troubled. Frowning perplexedly at Dido, he said, "Who are you, child? Why do I seem to know you? And what can you know of these high matters?"

It was evident that the three separate parts of his existence had not yet dovetailed together.

"Oh, *blimey*!" said Dido, hurt and cross. She felt ex-

tremely upset, but tried not to show it. She couldn't
help adding, however, "When I think of all the times
I fed Dora—and taught you the Battersea Basket—
and how you used to put cockroach lotion on my
toes—"

At the same instant Elen exclaimed in a tone of
horror, as though the reality had been gradually dawn-
ing on her, "You mean my cousin Gwydion is married
to that wicked woman—to Queen Ginevra?"

"*Was*—was, in a former life," corrected Caradog
fussily. "And as, although *he* has been reborn, *she*
has remained alive, of course the marriage is still valid.
Any court of law would uphold it. Not to mention
the ties of honor and obligation—since she has faith-
fully waited for him so many hundreds of years."

"I don't see how honor could tie him to someone
who's been eating people's bones all that time!"

"Really, Miss Twite, I feel this is none of your—of
our business!" exclaimed Lieutenant Windward.

"Our business is to fetch the lake back and have
Cap'n Hughes let out of the pokey," pointed out Mr.
Multiple matter-of-factly. "And then to get hell-for-
leather out o' this infernal country," he added under
his breath, rattling the diamonds in his pocket.

"If you are committed to reclaim the lake for Queen
Ginevra, of course you must do so," Caradog said
suavely. "The storm will abate very soon; you may
set out at daybreak."

Dido thought she noticed a calculating gleam in his
eye. There's one as'll bear watching, she thought;
cunning as an old weasel or my name ain't Twite.
Had poor Elen shut in a cave, was going to chuck
her in the lake—but we don't hear anything about that
now, oh, no! Butter wouldn't melt on his whiskers. If

Mr. Holy *is* King Arthur come back, what's it matter to Old Nibs there whether the lake is put back or not? And who does he remind me of? Who else has a long neb like that?

Her reflections were interrupted at this point by a tremendous fanfare of bocinas and bamboo trumpets outside the door, together with shouts of "Guardian, there! Ho, Guardian! Open up!"

"Who is it?" demanded Caradog suspiciously.

"Sextus Lucius Trevelyan, officer in command, second division, Wandesborough Frontier Patrol. You know my voice, you old spider! Come on, open up! We've heard a tale that you have the princess Elen with you."

"And who in the name of Nodens told you that?" muttered old Caradog, hobbling to unbar the door, which he had bolted behind him.

9

On the second day of Captain Hughes's captivity a new prisoner was thrust, cursing and struggling, through the door that led into the circular series of rooms at the top of the Wen Pendragon tower.

To the captain's surprise the newcomer turned out to be none other than Silver Taffy, who was equally startled at finding his commanding officer in the town jail.

"By jings, sir, I never expected to see *you* in such a place, and that's a fact! What reason did those sons of pigs fetch out for casting you in the lock-up?"

The discovery of the captain's incarceration seemed to have done a certain amount toward reconciling Silver Taffy to his own; he grinned broadly, displaying most of his well-polished teeth.

At first Captain Hughes felt inclined to stand on his dignity with this rogue, who had virtually gone absent without leave and who was, after all, originally a pirate. On the other hand, the captain was becoming heartily impatient with his confinement; Mr. Brandy-winde made a miserable fellow inmate, for he could do nothing but sit rocking back and forth, lamenting over his wife and child and his limp, paralyzed hands. At least Silver Taffy, though ruffianly, was lively and quick-witted, and might become a possible ally in a scheme that the captain was turning over in his mind; so, very much more amiably than might have been expected, he replied:

"The queen—who, I am persuaded, has windmills in her head—is holding me hostage while Lieutenant Windward undertakes a mission for her to King Mabon of Lyonesse. It is a perfectly disgraceful outrage that an officer of His Majesty's Navy should be used so—after all, I have ambassadorial status! But what use to protest? The woman is clearly unhinged. What of yourself, fellow? I trust that you are not incarcerated here for criminal activities?"

His voice did not suggest that he expected his hopes to be fulfilled.

Silver Taffy shrugged and winked.

"No, sir—but it's something of a different case from yourself. I've always been in the free-trading line, you know, fetching butter and astrolabes and woolen goods and such stuff from Lyonesse to Cumbria without troubling the customs! For Queen Ginevra, she levies a crool high rate of duty on all merchandise as comes in."

"You were a smuggler, in other words," snapped the captain.

"If you choose to call it so, sir," said Silver Taffy with dignity. "We prefers to call them benefactors."

"Very well!"

"I was a benefactor, bringing goods through the

mountains by a secret way. But them Cumbrian customs guards, with those damned red-and-white hell hounds of theirs"—here Mr. Brandywinde gave a shuddering whimper—"grew so active and fidgety that it became harder and harder to dodge 'em. So me and my mates got us a brig and took to sea, running up and down the coast from Santa Genista to the port o' Tenby. Well, then, by an' by, my auntie, she got in touch with me."

"Your auntie?"

"My auntie Ettarde, she as is first lady o' the bedchamber and mistress o' the queen's robes. My family is quality, Captain, I'd have you know," said Silver Taffy with dignity, "though for myself I've always been partial to a roving life." His teeth flashed again as he grinned, wearing the sly expression that had always made Dido mistrust him. "My auntie, she said to me, 'You've got a ship, David, and if you do a private errand for Her Mercy, I daresay she will be prepared to overlook certain activities of yours which are otherwise liable to get you dropped into the Severn River one o' these days for the pescadilloes to scrunch up.' 'Any way I can serve Her Mercy,' says I, 'o' course I'll be proud and willing.' So then she told me as how King Mabon's daughter fresh from boarding school had sailed out o' Bristol, England, on the *Maypole*, and how it'd be worth her weight in gold bezants to me if I could see this princess conveyed safe to Queen Ginevra, who would love her like an auntie."

"You abducted the princess, you villain?" exclaimed Captain Hughes. "So King Mabon was right in his suspicions! The queen did have the princess all along! But to what purpose?"

"As to that," said Silver Taffy cautiously, "he that

asks no questions don't get his tongue chopped out, like those poor gray ghosts o' sentries round the palace. Yes, I did pick up the princess, an' I had her conveyed to my auntie Ettarde. Well, just after that, I got tempted northeast'ards by a very pretty prize that was coming up from Patagonia—a Hanoverian merchant-man. I thought I'd slip her in my pocket afore travel-ing up to Bath City for to claim my reward from Her Mercy. But blow me, Cap'n Hughes, if I don't run up agin you in the *Thrush*, an' all my plans go aggly. And I get took prisoner and lose my ship and have to work as a common seaman. But then, what hap-pens? Why, the old *Thrush* herself runs down to Tenby, and I hear you're a-going to visit Queen Ginevra your own self. So all I have to do is sit tight, and I have a free passage to my own front door."

"And then, you rogue?" inquired the captain, inter-ested in spite of his strong disapproval.

"Why, when I did get to see my auntie Ettarde, she and I had a difference as to fee. I found out she was a-keeping four fifths o' what the queen had paid her, and passing on to me only a measly one fifth. 'If I was to pass word to King Mabon about what you did,' says I to her, '—for I'm in Lyonesse as often as not, and could easy drop word along, annie-nonnie-mousily —if King Mabon was to learn what you did, your life wouldn't be worth a lead bezant. He'd send his agents over into Cumbria somehow, and have you tressi-cated!' "

"Why, you treacherous dog!" said the captain indig-nantly. "You yourself were implicated just as deeply in the plot to steal Mabon's daughter."

"Ay, sir, but at least I'm an honest rogue," said Silver Taffy in an injured tone. "It was Auntie keeping four fifths of the takings when she's promised me half that I couldn't stomach. I'm a hard man to cheat, sir; I can't abear it. Howsumdever, my auntie Ettarde is a tough nut likewise, and deep as a well, furthermore. 'Oh,' says she, 'so that's your lay, is it? Well,' says she, 'I'll make a bargain. Fetch in that other lass, that young supercargo from the *Thrush*, liddle Miss Twiddletwite, and you shall have half the price for the pair.' 'Done, Auntie,' says I—sapskull that I am—and off I goes, thinking 'twould be an easy matter to pop Twite in the bag along with Mabon's lass. I had one try, and missed her; then, blow me if she didn't travel off into the wilds with Windward and the rest. And then blow me furder, if half a dozen o' them gray militia dummies don't grab me and sling me in here. And I know why, too—it's so Auntie don't have to pay me her lawful share. It's her doing! She has Queen Ginevra's ear—close as clams, they be. But I'll get even with her, so I will, when I'm out of the derwent house."

Captain Hughes looked at him thoughtfully.

"But how do you know you ever *will* get out?" he said. "Your aunt appears to be in a position of very great power. It might be in her interest to persuade the queen that you should stay here for a long time— perhaps for the rest of your life."

"Ay—don't think I haven't thought the same," said Silver Taffy. "But I'm a peevy man to diddle, as Auntie Ettarde will learn, and a hard man to fasten down. I'd not have stayed in the *Thrush* if it hadn't suited my book. It's odds but I'll find some way out o¹ the coop."

"If you are of that mind," said Captain Hughes, "you and I may yet be of service to one another. It's no use expecting aid or sense from *that* poor wretch"— he glanced exasperatedly at the lachrymose Mr.

Brandywinde. "Your aunt seems to have bewitched him—or he thinks she has, which comes to the same thing. He has lost the use of his hands."

"Ay, she can play that sort o' trick on a poor softie like him," said Taffy scornfully. Nonetheless, Captain Hughes noticed that he made the figure-eight sign, glancing nervously over his shoulder. "The sooner we're out o' here, Cap'n, the better pleased I'll be. Did you have any special notion in mind?"

"Why, yes. I have been exercising my wits to some purpose. Come through here and I will show you."

And Captain Hughes led the way to the chamber where there were paints, paper, and drawing materials.

"Look!" He indicated a mathematical diagram on a large sheet of paper. "I have not been wasting my time in here! The design is done. But the construction requires two people—because these struts here have to be bent and held in shape while the fabric is stretched over them. And poor Brandywinde is quite useless for that."

Silver Taffy bent over the design, and presently a shimmering silver smile split his face.

"Why, Cap'n!" he said. "You were wasted aboard the *Thrush*! You ought to spend your days a-visiting poor coves in prison!"

The journey from Lake Arianrod to the court of King Mabon was achieved in a considerably shorter time than Lieutenant Windward had reckoned. This was due to the fact that King Mabon, grief-stricken at the loss of his child and requiring distraction, had undertaken a tour of his kingdom, and was, the travelers learned, about to preside over the quarterly assize

sessions at his sheep capital of Wandesborough, hardly
fifty miles from the frontier.

At the spanking pace set by the frontier patrol on
their picked mountain mules, swift rangy beasts, short-
tempered and surefooted, it took the party less than a
day to reach the assize town. Wandesborough, like
Bath, lay in a great upland basin, but its surroundings
were green and fertile, kept temperate by balmy breezes
from the slopes of Mount Catelonde. For this reason
the last four hours of the journey were enlivened by
the continuous bleating of sheep, which were pastured
in enormous numbers on the high grassy slopes.

. "What a deal of wool and mutton they must export,"
remarked Lieutenant Windward.

He said this to Dido, kindly trying to divert her
mind, for he thought she looked very mopish and
down-pin. Not even the friendly escort of the legionaries in their short red tunics and mule's-hair–plumed
helmets, or being mounted on a crack cavalry mule,
seemed to put any heart in her. She only muttered "I
daresay" in reply to Windward's well-meant remark.

"Come, cheer up, little 'un," said Mr. Multiple. "I
reckon when King Mabon hears he's got his daughter
back, he'll hand over Queen Ginevra's lake without
any roundaboutation, and we'll be posting back to
Bath again in the twinkling of a pig's tail. And once
she has her blessed piece of water back, not to mention
her husband, if Mr. Holystone is really that—which I,
for one, take with a bushel of salt—then she'll let
Cap'n Hughes go, and we can all be on our way. And
I tell you what," he added generously, "I'll go cahoots
with you in some of my sparklers, for I've got enough
to make us both into nabobs!"

But even this promise failed to arouse any enthusiasm in Dido. She said, "Thanks, Mr. Mully," in a flat little voice, and continued to gaze glumly at her saddlebow, or sometimes ahead, to where Mr. Holystone and Princess Elen rode in silence side by side.

It is a considerable shock when somebody you have known (you thought) very well indeed, and have been fond of, not only proves to be a completely different person from the one you believed to be your friend, but also fails to remember you at all. If, on top of that, he turns out to be a king, reborn after thirteen hundred years, the shock is greater still. And if, into the bargain, he is married to one of the wickedest and most horrible people you have ever met, you can hardly help feeling very unhappy about it. Especially if he seems to be showing rather too much interest in a princess who certainly *isn't* his wife.

Not that Mr. Holystone talked much to the princess; but all the way on the journey, whether in motion or at rest, they kept near to each other, and there seemed to be a kind of wordless communication going on between them.

"What the dickens does it matter to *me*," Dido said to herself crossly, "if he rides beside her and helps her on and off her moke? *I* ain't in charge of 'em."

But she couldn't help thinking how very much Queen Ginevra would dislike it, if she knew that her newly recovered *Rex Quondam*, instead of making all possible speed back to Bath Regis to greet his long-lost queen, was riding in precisely the opposite direction, by the side of a much younger, and very beautiful, princess.

"The queen'll *never* let Cap'n Hughes out of prison at this rate," Dido thought gloomily. "And we can't go off and leave poor old Cap hobbled up in Cumbria. And it's bezants to breadcrumbs she'll grab the lot of us if we go back—have our heads shrunk, or our tongues cut out, or drop us in the river for those pesky fish to guzzle."

Dido's thoughts were far from cheerful.

But when they were about five miles from Wandesborough, they saw a mounted party approaching them at full gallop, accompanied by waving banners and the sound of bocinas; and the little brown-faced, roly-poly man on a fiery mountain pony in the lead proved to be none other than King Mabon himself, impatient for reunion with his daughter. He flung himself off his mount and ran to embrace her, then turned to address her rescuers in a flood of joyful Latin. As this was received by all except Mr. Windward and Mr. Holystone with blank faces, he switched to English.

"Heroes you are indeed, every one of you! My gratitude to the end of your days you will be having. Anything in Lyonesse is yours for the asking! Well, well, now—what a big bonny girl you have grown, cariad! I can see Miss Castlereagh fed you all those years on milk and honey, even if you are a bit skinny just now, with you," he added, giving Elen another hug. "And plenty of learning to go with the bonny looks, I am hoping?"

"Oh yes, Papa, I can speak seven languages, and Professor Crumhorn gave me AA for disputation, and I have reached the second part of the calculus."

"There, now! A bluestocking I have got myself! But as for that Ginevra," said King Mabon, suddenly becoming formidable, "as for that fiend in human form, boiling in oil would be too good for her. She should be—"

"But, Dadda—"

"Well, what?"

"Gwydion is married to her!"

"What?"

"They say that Cousin Gwydion is Queen Ginevra's *Rex Quondam*."

"Who say?"

"Caradog, the old guardian—and Gwydion himself says it."

The guardian, however, had prudently seen fit to make himself scarce and disappear during the bustle of departure from the Pass of Nimue.

King Mabon said to Mr. Holystone, "Is this so, my boy? Are you Mercurius Artaius? Are you the Pendragon?"

"Yes; it is true," said Mr. Holystone, who still looked very tired.

"Then I salute you, my liege lord, and offer you fealty," said King Mabon, going down without more ado on one knobby knee. This was not comfortable for him, since he wore a toga and short tunic, and the ground was stony; he kissed Holystone's hand, then briskly stood up again. "But, my boy, how is it you never knew that before? All those years when you used to visit us as a child, and play with Elen and her brothers—"

"His time had not yet come," interposed Bran, who now, greatly to Dido's astonishment, limped out from among King Mabon's escorting troop. I suppose it was him as passed word that Elen was up there in the stable, Dido thought. Bran wore a white tunic and purple toga. A page-boy carried his cockatoo. He went on, "No use to ask the chrysalis why it is not a butterfly.

The hour had not yet struck nor the hilt of Caliburn come to his hand."

"But—bless me—this puts an entirely new complexion on the matter." King Mabon ran a hand through his dark hair, which was cut short, Roman fashion. "Married to Ginevra, you are? Shocking pity that is, indeed! I don't mind telling you, some nasty rumors have been coming through about her, these twenty years and more. Still," he added, not very hopefully, "maybe now you are returned to her she will be a bit more neighborly. Closed her frontier, she did, years back, and the tales that trickle out from Cumbria I would sooner not be believing."

"I reckon they're all true, Mr. King," said Dido, who saw no reason why she should not take part in this discussion.

"And who might you be, my dear?" King Mabon turned his intense, dark, very intelligent eyes on her.

"Why, this is Dido, Papa, who rescued me; she helped me out of the cave."

"Then it's welcome you are as lambs in spring," said King Mabon. "But why are we all standing like this in the fosseway? Let us go back directly to Wandesborough so that the feasting may commence."

They remounted, the troop of legionaries riding ahead, the frontier patrol behind, and King Mabon and his daughter's rescuers in the middle.

King Mabon talked hard all the way.

"Now you are back, my boy—and delighted I am, though I won't say it wasn't a surprise—"

Wonder what Cap'n Hughes'll say when he finds his steward's a king, Dido thought.

"—unification of the three kingdoms—need for a

strong, guiding hand," King Mabon was continuing. "Danger from Biru, from Patagonia, and the Southern Incas—"

Mr. Holystone seemed to have little to say. He remained silent and listened.

Bran, who, despite his wooden leg, appeared able to ride a mule without any difficulty, came alongside Dido. Noticing her despondent looks, he broke into one of his little songs, sung very softly for her alone:

> *"I like the way*
> *You say my name*
> *None other says it*
> *Quite the same*
> *The syllables sing like the notes of a song*
> *When you say it, I wish it were five times as long!*
>
> *So when I die*
> *Pray don't feel glum*
> *But simply write*
> *Upon my tomb*
> *Forget his career; but tell this to his credit*
> *His name sounded best in the way that she said it!"*

"Your songs are downright silly sometimes," said Dido crossly. "And how did you get here, anyway? You belong in Cumbria. And the frontier is closed, King Mabon said."

"Smugglers, minstrels, and messengers travel where they choose," Bran said. "And a good storyteller is welcome anywhere. Shall I tell you a story, child? You appear somewhat despondent."

"Despondent?" said Dido. "D'you expect me to be as chirpy as a cricket? Cap'n Hughes is in jail, and Mr. Holystone says he's Arthur come back, so—so he's married to that hateful woman." Her voice wavered. To cover this she added quickly, "D'you reckon that's *true?*"

Despite his oddity, she felt sure that Bran would know, and give her a true answer. But instead of replying directly, he said:

"Once there was a wicked rich man who had gained all his riches by despoiling his neighbors. He had particularly abused a man called Abel, taking his land unlawfully, bearing false witness against him; in the end he had Abel turned out of his home. Abel, penniless, became a sailor, and was absent from his homeland for many years, and came back no richer than he had gone.

"But when he did come back, Cain, the rich man, was dying; all his ill-won riches could not protect him from death. And as he lay tossing and turning on his velvet couch, he was tormented by one desperate, feverish craving. 'In all my life I have never heard the sound of the sea! Oh, if I could but hear the sound of the waves beating on the shore, I believe I might recover. Or at least I could die happy.' But the sea was many thousands of leagues away.

"Now, as you know, you can hear the sound of the sea if you hold a shell to your ear. There was only one man in the town who possessed a shell, and that was Abel. The shell, indeed, was his only possession. But when he heard of his enemy's wish, he carried the shell to Cain's house and said, 'Here it is; listen to it by all means if you think it will ease you.' And Cain held the shell to his ear, and his face contorted with rage and envy. '*You have had this all these years, while I parched on the dry land?*' he cried. 'But I will take it from you now!' And he crushed the shell between his hands, and so doing, he died. But Abel said, 'I can still listen to the wind. Its voice is as sweet as the voice of the sea.' "

"Just the same," said Dido indignantly, "that rich man was a pig. A real pig! Did Abel get his things back after Cain died?"

"As to that," Bran said, "I can't tell you. But see, here we are, arriving in Wandesborough."

The assize town was very different from Bath Regis. It was laid out geometrically, a small walled town of neat thatched Roman villas, built strongly of clay and wattle, and all painted white. Mabon was staying in the governor's house, which was simply a bigger villa, with a large, square inner court containing the usual fountain and cactuses.

King Mabon instantly set his stewards to organizing a feast in the main hall, and dispatched messengers to Lyonesse City to make arrangements for the return of Lake Arianrod.

"Fair's fair," he said. "Let no one claim I don't keep my word. I have my child, the old woman can have her pond. And furthermore, I'll send it back faster than I took it." He chuckled. "My master of irrigation has hatched up a plan to ship it back by a series of air balloons, helped by the updraft over Mount Catelonde—which will be a deal quicker and cheaper than all those llamas."

"How did you manage to remove it without the guardian's knowledge?" inquired Mr. Windward.

"My spies picked a couple of nights when he was down in Bath reporting to the queen, which he does twice a month."

What a deal of trouble would have been saved, Dido thought, if the spies had only found the princess. I'd have been home by this time, and Cap'n Hughes wouldn't be in jail.

While the mutton was roasting for the feast, they all lolled on warm earthenware couches shaped like the letter *P* laid on its side. The villa was centrally heated by underground ducts from Pampoyle and Catelonde. They reclined against wool-stuffed cushions and drank mead, while Bran played his harp and sang, Elen and Mr. Holystone sat side by side, apparently listening to the music, not talking to one another. Dido felt a painful tightness in her chest, either at the music or at the sight of them, so she moved over and listened instead to King Mabon discussing with the English officers the state of affairs in New Cumbria.

"Bad as it can be, and no better in Hy Brasil," Mabon was saying. "Gwydion's foster brother Ccaedmon—lucky the relationship is no closer, proper tyrant *he* is—turned the whole country into a big-game preserve—evicted half his subjects from their homes. Cuts off the peasants' hands if they catch so much as a guinea pig."

"A guinea pig, sir?"

"Indeed yes! Cui, they call them hereabouts—because of the sound, you know"—King Mabon imitated a guinea pig's squeak so realistically that the governor's cat shot into the room and began searching suspiciously under the couches. "Or," the king went on, "some say it is short for *cui cui modo*. Guinea pigs used to be the staple diet in Hy Brasil until Ccaedmon declared that they belonged to the crown." He glanced over at his daughter and Holystone. His brow clouded slightly. He called, "Gwydion, my boy!"

Holystone rose a little reluctantly and came across the room.

"Sir?"

Dido caught a queer, polite echo of Captain Hughes's steward.

"Now, now, boyo, it is I who should be calling you sir," Mabon said, clapping him on the shoulder. "Only it comes hard with a lad I taught to cast his first trout fly. Queer it must be for you, indeed, and difficult to take it all in."

"Oh, *why*," burst out Holystone, looking harassed and miserable, "why must this happen to *me*? Why should I, of all people, be brought back in this way? To what end?"

"As to why *you*, bless me if I know!" said King Mabon frankly. "But it had to be someone, now, didn't it? And when you ask to what end—haven't I just been saying? Gracious to goodness, why this whole region—with the exception of Lyonesse, which, I pride myself, is as peaceful and prosperous a little country as you could hope to visit—the whole of Roman America apart from that is in a disgraceful condition of tyranny, anarchy, and misrule. Time it was the High King came back; someone who will be accepted by the people and set matters to rights.

"Are they still head-hunting in Cumbria?" he asked Windward.

"Indeed yes, sir; I gather it is a thriving practice."

"And the things that go on in Biru you'd never believe—brigandage, cannibalism—I believe they even sacrifice their grandmothers to Sul. Grandmothers! And in the streets of Manoa you daren't go out at night because robbers make off with the silver manhole covers; you could fall straight into the sewers and get washed away. No, no, my dear Gwydion—Artaius—

time it is you came back, not a moment too soon indeed. And then there's your good lady over in Cumbria—time some of *her* habits were taken in hand."

Holystone looked even more unhappy.

"Have you ever met her, sir?"

"Not I, my boy! Won't cross her frontiers; won't receive foreign rulers. But these gentlemen have met her, I believe."

Multiple shook his head. The lieutenant said, "The young lady has talked to her more than I have."

"Have you indeed, my dear? And lived to tell the tale? Uncommon, that is," King Mabon said. "Tell us what she is like, then, eh?"

How to describe someone who is both wicked and sentimental, self-centered, silly, and terrifyingly powerful? Dido's usual readiness of tongue deserted her. And besides, it was, after all, poor Mr. Holystone's wife they were talking about; and he looked glum enough already.

After some thought, Dido muttered, "She sure wants Mr. Holy back. She don't think of much else. She wanted me to try and gull King Mabon into believing I was his daughter. So she'd get the lake back."

She looked up into Mr. Holystone's sad gray eyes.

"You have seen Guinevere?" he said slowly. "Is she—is she much changed?"

"How'd *I* know?" Dido said crossly. "I dunno what she was like afore, do I? All I know is, she's been waiting a plaguey long time and it's—upset her. She'd be the better for not having that mess o' havey-cavey old witches round her, too—Lady Ettarde, and Morgan, and the other one. Well, one of 'em's dead," she added thoughtfully, remembering the scene at Elen's rescue.

"Which one?" inquired Bran, who had joined the group. His voice was sharp with interest. Dido glanced at him in surprise.

"I'd have thought you'd know, mister! It's the one as called herself Mrs. Vavasour."

An odd look came into Bran's face—sorrow compounded with relief. He lifted his shoulders as if a weight had fallen from them. And his cockatoo flew across the room and perched on his wrist.

Dido wondered what Bran's connection had been with the witch-dressmaker. But Princess Elen had now followed Holystone, and sat down by her father, who tucked his arm round her affectionately. She said, "Mrs. Vavasour is dead? I am glad of that."

She shivered, and went on: "She told me she had set a snake to watch me, outside the cave entrance, and that it would grow and double its size every day, and could see me through the crack and would bite me if I tried to get out. I—I didn't really believe her, but I used to think I could hear it hissing."

"Ugh! How could you bear it, ma'am?" said Multiple with a shudder. "I can't abide snakes."

"I daresay most of their witcheries are no more than mumbo-jumbo, done to frighten credulous folk," said Mabon.

"But that owl did turn into Mrs. Vavasour," said Dido. "It ain't all mumbo-jumbo." And there was my reflection in the mirror, she thought.

Elen said, "Bran used to tell us when we were children that witchcraft was the wickedness in several people's minds combining to form something worse still. Like making poison by mixing things that are harmless taken singly." She looked into Holystone's face wistfully. "Artaius? Gwydion? Can you really remember nothing of when we were children?"

He shook his head. "Only a vagueness—like a dream, half-caught."

"You don't recall how you used to stay with us? Or that Bran here was your tutor?"

"The best pupil I ever had," Bran said. "*He* never had to stay in to learn his principal parts, as you and your brothers did, Princess."

"*Why* can't I remember?" muttered Holystone, pressing his brow, as if to make a hole and let air into his brain.

"Some external force is blocking your mind for its own ends," Bran told him. "It is of no consequence. You know that you are the High King. Other memory will return in time."

The governor's cat had followed Elen and now jumped into her lap.

"They still follow you, eh?" said her father. "Did they do so in that English Bath? And what did Miss Castlereagh say to that?"

"Oh, she was a very kind lady, Dadda. She sent her dutiful respects to you, when I left, and gave me a pomander ball and a copy of Dr. Johnson's *Dictionary of the English Language*. The pomander ball I lost when the pirates captured our ship, but the dictionary has proved very useful."

"Nothing like a good vocabulary, I always say." King Mabon beamed at his daughter. "But look, supper's ready—all your favorites, my dear. Roast mutton, bara brith, and syllabub!"

10

Since he had had no expectation of meeting his daughter when he first began his tour of the kingdom, King Mabon had brought no ladies-in-waiting with him. Dido kindly offered to perform this office for the princess until they reached Lyonesse City.

"As to that," said Elen, "personal maids weren't allowed at Miss Castlereagh's, so I managed for myself all the time I was at school. But I'd be glad if you would share my room, Dido. I still feel nervous when I think of that cave; if I listen, I think I can hear those old witches flapping and hissing outside." She shivered uneasily.

"I've never been to school. Did you like it?" asked Dido, hoping to distract her.

"All but the embroidery. I must have stitched at least eighteen miles of it in the nine years I was there! I made a vow that when I got back to Lyonesse I'd never touch a needle again."

They were brushing each other's hair with bunches of ichu grass. There was no looking glass in the room, but Dido suddenly recollected that she still had Queen Ginevra's little diamond-studded hand mirror, and pulled it from her jacket pocket.

"Why!" she said, pleased, "my reflection's come back."

"What *can* you mean?"

"Queen Ginevra took it." Dido explained how her image had gone from the bowl and glasses.

"I daresay her power grows less the farther you are from Bath," Elen suggested.

Dido wondered rather dismally what would happen to Mr. Holystone when he returned to that city.

"Oh!" cried Elen, as if catching this thought, "I can't *bear* it that he's married to that hateful woman. When he has gone back to Cumbria—I shall probably never see him again."

Dido saw that there were tears in the princess's eyes.

Poor thing, she thought. I used to reckon it'd be all jam and high jinks being a princess, but I guess that ain't so; they don't have it much better than ordinary folk.

"Come, cheer up," she said gruffly. "You can't ever tell how things'll turn out. Maybe they'll look better in the morning. Us had best get to bed."

In the middle of the night, however, they were woken by a tap on the door. Dido, opening it cautiously, saw Mr. Multiple, who had been posted outside to keep guard. He looked very strange—pale, ghastly, and staring eyed.

"Why, what's up, Mr. Mully?"

"*Quick*—don't make any noise, but follow me, both

of you!" he whispered. "There is horrible danger!"
His freckles were black dots against the pallor of his
cheeks, his red hair was dark and lank with sweat.

"What the blazes can it be? Where's Mr. Holy—and
King Mabon—and Bran?"

"*Hush*! Come outside and I will tell you! The princess too!"

Dido was disturbed and dubious, but Mr. Multiple
whispered, "*Please* come!" with such urgency that Elen
said, "Very well, we will follow you," and the two
girls wrapped themselves in togas and tiptoed after
him. He led them swiftly but silently to a side entrance
that opened into a narrow lane beside the governor's
house. Dido, following him, noticed that he seemed
oddly bulky. How'd he ever get so fat so fast? she
wondered; he must have fairly tucked into that roast
mutton and syllabub.

Outside, in the alley, "Now then, what is—?" Dido
began, but before she could utter another syllable her
hands were grabbed and tied behind her and she was
lifted up and bumped down uncomfortably onto the
crupper of somebody's saddle. "Make no sound!" a
voice hissed in her ear. "Do you feel this blade?" Dido
nodded. A sharp point was jabbed between her ribs.
"It will gut you like a herring if you let out a single
squeak." Elen had been similarly pinioned and
mounted. Looking in horror and outrage for Mr. Multiple—how *could* he have been capable of such treach-
ery?—Dido gasped with astonishment. An enormous
snake which had been coiled round him under his
jacket now dropped to the ground and slithered away
into the shadows. Half fainting with terror, the
wretched midshipman was also tied up and dragged

onto a pony; then the troop of their captors—there seemed to be nine or ten—set off silently and speedily through the dark streets of Wandesborough.

The ponies' hoofs were muffled in sacking and made no sound. Dido thought they must surely be stopped when they came to the town gate, but no: evidently the sentries had been poisoned or drugged, for they lolled in their guard boxes like limp marionettes and never stirred as the riders passed by. Once outside the wall, the ponies' pace was increased to a gallop.

There was a little light from the old moon, which hung like a sliver of coconut in one corner of the sky, and Dido could see that they were taking a course at right angles to that followed by King Mabon when he and his legionaries returned to the town. Best keep a watch for landmarks, Dido thought; not much else to be done just now.

There were few landmarks to be seen in this huge, grassy basin, but they rode with the four stars of the Southern Cross behind them and to the right, which must mean that they were heading northeast; and away to the left a red glow, and occasional sparkles in the sky, suggested that Mount Catelonde was fretting and fidgeting as Mr. Holystone had done in his haunted sleep.

Blister me, thought Dido angrily, I'll never trust *anybody* ever again. I reckon this must be more of Queen Ginevra's doing; wonder how she knew that Mr. Mully was so scared of snakes? Poor thing, he must feel terrible bad.

She half wished she could get near him to comfort him, but felt impatient with his cowardice, too. He mighta managed to give us *some* hint, so we could have raised the alarm. But then, in fairness, she thought, I've never had a snake wrapped round my midriff. I mightn't feel so devil-may-care if I had.

After an hour's hard riding the party reached a region of steeper hillsides and small deep valleys. By now dawn was beginning to pale the sky and a faint glow showed where the sun would rise, over on the right. Dido was confirmed in her guess that they were traveling toward New Cumbria. By a different route, evidently, not through the Pass of Nimue; and indeed, approaching a high crag, where cascading lava from Mount Pampoyle had hardened into a kind of rock ladder, they dismounted and climbed up to an entrance in the cliff face above them. The three captives were prodded forward at dagger point, and some of their guards stood below as they climbed, pointing crossbows at them.

"Don't try to jump," Dido's guard warned her, "or you'll come to ground spitted like a pigeon."

He wore a hood, but she thought she recognized his voice.

Having entered the cave, their captors lit candles in glass lanterns and urged the prisoners forward at a rapid walk. At this point Mr. Multiple managed to get near the two girls.

"I'm sorry, Your Highness, I'm *sorry*," he muttered miserably. Dido saw that tears were running down his cheeks; he looked utterly wretched. "Oh, I could kill myself," he cried. "But what good would that do?"

"None at all." Elen gave him a stony look. "I hate a coward," she said haughtily.

Dido had more sympathy toward the wretched lad. She remembered how she herself felt about spiders.

"Never mind, Mr. Mully," she said. "Done's done.

Best you can do now, if there's ever a chance, is get away and give the alarm which way we've gone."

However, it seemed, he was not to be given the chance. After they had walked what felt like three or four miles (but was probably less) along dark, narrow ascending galleries, they came to a much larger cavern, where the high, regular walls showed the scarred signs of workings. Probably silver mines, Dido guessed; there were pickaxes and sections of machinery lying here and there. An underground river crossed their path and had to be forded by a series of square stepping-stones which had evidently been set there for the purpose.

Not far from this point the river apparently plunged over a cliff into a gorge; they could hear the roar of a waterfall and see spray rising. Dido's hooded guard nodded toward Mr. Multiple and indicated the falls.

"Toss him over there. He is no further use to us. His body will never be found in here."

"*No!* You can't do that!" exclaimed Dido in horror.

Mr. Multiple yelled and struggled unavailingly as four of the hooded captors dragged him toward the gorge, while the rest of the party proceeded swiftly on their way. Dido heard the unfortunate midshipman's voice raised in a final shriek of despair.

Soon afterward his assassins rejoined the other group, which had reached the terminal point of a strange little conveyance evidently used for transporting ore through the galleries of the mine. It was a series of open cars, linked together, which ran along above a single track, or rather groove, in the rock floor; this groove emitted steam, which somehow propelled the cars by turning a rotor which engaged with the wheels. Cap'n Hughes would go crazy over it, Dido thought glumly, as she and Elen were thrust into a car with two of their captors (each car held no more than four persons, and that was a tight squeeze); a lever was pulled to start the train, which moved off slowly, but by degrees built up a terrifying speed, so that they hurtled hissing through the darkness, rocking and swaying from side to side.

"Keep your head down," Dido's guard curtly warned her, "or you're liable to get your brains dashed out."

She followed this advice and huddled on the floor of the car, a prey to the most dismal thoughts. Mr. Multiple's dreadful fate had upset her horribly; he was a decent, kindhearted boy, she thought, not a mite of harm in him, not his fault he didn't like snakes; and they tossed him over the cliff without giving two thoughts to the matter, as if he'd been an apple core!

It was stiflingly hot in this part of the mountain. The air, such as there was, smelled very bad, of hot metal, aged rock, and sulfureous steam; what with that, and the train's seesaw, oscillating motion, Dido began, after an hour or so, to feel very sick indeed. Her head throbbed, and she had to keep swallowing; but she had nothing to swallow *with*—her mouth felt as dry as stale bread. The guards' lanterns had long ago blown out, in the wind of their progress, and she could not even see Elen, but groped about and found her hand. She feared that the princess—only just rescued from that cave—must feel even worse; and indeed Elen's hand seemed alarmingly cold and limp, returning only the faintest pressure in response to Dido's.

After an immense interval—Dido thought she might have slipped into a kind of faint; the time slid past in feverish fits and starts, as it does during illness—they came out into larger, lighter galleries, past gleaming piles of silver ore and uncut gemstones awaiting carriage to the outer world. At last the train began to slow down, and finally it drew to a stop. The lanterns were lit again.

Dido's guard had pushed back his hood during the journey, and she saw that he was the grand inquisitor, Daffyd Gomez. The person holding Elen was likewise revealed as the vicar general, Fluellen. Might have guessed those old ravens would get in on it somehow, Dido thought dejectedly, letting herself be pushed out of the car onto a rock platform.

The hiss of the train died away, and instead Dido heard another familiar voice.

"So you have got them! Just as well one part of the business has gone right."

Another masked, cloaked figure, unmistakable nonetheless by its smallness as Lady Ettarde, hobbled along the platform. She took off her mask to glower at the two exhausted girls. She was accompanied by old Mrs. Morgan.

"Why, what has gone wrong?" demanded Fluellen.

"Those fools have let Hughes and my nephew escape from the Wen Pendragon."

"Holy Sul! I didn't think it could have been done. Where are they now?"

She shrugged.

"Who knows? Gone into the mountains. Very likely the aurocs will get them. But on account of that, Her Mercy needs new hostages, as a lever against anything Mabon may try. And she is becoming very impatient. *Come* along, you!" she said to Dido and Elen.

The girls were jerked and jostled to the foot of a steep, winding stairway, and obliged to climb it. In their dazed and fainting state they made very slow

progress; Mrs. Morgan, behind them, kept up a continual angry mutter: "*Git* along, *git* along, then, me
little runaway darlings"—on the word *darlings* she
poked Dido with what felt like a bodkin—"Her
Mercy'll be happy to see *you* again, that's one thing
certain."

They arrived at the top of the long climb with knees
that felt like wool.

Now, to Dido's utter amazement, she recognized
her surroundings; the stair had brought them into one
of the antechambers of Bath Palace. Who'd a thought
we had come so far? she said to herself. So the queen
has her own private way into the silver mines. Very
handy for her anytime she wants a new pair of earrings.

Lady Ettarde halted her prisoners at the foot of the
grand staircase.

"Now listen to me, you two!" she hissed. Despite her
small stature she looked extremely formidable. "First,
don't think you will be so lucky as to escape a second
time! My brother himself will guard you this time.
Clever as you may think you are, once you are in the
city of Sul, he and his cat-a-mountain will be more
than a match for you."

Neither of the girls made any reply. They were still
getting their breath after the punishing climb.

"Idiot!" snapped Lady Ettarde to the grand inquisitor. "Why did you not take some rumirumi flowers
with you? Her Grace will not be best pleased to see
them so fatigued."

Dido had a recollection of Mrs. Morgan saying, "*She*
don't like them if they're droopy."

When Lady Ettarde turned to continue on up the
grand stair, Dido whispered to Elen, "Droop as much
as you can. Pretend to feel even worse than you do!"

They were led along the curving gallery toward the throne room. But halfway along the gallery Lady Ettarde halted them once more, ostensibly to let them get their breath, in reality to whisper menacingly, "Don't tell the queen that the Rex Atahallpa is back."

"*Who?*"

"Atahallpa. Artaius. Don't tell her."

"Why not?" said Dido sourly.

"Because if she knows that he is back and has not made haste to join her, she will be so angry that she will probably have your tongues cut out on the spot."

"But why should you care?" said Dido. Partly she was playing for time—anything to keep the old witch talking; but she did wonder why it mattered to Lady Ettarde.

"Never you mind!" rasped the mistress of the robes, and hobbled on again.

As Dido followed, the answer came to her. Of course *she* don't want Mr. Holystone to turn up here and settle down as Queen Ginevra's ever-loving husband. Because when he does, it's crowns to cake crumbs as her turn'll be over; the queen won't pay heed to her anymore. Likely she's sorry he ever came back, and wishes him at Jericho.

Now they were led into the queen's presence.

Ginevra hardly seemed to have moved since Dido saw her last. She still reclined, fatly, in her loose white gown, among cobwebby gray curtains. But she looked older, Dido thought; her face was drawn and haggard, there was no coyness or sentimentality about it today. Her eyes were strangely dull, except that every now and then, even though she was not wearing her glasses, they suddenly, for a moment, would become purely reflectors and mirror the scene in front of her. This,

when it happened, was horribly disconcerting, as if
the queen had stopped being a real person at all and
was just a piece of machinery, mechanically carrying
out her own wishes.

"Here are the two girls, Your Mercy," said Lady
Ettarde. "Mabon's daughter and the other one."

Ginevra did not show any particular triumph or
pleasure. Her head turned slowly, surveying the girls.
Her eyes played their odd trick, shining, turning glassy;
then, after a moment, they became eyes again, and she
said, "Has Mabon returned my lake?"

Lady Ettarde looked inquiringly at the grand inquisitor, who had followed them. He said, "Your Mercy,
he has begun sending it back. It is being flown over
the mountains in leather water-skins, borne by small
air balloons. The thongs are waxed, so that they melt
and discharge their contents into the lake basin." He
had made this report in a dispassionate, formal manner, but he concluded with some enthusiasm; "And I
must say, it was a capital notion of King Mabon's!
Highly ingenious! He must have some excellent de-
signers. As I have often said to Your Mercy, if he were
only our ally—"

"Quiet, fool! How long will it take? How soon will
the lake be filled again?"

"At the rate the water-skins are discharging, I would
guess, about thirty-six hours, ma'am."

Now Elen spoke up.

"How dare you take us prisoner, when my father
has honorably fulfilled his undertaking to return the
lake?"

Her voice was brave, but she flinched a little when
the queen turned those glassy eyes on her.

Ginevra did not address her, however, but said to Lady Ettarde, "When is the new moon?"

"In three days, Your Mercy."

Ignoring a sick feeling in her inside, Dido bluntly addressed the queen.

"If you were thinking of having us tossed in the lake, Your Royalty, you might as well know that your *Rex Quondam* is back; so there ain't no need!"

She heard a sort of growl from Lady Ettarde, behind her, and thought she saw something black and furry detach itself from that lady's full skirts and scurry in Dido's direction.

Now the queen's shining, sightless eyes were staring at her. To avoid their unnerving stare, she looked down at the floor. Yes, it was a spider the size of a hairy grapefruit; it was on the point of climbing up her leg.

On a step of the dais, lying disregarded where Ginevra had dropped it, was the chunk of raw sapphire that Bran had given the queen. Dido snatched it up and used it to deal the spider a satisfactory, crunching thwack. The spider rolled over, its legs thrashing, then folding in death.

Don't I just wish Bran was here, Dido thought, clutching the stone. But even the memory of him was comforting.

Queen Ginevra said, "*The High King is back*? Back *where*?"

"He was up at Lake Arianrod," Dido said. "Now he's in Lyonesse."

"Is this true?"

"Oh yes, it's true," said Elen wearily. "My father has sworn fealty to him."

The queen turned her mirror eyes on Lady Ettarde.

"Why was I not told?"

"Ma'am, how do we know whether the girls are speaking truth?"

"It may be only a rumor," Lady Ettarde and the grand inquisitor said together.

Ignoring them, Ginevra clapped her hands.

"Have the coronation regalia brought out, so that I may inspect it! Send my chief herald to me. Where is my soothsayer? Fetch him here!"

"Your Mercy, nobody knows where he is."

Lady Ettarde was red-faced, flustered and gasping.

"Have those two girls sent up, under double escort, to the city of Sul," the queen went on. "Give this message to the guardian." She scribbled on the tablets a scribe brought her. "Ettarde! I shall need ten new gowns. And my lord will doubtless require a royal wardrobe—and a coronation robe. Let tailors be sent for."

"Of course, Your Mercy." Lady Ettarde looked relieved at this evidence that her sphere of usefulness was not yet ended. "What shall I—?"

"Quiet! Leave me now. I must have rest and quiet. I must think. I must remember." She lay back on her cushions.

The girls were hustled away. Once they were out of sight, Lady Ettarde gave Dido a box on the ear that rattled her teeth together.

"That's for disobeying me, you little hussy!"

Their journey to the Temple of Sul was also taken by underground train through the silver mines. Too bad the queen didn't tell us this way before, Dido thought; saved us a deal of travel, that would, and poor Plum wouldn't have been took by the aurocs. But then, she reflected, I wouldn't have found the sword, and Elen wouldn't have been rescued. Though what's the good of that now?

Dido felt very low-spirited. The death of poor Mr. Multiple had upset her dreadfully; the interview with Queen Ginevra had not cheered her at all. And besides that, it was now three quarters through the day, and she felt hollow and light-headed from lack of food and sleep.

The train they rode on this time, however, was far more comfortable, apparently the queen's private conveyance to the Temple of Sul. The cars had glass windows like small hackney coaches, and wool-stuffed cushions. These pits were still being actively worked, and miners could sometimes be seen through the windows hacking at rock faces or carrying the ore in baskets strapped to their backs. There were a great many women and children at work, too. Elen was shocked to see this.

"Small children pulling those heavy trolleys along the rails? It is disgraceful!"

"Keeps them out o' the way of the aurocs," Dido pointed out.

"It should not be allowed. It is not so in Lyonesse."

"It is in England." Dido had never set foot in an English mine, but she knew that quite small children did work there.

"Well, when I see—*if* I see Gwydion again, I shall tell him he should have it stopped."

"Yes, you do that," said Dido soothingly, and then both girls fell into a despondent silence.

One thing, though, thought Dido, her spirits picking up again—it's good to know that old Cap'n Hughes got himself out o' the pokey. I wouldn't a thought he had the gumption! I wonder who Lady Ettarde's nephew is, that she spoke of, and why he was in there? Could it be—? But no, the idea was too preposterous.

Lady Ettarde had accompanied them on this journey, along with a troop of the silent, gray-uniformed guards. But the mistress of the wardrobe was preoccupied, and sat in a separate car, busy making sketches of coronation robes. Dido and Elen traveled in a car with two guards, who sat facing them but did not speak.

Toward the end of the journey the train evidently began to climb an exceedingly steep ascent; the guards had much ado to keep from sliding off their seat, and the girls were tipped against the back of theirs. The train labored more and more slowly, wheezing, hissing, and wailing. At last it ground to a stop.

"Hope we ain't going to slip backwards," said Dido.

However, it seemed they had reached their destination. The guards, who carried pikes, gestured that the girls were to alight, and they did so, finding themselves in a large, cold cave, dimly lit by oil lamps hanging on the walls. They were led out under an imposing arched entrance, past piles of crushed rock, and then up a steep but well-paved road. As they climbed higher they could see, below and to the right, the familiar star-shaped basin of Lake Arianrod. But what a drop! It must be well over a thousand feet below.

The paved road zigzagged to and fro over the mountainside, and now, looking up, Dido could see high walls above them, built from huge, massive blocks of stone, each probably weighing more than four hundred tons. The walls were fortified with towers at regular intervals and circled the mountain, crossing gullies and ravines, perching on the edge of precipices.

"Not a place you'd get into if they didn't want you,"

panted Dido to Elen, as the party turned to take breath on a hairpin curve. "But I thought it was a temple? That place looks twice the size of Bath."

"It is a town," said Elen. "But nobody lives there now."

"Be quiet, girls!" snapped Lady Ettarde. "You are entering Sul's sacred city."

Lady Ettarde was being borne upward in a sedan chair. Lucky for the carriers that she's so short, Dido thought. They must need a half a dozen to tote the queen along when *she* comes up.

A great stone stairway led down into a dry moat, then up again to a huge gateway. They passed through this, and on up a steep, silver-cobbled hill.

"Mystery me," muttered Dido to herself. "I never thought I'd see a whole empty town. Wonder what *happened* to all the folk?"

It was plain that the city of Sul had been uninhabited not for ten, or a hundred, but for many, many hundreds of years. Great forest trees had grown among the temples, palaces, baths, and blocks of dwellings. Near the outer wall the houses were mere cobblestone hovels, but farther in the buildings were splendid, constructed from huge chunks of white granite, roofed with masses of peaked gables, interwound with countless stone stairways. What a deal of years the place must have taken to build, thought Dido; it covers the whole blessed mountaintop. Looking back, as they toiled ever upward, she could see three different mountain ranges in the distance, and great masses of white cloud, tinged with sunset pink, floating far away, over what must be the forest of Broceliande.

The whole city was completely silent.

They reached a sloping oblong space, five hundred

yards in length, evidently the main square of the city.
At the upper end of this was a massive building with
no windows at all, and but one entrance, a plain
square doorway, on the broad lintel of which was
carved the same woman's head, with snakes for hair,
that Dido had seen in Bath. The guards bowed rever-
ently before it, and Lady Ettarde clambered out of her
sedan chair to make a stiff curtsey. Apparently this
was the Temple of Sul.

The entrance was approached by a flight of steps.
At the top of them old Caradog the guardian stood
waiting.

"Welcome," he said simply, and to Elen, "Those
who were once lost are doubly welcome."

Lady Ettarde hobbled up the steps and kissed him.
Seeing them together, both short, long nosed, narrow
lipped, with deep-set eyes, Dido realized they must be
brother and sister. What a clunch I am, she thought;
they're as like as two peas in a pod. Why didn't I
notice before?

In fact Caradog was saying, "Will you stay the night,
Sister?"

But she replied, "No, I thank you, Brother, I must
return to the queen. *That* ill-conditioned child"—she
cast an angry glance at Dido—"revealed that Artaius
had returned, as you had already told me by carrier
pigeon; Her Mercy wants coronation robes prepared."

"The news could not have been withheld from her
for long," Caradog said calmly.

"Where is Artaius now?"

"With Mabon."

Both of them glanced at the sky. Dido, following the
direction of their eyes, saw a tear-shaped globe drifting
over the peaked and gabled roofs. It was pale yellow

in color; below it, on cords, swung a barrel-shaped leather vessel. It was hard to guess how big the balloon was, up there in the sky; perhaps about the size of a pig. "Look!" Dido said, nudging Elen. But the princess, at this evidence of her father's honorable nature, appeared very downcast.

"I wonder he hasn't stopped sending them," she said.

The balloon vanished from view behind a high, round tower at the top of the town.

Now Dido watched with astonishment as a dozen of the gray-clad guards came staggering across the square carrying an upright piano, which had evidently been brought up on the train along with the prisoners.

"What you want a *piano* for . . ." said Lady Ettarde to her brother, in a tone of mystification, as it was heaved up the steps of the temple.

"It is so silent up here, just myself and Grandmother Sul," explained Caradog, inclining his head to the carving above the lintel. "I thought she might enjoy a different music."

Lady Ettarde sniffed. "Fanciful nonsense! The old ways were better—nothing but bocinas when I was a young gel. Good-bye, brother—I must be getting back to the queen. Her Mercy won't be best pleased at being left alone all this time with no one but old Mag Morgan. I'll leave you the guards."

"No need; I don't wish for them," he said. "Tell them to lock the town gate as they go out. Then the young ladies will be safe enough—unless they have a taste for flying."

"Are you *certain*?" His sister looked very doubtful. "We want no repetition—"

"Whose idea *was* that cave? They will be far safer

here. Hapiypacha will watch over them. Farewell.
Until the Day of Sul."

"Until the Day of Sul," Lady Ettarde said, and
climbed back into her sedan chair. The guards, having
delivered the piano somewhere inside the building,
carried the chair across the square and disappeared
down the hill.

Caradog turned and surveyed his prisoners.

"Are you hungry?" he asked unexpectedly.

"Ain't we jist!" said Dido.

"Then you had better come inside."

The interior of the temple was a huge space shaped
like a long isosceles triangle, tapering not quite to a
point but to a high narrow wall at the far end, pierced
by three lancet windows. These were the only windows
in the place, which was very dim; the long side walls
were blank, broken only by niches alternating with
protruding cylindrical stones.

Under the three windows—which admitted pink
sunset light—stood a huge stone altar block, fourteen
feet long by five feet high. On this, rather unexpectedly, lay various musical instruments: bamboo flutes,
a harp, a lute, several crumhorns, and a rebeck.

"Material offerings are of little interest to Sul,"
Caradog explained, as Dido glanced inquisitively at
these. "The sound of music, or the human voice, is to
her what burnt offerings are to lower gods." He gave
an explanatory nod at the piano, which had been set
down not far from the altar.

What about chucking us in the lake? Dido wanted
to ask. What does Sul think about that? It ain't Sul
who wants us in the lake, it's that greedy queen.

Caradog led the girls on through a door beside the
altar into what was plainly the priest's house. This

was a bare stone building, scantily furnished with carved stone couches and tables; however, there was a fireplace, where blazed a fire of thorn and fig branches, filling the air with aromatic smoke. Ordering the girls to sit down on one of the stone couches, Caradog presently handed them each a bowl of rather tasteless bean-and-yucca stew. This was accompanied by ancient, slightly moldy bread and weak willow-leaf tea. Being exceedingly hungry, the prisoners ate uncritically and began to feel, if not cheerful, at least somewhat better.

The meal finished, Caradog led them back to the temple again. Here he began to play on various of the instruments, fetching strange quavering sounds from the bocinas, plucking on the harp and lute, blowing through the crumhorns; the noises he made were very uncouth. Dido did not think highly of his performance; nor, to judge from the grimace she made, did Elen, who presently volunteered, "I can play on the piano, if you would like me to. I learned in England."

"Can you, though?" Old Caradog's deep eyes lit up; he dragged a stone block up to the piano, since a stool had not been provided. Elen sat down on this, rather uncomfortably, and proceeded to play a waltz.

The guardian was amazed. He stood with his eyes shut in ecstasy, swaying the upper part of his body about in time with the music. When it was ended, he opened his eyes again and sighed, as if his spirit had returned from another, far-distant region. Dido, too, was greatly impressed with Elen's proficiency. She herself had not the slightest notion of how to play on the piano.

"Oh!" sighed Caradog. "If I could but keep you here long enough to teach me that art!"

This depressing remark spoiled the more cordial

atmosphere that had been building up between the guardian and his prisoners. Looking at the light, which was almost gone, he said shortly, "Come; it is time you retired for the night," and took them back into his house.

"This is your room"—indicating a small chamber, stone floored, and with no furnishings at all except what looked uncomfortably like a large heap of human hair in one corner. "There is water in the room next door," said Caradog; and there was, a large stone tank of it. "Now," he continued, "I will introduce you to Hapiypacha, who will watch over you from now on."

At the end of a passage he pulled back an iron-barred gate as big as a door. From the darkness beyond came a loud, yawning growl—the sound made by someone who is roused too suddenly from sleep and not best pleased about it.

"Hapiypacha is kept hungry through the night," said Caradog. "I feed him at dawn."

As Caradog said this, Hapiypacha emerged from his sleeping quarters in one long, fluid bound. He snarled and spat sideways at the guardian as he passed; the old man stood his ground, remarking calmly, "Hapiypacha has an unfriendly disposition; but he knows I am his master."

Hapiypacha was an ounce, or mountain leopard; he stood four feet high at the shoulder and was about nine feet long, including his tail. He had a pale gray coat, dotted over with large, dark rosettes, and three black stripes along his back; his black ears were tasseled, and he had two dark "tear marks"—stripes—down his cheeks, white whiskers, green luminous eyes, and a no-nonsense expression. Wrinkling up his black nose as he snarled again, he loped to the temple entrance, passed through, and could be seen in front of the altar, pacing up and down as if he were keeping guard over it. A strong musky smell came from him: like cheese with dried fish, Dido thought.

"Now," said the guardian, "behave yourselves, keep quiet, and Hapiypacha will do you no harm. But if you make any sudden move—or shout—or break into a run—he is trained to overtake a running quarry, and he can catch anything on four legs or two. I do not advise you to try it. . . . Good night."

He left them at the entrance to their room and returned to the temple.

There was no means of fastening their door, they discovered; if they pushed it to, it merely swung open again. In the end they managed to wedge it shut with a handful of hair from the heap—which was indubitably human. Deeply depressed by this circumstance, they spread out their cloaks on it, and combed their own hair with their fingers. "We'll look for some ichu grass tomorrow," said Dido. Then, silently, they lay down to sleep. They were in no mood for chat.

Their bed was soft enough, despite its frightening implications. But Dido's sleep was broken by miserable dreams. She heard Mr. Multiple scream as he was thrown over the waterfall; she saw poor Plum carried off by aurocs; fiery-eyed owls dashed at her; snakes wriggled among the heap of hair. Mr. Holystone stood on the far side of a ravine, with Caliburn in his hand, but looking away from her, in the wrong direction.

Toward dawn she woke, parched with thirst, and, in some trepidation, padded next door carrying a wooden cup Caradog had left them, to fetch herself a drink of water from the stone tank. As she came back, it struck her that their bedroom door had been ajar;

someone must have opened it while they were asleep.
And, returning to bed, she discovered who: sprawled
out beside Elen, with his chin comfortably supported
by her ankles, lay Hapiypacha, fast asleep.

Dido regarded him rather doubtfully for a moment.
Then she knelt and set the wooden cup of water down
on the ground. As she did so, for some reason, she
remembered Mr. Holystone saying, "Never drink the
first cup of liquid offered you by a stranger."

Maybe things'll somehow come right, she thought.
Though dear knows how!

Then she curled up on the far side of the heap from
Hapiypacha and went back to sleep.

11

When Dido next woke, it was to see Elen thoughtfully scratching the thick, soft fur between Hapiypacha's ears, and pulling out the loose fluff over his eyebrows, while he purred like the distant rumble of Mount Catelonde.

"It's going to be awkward," Dido remarked, "not letting old Caradog find out how thick you and Happy Pussy have got. Or he might think we'd need another keeper."

But in fact it proved not too difficult. Most of the daytime hours were passed by the old guardian in front of Sul's altar, where he blew or plucked on his various instruments. During the afternoon he went to feed his animals stabled in the valley below, and was absent for a couple of hours, departing through a postern gate in the massive wall, which he locked behind him. At noon and in the evening he fed the girls some more of his bean-and-yucca stew. If Elen chose to come and play the piano in the temple—which she did from time to time—he was happy to desist from his own performances and listen to hers, rapt in a trance of pleasure; sometimes, indeed, after these interludes, it was quite hard to rouse him. Otherwise he paid little attention to his prisoners; they might wander where they chose through the cold, sunny, deserted city, climbing stairs, coming out onto terraces, peering over terrifying drops. As Caradog had said, they were free to fly out if they chose; there appeared to be no other way out.

Everywhere they went, Hapiypacha accompanied them, loping at their heels, or sometimes bounding ahead, leaping up onto some balustrade or rock platform if a merlin or rock dove chanced to alight. Caradog had warned them about aurocs, which, once or twice, they saw planing about the sky with their hideous triangular wings outspread. "But," the guardian said, "so long as Hapiypacha's with you, no auroc's going to come near; they won't tangle with *him*." Indeed, the great leopard often snarled upward, wrinkling his nose and hissing, when the shadow of an auroc passed over.

Up at the top of the town, beyond the Temple of Sul, there was a round tower, which Dido had noticed on their first arrival. Exploring in this direction, they found that the tower was not a tower at all, but simply a huge rock, the upper part of which had been cut and shaped into a single stone shaft some twenty feet high. At the top of this the familiar face of Sul was carved. Beyond the pillar extended a balustraded terrace from which the whole of Lake Arianrod could be seen. There was now a fair amount of water in the star-shaped basin, and more of the yellow balloons kept arriving.

"They are made of wild silk," Elen said sadly. "Used for irrigation in the highlands. Why doesn't Papa stop sending them? I don't understand it."

Dido was visited by a depressing idea.

"Perhaps old Gomez, when he nabbled us, left a note, as it might be from you or me, saying, 'Don't worry, gone off with Mr. Mully to pick up diamonds in the lake bed,' or summat of the sort."

"Surely Papa would not be so foolish as to believe such a story?"

But no other possible explanation occurred to them.

Most of the balloons came drifting over the shoulder of Mount Catelonde, the heat of which was sufficient to melt the wax on the fastenings and make them discharge their contents into the lake bed. But a small number floated over the crater itself, through the reddish-black column of smoke that came coiling sluggishly from the volcano's open jaws. Then that particular load of water never reached the lake, but fell down into the heart of the volcano, like a teacupful of water dropped into a furnace. And as the furnace sizzles and spits when water is dropped into it, so Mount Catelonde rumbled and hissed and spat out jets of red-hot ash and lava each time this occurred.

"If enough water got spilt into the crater," said Elen thoughtfully, "I shouldn't wonder but what it might start a full-scale eruption."

"What would happen then?"

"It would be like a saucepan boiling over. Only what comes out of a volcano is lava—boiling rock, thick as molasses, rolling down the mountain. Of course, it might just roll down into Lake Arianrod; but if it went down the other side of the mountain—or if there were a big explosion and part of the mountain blew off—it might be dangerous for the city of Bath. Oh, *how* I wonder if Gwydion has got there yet! If he has— if he learns what has happened to us—he will surely come to rescue us!"

"I wouldn't depend on that," Dido said. "Who'd tell him? If you ask me, it's no use expecting other people to help you. . . . What's that thing down there, d'you suppose?"

A flight of steps led down the steep hillside from the terrace on which they stood. Below, extending outward from the hillside, rather like a diving board, was a narrow natural tongue or spur of rock, perhaps ten feet long and three or four feet wide. Below it, the cliff fell sheer, more than a thousand feet, to the blue waters of Lake Arianrod.

Elen looked down and shivered.

"Can't you guess? That's the Tongue of Sul—where we shall be thrown into the lake. I believe we aren't really thrown—just pushed out along the rock and left to stand there until we fall off. I should think it would not take long—you would soon become giddy on that narrow tip. Some people jump off, I've heard, so as to get it over sooner."

Now it was Dido's turn to shiver.

"Brrr! What a spooky spot. Let's get away from here. I'm sorry I asked—I wouldn't have come this-away if I'd known. Maybe it's dinner time—the sun's moved quite a bit since we've been here."

But Elen, walking dejectedly after Dido, burst out, "I don't know that I *mind* being thrown into the lake, Dido! I really love Cousin Gwydion. I always have. I can feel it *here*"—she thumped her chest. "If I can't marry him, I might just as *well* be in that lake. Or— or go back to England and teach mathematics! I'm certainly not going to stay in Lyonesse and marry one of those Ccapacs."

"But Elen," said Dido, shocked, "how *can* you marry him? He's married already. And anyway, you've hardly met him—how can you be sure?"

"You forget. I was partly brought up with him. I loved him then. Oh, if only he were just Cousin Gwydion!"

If only, thought Dido sadly, he was just my Mr. Holystone.

Trying to retrace their steps to the Temple of Sul, they became confused among a maze of narrow, cobbled ways, and came out on a dry, dusty shelf above a ravine which was quite narrow—only about ten feet across—but unbelievably deep.

"Watch out, Elen," Dido said anxiously. "Don't go too near that gritty edge."

A mountain hare, sunning itself among a tangle of wild fig and cactus on the far side of the gully, started up and bolted away across the mountainside. To the girls' utter amazement, Hapiypacha cleared the gully in one effortless bound and shot off in pursuit of the hare, going so fast that he seemed to float over the ground. In twenty seconds he had caught it, and he returned with it in his jaws, leaping back over the gully with the same unconcerned ease, before settling down in a patch of shade to demolish his prey in four bites.

"*He*'s got his own way out, at all events," Dido said. "Guess the guardian don't know that."

An idea seized her so suddenly that her jaw went stiff and she stammered in her excitement. "Hey—P-P-P-Princess! He—he *likes* you!"

"Who does? What do you mean?"

"Why, old Puss there—" as Hapiypacha, having finished his lunch, came to rub his head against Elen's arm. "D'you reckon you could ride him? Get him to take you out of here?"

"You mean—over *there*?" Elen's eyes went huge with fright. She looked down into the terrifying gully.

"Go on! You said just now you wouldn't mind being thrown into the lake. At least there'd be some *point* to *this*!"

"But—but what about you?" Plainly, though, Elen had begun to consider the idea, instead of just dismissing it.

"Well," Dido said reasonably, "it'd be no use *my* trying to ride him. He don't like me above half. It's you he's took sich a fancy to. So it's a case of you or nothing, ennit? But he's a right fast goer, our Happy Pussy; if you could get across that gully on him, and ride him over the mountain to Wandesborough, maybe you could give the alarm in time to send somebody and stop old Stone Eyes from dropping me in the lake. Or—or if not—it's better *one* should get away than both of us get polished off. And then—and then—you can tell your cousin Gwydion about Queen Ginevra's goings-on." She had to reiterate this argument a good many times before Elen could be brought to consider it.

But presently, after they had eaten their noon meal and Caradog was away feeding his beasts, Elen did try riding the leopard. At first it was doubtful whether he would sanction the idea at all; he hissed and spat and started away when, nervously tucking up her skirts, she attempted to bestride him. But by the end of the day he was cooperating tolerably well, though he did not look pleased about it; his ears were set back flat against his head and he mewled angrily to himself all the time she was on his back.

"Still, we're a-getting somewhere!" exulted Dido. "Who'd a thought, this morning, that he'd let you ride him so biddably? And it's still two days to the new moon. If you practice all day tomorrow—"

"All day!" shuddered Elen. "If you knew what it was like sitting on his back! There isn't any saddle hollow—nothing but bony spine all the way along. It's all very well for you—"

She bit her lip and stopped suddenly.

"Don't you worry," said Dido. "Maybe the old boy will be so sore when he finds he's lost you *and* Hapiy-pacha that he'll be out a-hunting over the mountain, and I'll have a chance to get away too."

Though what could I do? she wondered. Steal a ride back on the silver train? Her private thoughts were not hopeful.

By the evening of the next day Elen was getting on much better with her wayward mount. She had learned that the usual taps or kick used to urge a horse to greater speed only put him in a bad temper, but he would respond very well to coaxing words if she leaned forward and whispered in his ear.

"I reckon *now*'s as good a time as any," said Dido, who had discreetly removed Hapiypacha's breakfast of dried guinea pig when the guardian's back was turned, so as to render the leopard extra-hungry by evening. "Let's go up to that gully spot and hope for another hare."

At first they were afraid they were not going to be

able to find the place again, as they wandered to and fro in a network of dusty silver-cobbled alleys, with late swallows and mountain falcons wheeling overhead in the last of the sun.

But at last they came out on the edge of the gully, and, as luck would have it, there was another hare, drowsing in exactly the same spot on the other side.

"*Quick*, Elen—before you've got time to get scared— hop on him!" said Dido. Impulsively she gave the other girl a hug. "Go on now—don't be frit! Give my best regards to Mr. Holy if you find him—"

Elen scrambled herself onto Hapiypacha's bony withers. Leaning forward, she took a firm grip of the thick fur on his neck with both hands and whispered, "Go on now, Tomkin—after him!"

The leopard bounded, checked an instant, and then shot away, clearing the ravine with his usual carefree power, landing well over on the other side, despite the rider on his back.

"Grip with your knees!" shouted Dido, as Hapiypacha raced after the hare. "Good luck!"

And then she turned round to find herself staring straight into the indignant face of Caradog.

"You are a very, very wicked child!" he said wrathfully.

"Oh, come on, mister!"

"My sister said you were a troublemaker! She was right!"

"Now listen here—"

"I let you and your companion go free, instead of locking you up, as I should otherwise have done (it is true," he added in parenthesis, "that Sul prefers a healthy, willing sacrifice; or so I have always thought) —and what happens? You act with outrageous deceitfulness and ingratitude—you seize the first opportunity to escape!"

"Well," Dido said reasonably, "what would you have done? Just sat down and waited to be chucked over the cliff?"

"If Sul wished it—yes!"

"Mister," said Dido—by this time the old man had grabbed her by the scruff of the neck and was marching her fiercely back in the direction of the temple, a most uncomfortable progress—"Mister," she said, screwing her neck round to look at him, "has it ever strook you that perhaps it was meant for Elen to escape?"

"Meant? What can you possibly mean?"

"Well, she managed it twice, didn't she? Once we and your High King just happened to be on the spot; and as for this time—well, no one but a noddy woulda left the girl to be guarded by a cat, when I'd a thought the whole population around here might know she dotes on the whole tribe o' cats and them on her—*ouch!*"—for the old man had now taken a firm grip on her ear.

"I wish to hear no more of your irreverent rubbish," he snapped. "Sul needed that girl. Nodens is angry. See how Catelonde burns and sulks—" gesturing across the valley to the volcano, which had just received two water-skins in its hot gullet and was vomiting out a fiery spray of lava.

"But don't you *see*, you old fossil, that's because—oh, well . . ."

Looking at his angry, implacable old face, Dido decided she might as well save her breath. He was not going to be convinced by anything she said. Instead she asked, "Who's Nodens?"

"He is the husband of Sul. He must be propitiated.

Or he may wreak his vengeance on the whole city of Bath."

"If you ask me, the whole city of Bath could just about do with a tidy-up—hey! That hurts!"

Grasping her by both ears, he pushed her past the altar and with a final heave propelled her sharply through the door of her bedroom so that she fell on her face onto the stone floor. By the time she had picked herself up, he was nailing the door shut with furious bangs of a hammer.

"And there you stay!" he shouted through the door, "until tomorrow evening, when it is time for you to go to Sul. *Hodie mihi, cras tibi! Nota bene! Respice finem! Suaviter in modo! Experto crede!*"

And she heard him stomping off back into the temple, where he soothed his feelings and allayed his temper by making a lot of noise on various instruments and thumping some very cacophonous chords on the piano. Poor old boy, thought Dido, he ain't *half* sore that he lost Elen. I guess those old girls will be right mad with him.

And then Dido began to wonder and worry as to whether she had done the right thing in encouraging the princess to escape on Hapiypacha. Would the leopard really consent to be ridden all the way over the mountains to Wandesborough? Or would he toss Elen off into a sigse thorn thicket and then eat her? Or would she fall off his back? Or would they get lost, and fall asleep on the bare mountain slopes, and become the prey of aurocs?

Still, thought Dido, anything's better than waiting here to be chucked off a blessed rock into a perishing lake.

She had ample time to think this. It was a miserable

night. The room was extremely dark with the door
shut, since there was only one window, about the size
of a brick, very high up. Dido groped her way to the
heap of hair and curled up on it miserably. She felt,
for the first time, horribly lonely—for Elen, for Mr.
Multiple, for Holystone, for Noah Gusset—even for
Captain Hughes and Hapiypacha. Where were they
all, this night? Dido was very tired indeed, but it was
a long time before she slept.

She woke up hollow with hunger—for the guardian's
bean stew was not very nourishing, and it was many
hours since she had eaten it—and also parched with
thirst. She thought longingly of the water in the tank
on the other side of the nailed-up door. The sun was
up—she could tell that by the light in her window
hole. Banging on the door, she shouted, "Lemme out!"
For a long time there was no answer; then Caradog's
voice replied, "Quiet, child, you interrupt my devo-
tions. And in any case you cannot come out till moon-
rise. You had better think, meditate, put yourself in
a proper frame of mind to go to Sul."

"I don't want to go to flaming Sul!"

But nothing she said could elicit any further response from the guardian; she heard him from time
to time chanting and playing on his instruments. Then
there was a long silence; perhaps he was away seeing
to his beasts.

The day dragged. It is bad enough at any time being
shut up in a room in the dark with nothing to do;
but the prospect of being a human sacrifice at the end
of it makes the whole situation incomparably worse.

Dido's thirst, hardly bearable at the beginning of
the day, was so acute by nightfall that she could hardly
speak when at last the guardian wrenched open the

door and let her out. She had to work her sore throat several times before she could get out the word *Water* in a hoarse wheezing whisper.

"Thirsty, are you?" said Caradog sourly. "No more than you deserve. Water's not what you need, with a thirst like that; what you need is a cup of my willow tea." He had a cup ready brewed, which he handed to her; for the second time within two days Dido thought of Mr. Holystone's admonition: Always throw away the first cupful from a stranger. But she was too thirsty to throw away this cupful; she grasped the cup with shaking hands and tipped the contents eagerly down her painful throat, which was almost closed up with dryness. The willow tea tasted stale and metallic, like water that pennies have been soaked in. But then, all the guardian's concoctions tasted peculiar; Dido thought nothing of it.

"Now I want some cold water," said she, and before he could stop her she walked into the room with the tank and swigged down about four cupfuls, one after the other. Caradog wagged his head angrily.

"Not good, not good!" he said. "You should go empty to the sacrifice!"

"Croopus!" said Dido. "I'm the one as is going to be sacrificed. You oughter be giving me crumpets and plum jam and haddock kedgeree and pancakes."

Caradog looked at her as if she had gone mad.

"Condemned person's breakfast," explained Dido. "Who's a-coming to the ceremony?"

The one thing that had cheered her (and that not much) during her hours of incarceration had been the thought of a huge crowd with the queen, the grand inquisitor, the mistress of the robes, and the rest of them, come to see her jump to her doom. She would make a speech, which she had been preparing, giving them a piece of her mind, telling them what she thought of them. But the guardian undeceived her.

"Ceremony?" he said. "You mean the sacrifice? Nobody comes. Only you and I. Come along—it is time."

He picked up a thing like a witch's broom, a long stake with a bundle of ichu grass tied at one end, and with it gestured Dido toward the doorway. She had intended to put up a vigorous struggle, but to her surprise and rage she found herself obeying him with dreamy docility, walking peacefully along, putting one foot in front of the other.

"Blister it, mister," she muttered, yawning, "I reckon you put some hocus-pocus in that cup of tea, you wicked old wretch, didn't you? What a noddy I was to go and drink it. Mighta known you'd be up to tricks. Should have remembered what Mr. Holy told me. . . ." She yawned again.

"Just keep walking," said the guardian.

Outside, it was not so dark as it had seemed in Dido's room; a mild blue dusk filled the silver-cobbled streets. Beyond the twin peaks of Ertayne and Elamye the evening star shone clear, and the slopes of Mount Catelonde were turning a soft velvety red. A few birds still keened and whistled overhead; and, when they climbed higher, Dido, looking down, saw that Lake Arianrod had been completely refilled, and now lay among its mountains like a calm, steel-blue star.

"When you think about it," she said to the guardian —she could still argue, though she seemed to have lost command over her arms and legs—"when you think about it, there wasn't no need for Mabon to send back the lake."

"Why not?" grunted Caradog.

Dido, turning to look at him, observed that he had donned formal clothes for the ceremony—a frock coat and black stovepipe hat.

"Why not? She wanted it back so her *Rex Quondam* could come out of it, didn't she? But he'd already come! And you're throwing me in, like you did all the other poor gals—and hundreds of other guardians before you, I suppose—so as to keep her alive till he gets back. Well, he's got back. And she's still alive. So what's the point?"

"Keep moving," the guardian said. He gestured with the hand that held the broom. The other clasped a silver-tipped wand of office. He added, "Even though Artaius has returned, his lady is still of immense age. Married to a much younger king, she will need more care and support than ever before."

"Well, *I* reckon she's lived quite long *enough*," said Dido. But despite her indignant feelings she could not prevent herself from obeying the guardian. They came to the high stone shaft with the face of Sul; they descended to the terrace below. And here Caradog waited, leaning on his silver-tipped rod and eyeing the horizon, until the delicate slip of the new moon moved out from behind the shoulder of Mount Damyake, with the mysterious, shadowy ghost of the old moon cradled inside it, like an egg inside its egg cup.

"Now it is time," he said.

"Blame it!" expostulated Dido. "It ain't *right* for me to die! Have you thought of that, mister? You're an *old* gager; you've lived nigh on fourscore years, I shouldn't wonder. You did a whole lot of things and learned a lot o' stuff—though mussy knows, you ain't put it to very good use. But I haven't hardly done *nothing*! And I ain't learned much, neither, except the use of the globes that Mr. Holy taught me, and how to curtsey and cut up whales.''

At the thought of Mr. Holystone her voice, to her shame, began to wobble dangerously; she stopped speaking and drew a deep breath.

"Cease repining, child, and go down those steps," said Caradog. "Do not quarrel with your destiny. If Sul wishes you to die, then it is your time."

Dido remembered the story that Bran had told about the man who picked up the necklace. Well, if it is my destiny, she thought, best not to make a pother about it.

She walked slowly down the long flight of stone steps and out onto the rock spur. It was much longer and wider than it had looked from above; it took about twenty steps to reach the end. There she stood, feeling the mild evening breeze, gazing down at the waters of Lake Arianrod a thousand feet below. One thing the old cuss has forgot, she thought—there ain't any fish in the lake now. Their bones was lying all over the sand. So no one's going to nibble me to a skellington; I shall just drown. But still, I don't much want to drown.

A red light began to glow behind her. She half turned, cautiously, and saw that the guardian had set light to the end of his broom, which was a kind of long-handled torch. He stood at the inner end of the rock spur, holding the flaming brand, presumably to prevent Dido from trying to go back, should she have any thoughts of doing so. He was waving the torch in slow circles so that it plumed and sparkled. The sight made Dido dizzy, so she turned her back on him again.

How long will it be before I get so fuddleheaded that I topple off? she wondered dismally. Maybe it would be best to jump?

But I don't want to jump!

And then, looking up, she thought with a pang of dismay, Blister it, there's aurocs about. I thought they wasn't supposed to come out after dark? For an un-mistakable triangular shape was floating down toward her, silhouetted black against the twilit sky; it must have launched itself from a crag somewhere higher up the hillside.

"No, really, that's a bit much!" Dido exclaimed. "Drowning's one thing, but I ain't a-going to be a bedtime tidbit for no auroc!" and, taking a deep breath, she tensed her knees, preparing to launch her-self off the rock pinnacle, when she was startled almost out of her wits by a very familiar voice.

"Keep quite still, pray, Miss Twite," said Captain Hughes. "Don't kick; don't cry out. Above all, don't wriggle. Just remain calm, and I promise you that in a very short time I shall convey you to a place of safety."

And he gripped her very firmly indeed under her arms, and floated off with her above the dark waters of Lake Arianrod.

12

Dido and Captain Hughes talked their heads off all the way across the mountains.

"What a *naffy* idea, Cap'n. A flying machine! How in the world did you ever come to hit on it? Was that how you got out of prison? But how'd you ever *make* it?"

"Ahem!" he said. "As you know, I have always been interested in aërial appliances and such things; I had considered for a long time whether a device might not be constructed, by means of which, if a person were able to commence his flight from some lofty eminence —say a tower, or a mountainside—"

"But how'd you ever manage to make it in *prison*?"

"Very fortunately, all the facilities were to hand— materials, drawing implements, besides a skilled and willing helper. But, Miss Twite—I must delay no longer in telling you how creditable—*exceedingly* creditable, indeed—are the accounts of your behavior during this expedition that I have received from—"

"You had a helper in prison? Who was that, then?"

"In point of fact I had two companions during the period of my confinement. One of them, that dismal fellow Brandywinde, I found to be wholly ineffectual —a wretched milksop! But the other, the man David Llewellyn, known as Silver Taffy to his companions, though a shocking rogue in many ways, proved a most proficient assistant."

"Silver Taffy was in the jail too? Did he escape as well?"

"Why, yes. I do not know where he has got to now, however; I believe his intentions were to enter the city of Bath in disguise. He also undertook to look after poor Brandywinde—though I *did* wonder whether his intentions in that respect were wholly straightforward and trustworthy," said the captain, sounding a little doubtful for the first time. "We had to strap Brandy-winde into his aërial floater with great care, since he had lost the power of his hands. So what use he could be to Silver Taffy I fail to see. . . . But is it not a capital device?" Inventor's pride swept away his doubts. "Made of silk, you see, stretched over cane struts. I shall take out a patent when I return to England; what do you think of the 'Owen Hughes Patent Aërial Floater' as a title?"

"That sounds first-rate, Cap; you'll make a fortune. . . . So you jumped outa the windows of the Pendragon Tower and floated away—then what happened?"

"Why, hearing from Mr. Multiple that you and King Mabon's daughter had been recaptured by Queen Ginevra—who, I am shocked to discover, is a *wholly* discreditable personage—I shall indite a memorandum to His Majesty's government in the strongest terms as soon as I am back aboard the *Thrush*—"

"You heard from *Mr. Multiple*?" Dido's voice almost cracked with wonder and joy. "But I thought he was dead?"

"No. I understand that he was on the point of being assassinated—some villains were about to toss him into an underground chasm—when he, very fortunately, recollected that he had a considerable quantity of diamonds about his person; by bribing his assailants with these they were persuaded to release him, and so he was enabled to make good his escape."

"*Croopus*! *Am* I pleased about that!" said Dido.

Her position was becoming very uncomfortable indeed. As they floated along the valley between the huge dark shoulders of Mount Catelonde on one side and Calabe on the other, the captain had contrived to pass a leather strap around her, under her armpits, and had buckled this to bevels on the understruts of his aërial floater, so that she was tolerably safe, but the strap cut cruelly into her shoulders. Still, the good news about Mr. Multiple made her able to disregard such discomfort with ease. She asked, "Where'd you come across Mr. Mully, then?"

"I met him in the mountains. He, it seems, had retraced his way from the cave where he was nearly murdered, purchased a peasant's llama with his last small diamond, and was journeying to Lyonesse City to inform King Mabon of the princess's recapture."

"Good old Multiple! Those diamonds came in real handy. I guess he got there too late to stop King Mabon sending back the lake; still, at least they knew about the princess. They'll be out after her by now."

"I daresay they will have encountered her by this time," said Captain Hughes. "When I met her—"

"You met her *too?* How in the name of Nodens did you do that?"

"If you would not keep interrupting me, Miss Twite, I might be enabled to recount a consecutive narrative," said Captain Hughes.

"Sorry, Cap! You go right on. Where'd you meet Elen? Was she all rug? Was she still riding old Lepper?"

"I was informed by Mr. Multiple," said the captain, "who had learned it by listening to the conversation of his captors, that your ultimate destination, and that of the princess, was the city of Sul, where you were to be thrown into the lake—a most disgraceful procedure; I shall write another memorandum about that to H.M. government. Since the matter appeared one of extreme urgency, I directed my course toward that location, having a very tolerable recollection of its whereabouts, due to my careful study of the map of New Cumbria."

"Yes? And then what?"

"I was steering a course northwestwards—one can direct these aërial floaters with admirable facility and precision hereabouts, owing to the abundance of volcanoes emitting convective thermal currents into the atmosphere—I daresay it may not be *quite* so easy in Britain," said Captain Hughes, a certain melancholy entering his voice as he recollected the scarcity of volcanoes on that island.

"You were steering northwestwards, Cap, yes? And then?"

"Why, then I observed a young lady scuddling across the countryside at a remarkably fast pace upon a snow leopard. This, as you may know, is a beast of considerable rarity and zoological interest, which, hitherto, has been believed to be resident only in the eastern hemisphere, especially in central Asia, where it is found in some profusion. Even young Mr. Darwin failed to discover its presence in these regions, so I shall take considerable pleasure in writing a report to the Royal Society—"

"You saw Elen riding on Happy Patchy? Did you talk to her?"

"Indeed yes. She, not unnaturally, was somewhat amazed at being hailed by a voice from the empyrean. And so was her mount; indeed, she had some ado in pacifying him—apparently he took me for an auroc, for which creatures, it seems, he has an intense aversion," said Captain Hughes, sounding a little ruffled as he recalled the episode. Dido chuckled; she wished she had been there to see it.

"You talked to Elen?"

"The princess of Lyonesse," replied Captain Hughes repressively, "was so good as to inform me of the practical sense and unselfishness—I may go so far as to say heroism, Miss Twite—which has distinguished your conduct; of how you planned this means of escape for her and urged her to avail herself of it. I shall certainly indite a note to H.M.—"

"Oh, bother the note! Do you suppose Elen got to Lyonesse all right and tight?"

"I should judge so," replied the captain, "since the foothills which remained for her to cross presented no particular hazards and were wholly unpopulated so far as I could judge from my aërial viewpoint. I was considerably exercised in my mind over conflicting duties at that point, I must confess; some would say that I should have escorted the princess to her father. But since she appeared perfectly capable of continuing *un*escorted, whereas *your* plight, so far as I could judge, was more perilous—"

"It was a right near squeak," agreed Dido. "I sure thought I was a goner. I'm real grateful to you, Cap'n Hughes; I'd never have thought I'd be so pleased to see you! And I'll never borrow your spyglass again without asking!"

"I beg your pardon?"

"So what's the plan now?" pursued Dido.

"Mr. Multiple also informed me—though I could hardly believe my own ears—that Holystone—that my own *steward*—has been acknowledged by several persons of repute, including King Mabon of Lyonesse, as the returned, or reborn, prince of these regions, Mercurius Artaius Ambrosius, and husband of Queen Ginevra of New Cumbria."

"Yes, that's so," agreed Dido sadly, wondering, however, if Captain Hughes would call the old guardian a person of repute.

"If this is so, it is certainly my duty to H.M. government to report on such a state of affairs, and discover what occurs when the personages concerned encounter one another."

"You mean, when Holystone meets the queen?"

"If a change of government is indicated," said the captain, "H.M. should know about it. After all, New Cumbria is our oldest ally."

"I daresay Mr. Holystone will go to Bath quite soon." Dido's tone was glum. She added, "But we better not get there before him, or dear knows what the queen'll do to us. I saw her a couple of days ago, Cap'n. She was in a real rum state—all trembly, and eyes like bits o' looking glass. You couldn't trust her not to fly right off the handle. The only person she seems to pay heed to is that there Bran, and he was over in Lyonesse."

"Well, I daresay that King Mabon, and Holystone— or Artaius, as I suppose one should designate him— will lose no time in sending an expeditionary force to Bath, once they are assured of the safety of the princess. I learned from the man Silver Taffy that in Lyonesse there are a large number of malcontents from the kingdom of Hy Brasil, escaped from the tyrannical regime there, who may well rally under the leadership of Holy—of Artaius. If you recall, he informed us that he was brought up in that country."

"He certainly better not go back to Bath without taking some pals with him," Dido said thoughtfully. "It's my belief that it was the witcheries of those old hags—Ettarde and the others—that made him sick when he went there before. I reckon they didn't want him back, because then the queen mightn't pay such heed to them. And when he does go back—you never know—the queen herself might take a dislike to him."

"The reality might disappoint her," agreed the captain. "Having cherished a figment in her imagination for so long—"

"What's a figment, Cap? Hey, look on down there!"

They had come gliding round the shoulder of Mount Damyake, and were now floating, in icy darkness, above the stony upland saucer of plain that surrounded Bath Regis. Away in the distance Mount Catelonde glowed and coruscated; closer to hand, Mount Damask seemed to have caught the contagion, and was shooting a vertical stream of sparks up into the black heavens to join the cold, glittering stars that spread a spangled canopy there. And down below on the plain, like a reflection of the Milky Way, a brilliant procession of lights wound slowly in the direction of Bath.

"I bet that's King Mabon and Mr. Holy!" cried Dido joyfully. "Shall us go down and see?"

"We had better exercise considerable caution," said the captain. "Firstly, if they are coming from Lyonesse, they are taking a singular route; one would have assumed they would go through the Pass of Nimue and be approaching from the other direction."

"Ay, that's true."

(In fact, as they subsequently discovered, King Mabon's troop had made use of a secret smugglers' route through the silver mines, revealed to them by Bran.)

"Secondly, if we take them by surprise, they may open fire, believing us to be aurocs."

Fortunately, this misadventure did not occur; when, by the captain's skillful direction of his floater, he and Dido were hovering almost directly above the marching column, she was able to recognize the eagle standards of the Wandesborough Frontier Patrol, and she hailed them shrilly from overhead:

"Hey, Sextus Lucius Trevelyan! Have you got Mr. Holystone with you? I mean King Artaius? And the folk from the *Thrush*?"

Some natural surprise was caused by a voice apparently addressing them from heaven, and the more superstitious soldiers in Captain Trevelyan's troop fell flat on their stomachs. But Captain Hughes was now low enough to recognize the familiar face of Lieutenant Windward, riding with Mr. Multiple in the rear of the advance guard, and so he brought his floater to the ground, exclaiming briskly, "There you are, then, Windward! I'm devilish glad to see you again, sir! I have with me Miss Twite, who, I am pleased to say, I have been able to extricate from captivity."

The whole procession came to a halt amid cries of joyful recognition and congratulation.

"Miss Twite! Dido! Thank God you are safe. Who would have thought of encountering you here! Bless my soul, missie, we thought you was at Kingdom Come!" (That was Noah Gusset.) "Gadzooks, Miss Twite, I am delighted to find you at liberty—and Captain Hughes too!" (That was Lieutenant Windward.) Mr. Multiple fairly hugged Dido in his joy and relief.

"I'm real sorry about the diamonds," she whispered to him.

"Oh, never mind it! The princess got back safe to her father—here she comes now, in fact!"

King Mabon, riding in the rear, had sent forward to learn the cause of the stoppage, and, being informed what it was, now hurried forward with his daughter and Mr. Holystone. They were all mounted on Patagonian ponies, but Dido observed that Hapiypacha (whose devotion to the princess had apparently remained unimpaired despite being ridden by her across country) kept close at the heels of her pony, causing the latter no little uneasiness, and snarling if anyone chanced to come what he considered unsuitably near to his mistress.

King Mabon hopped off his pony and came to give Dido an unaffected hug. So did his daughter.

"Oh, I was so *wretched* about you!" said Elen. "All the way over the mountains I was thinking I should never, never have let you persuade me—"

"Anything you want, child, in the kingdom of Lyonesse—it's yours, indeed to goodness," said King Mabon.

"Oh, it weren't nothing," said Dido gruffly. "Arter all, what else was there to do?"

Mr. Holystone was standing quietly behind Elen. A whole ring of torches now surrounded the group, and in the flickering light Dido saw that he was very grandly dressed indeed in a red tunic, gold-bordered toga, sparkling diadem, and sandals with gold buckles. Caliburn hung at his side in a silver-studded scabbard. But he looked, surprisingly, much more like the old Mr. Holystone, and his voice, when he spoke, confirmed this.

"I am very happy to see you alive, Miss Twite. Pray, ma'am, from which tradesman do you obtain your tay?"

"Oh, Mr. Holy! You remembered me! Oh, that beats cockfighting!" Dido cried out joyfully. She was so happy that her spirits could hardly rise higher when Artaius, too, gave her a welcoming embrace and kiss on the cheek. Her delight was so profound that she thought, Now I don't care *what* happens.

"Well, well, well, Holyst—I mean, sir, King Artaius," Captain Hughes was saying, somewhat awkwardly. "This is a bit of a change, hey? Ahem!"

"I shall always remember, Captain, the kind treatment I received as your steward," Mr. Holystone said.

"When did your memory come back, Mr. Holy?" cried Dido. "When did it all come together?"

"Quite suddenly—about twelve hours ago. It was as if a shutter clicked open in my mind—I remembered the *Thrush*, and how you used to cut curls of coconut for me. . . ."

"Some influence that had been blocking his mind was suddenly removed," said Bran, appearing with his usual unexpectedness.

"Yes, you old schoolmaster!" said Holystone, clapping him cheerfully on the back. "But what influence?"

"That we shall no doubt discover when we reach Bath."

As dawn was approaching, King Mabon now suggested that they should halt and take breakfast where they were, in order to arrive at Bath tolerably rested and refreshed, since nobody had any idea what kind of reception might be waiting for them there. Accordingly fires were lit, wine was mulled, yams thrust into the embers to roast, and sausages toasted on sticks. Dido, who was ravenous after her day's solitary confinement and starvation in the city of Sul, could hardly bear to wait for the food to be ready.

"Was he very angry—the old guardian? When he found I was gone?" inquired Elen, coming to sit by Dido on a folded toga.

"That he was! Poor old Whiskers."

> *"When you are gone*
> *I'll cry all day—*
> *My tears will wash*
> *My feet away—"*

sang Bran, coming to lower himself on the ground beside the girls.

"Mister Bran—why *do* you think Mr. Holy got his memory back?" Dido asked.

"I expect we shall discover that one of the people attempting to prevent his return suddenly lost the power to do so."

"Why should that happen?"

Bran shrugged. "In several ways. We shall see soon enough, no doubt."

When they resumed the march, Bran rode alongside the two girls. Dido would have liked a long conversation with Mr. Holystone—there was so much she wanted to ask him!—but she could quite see that he had a lot of important affairs to discuss with King Mabon and Captain Hughes. Bits of their conversation came floating back: "Dissident elements in Hy Brasil . . . abolish practice of head shrinking . . . joint action to exterminate the aurocs . . . improved conditions in the silver mines . . ."

"Bran," said Dido, "do you think Queen Ginevra will *let* him do all those things? I reckon she quite *likes* those shrunken heads."

"Who can tell?"

"I'd a thought *you* could. Can't you tell the future?"

"After a fashion, yes, I can. But, if you recall, I can do nothing to affect it. Only continue to remind people that free will exists."

"What's free will, Mister Bran?"

> "In Bath's happy city
> Where the girls are so pretty
> How free was my will
> As I freewheeled along
> Why, even a sparrow
> Can choose broad or narrow
> And a man can choose daily
> Between right and wrong . . ."

sang Bran.

"You'll never get a sensible answer out of him," said the princess. "Not when he's in this mood."

"Bran," said Dido, "how come you knew Mrs. Vava-sour so well?"

The princess looked doubtfully at Bran, as if won-dering how he would take such a personal question. But he answered readily enough. "Why, who should know her better than I? I was married to her for five hundred years or so—sweet Nimue! Dear Nynevie! And to show her wifely affection she threw me into an enchantment and shut me up under a stone—rather like you, Princess, but for a deal longer."

"You were *married* to Nynevie? Then are you sorry she's dead?"

"Of course I am. You can't be married to somebody and not have *some* feeling for them—however wicked they may be, or how badly they treat you."

Elen rode in silence for a long time after this ex-change.

Now they were very close to Bath, approaching it from the southern aspect, over Odd Down, one of the foothills of Mount Damyake.

As they came near enough to distinguish individual objects, Dido saw that the walls of the city were lined with silent watchers; news of their approach had evi-dently gone ahead of them to the city. The great south gate was closed; but when they came within fifteen hundred yards of the walls, it slowly swung open.

"Humph," muttered Lieutenant Windward, who happened to be riding beside Dido at that point (she and Captain Hughes had been provided with ponies). "I don't much care for the look of Mount Catelonde. *Or* Damask, come to that." Great, thick, oily black piles of smoke kept knotting and piling upward from

Catelonde's crater, every now and then pierced by a gush of sparks or flame; and a distinct bulge had appeared on the shoulder of Damask—"like a boil about to burst," as the lieutenant pointed out.

He went on: "I only hope the superstitious folk in Bath don't connect it with Holystone's return and decide that he's a bad halfpenny and Grandmother Sul don't want him. Or we'll *all* be in the basket!"

Now there was a change in the order of march.

Holystone rode out ahead on his lively black pony. The fitful sunlight (coming through immense clouds of black volcanic smoke) fetched gleams from his diadem and the hilt of Caliburn; he looked very kingly.

But Captain Hughes muttered testily, "All very well, but, bless my soul, I wonder if that's wise? It only wants one marksman with a musket—or crossbow . . ."

Holystone, however, rode on steadily across the stony plain, and his troop quietly followed him.

When he reached the gate, he looked up, without speaking, at the black heads of the watchers, crowded like starlings on the walls at either side.

One of King Mabon's heralds spurred forward and blew a loud blast on a bocina, then bawled resonantly through a trumpet-shaped wooden mouthpiece: "The High King, Artaius Mercurius Ambrosius, true son of Uther Ambrosius, Pendragon of Cumbria, Lyonesse, and Hy Brasil, returns in peace to his city of Bath Regis."

There was a long moment of hushed silence following this announcement; then the whole city of Bath almost lifted off the ground in deafening response. Bells clanged till the steeples rocked, muskets were discharged, bocinas clamored, horns rooted and tooted, rattles clacked, and over and above and through all the other sounds, human voices could be heard shouting joyfully, "Welcome, welcome to our *Rex Quondam*! God bless Mercurius Artaius! God bless King Arthur!"

Holystone was evidently much moved. He got off his pony for a moment, knelt to kiss the threshold of the gate, then, quite simply, wiped his eyes on the pony's mane. As he was about to remount, a boy, still blackened from work in the silver mines, came running to offer him a huge key, shaped like a basilisk, which was apparently the key to the city of Bath. Holystone received the key on its cushion, made some remark which set the boy laughing, then handed it back, swung himself into the saddle, and rode on up Damask Street.

It was as if no one had been sure that he was really coming; as if they could not quite believe their luck until they had the evidence of their own eyes. Now, as he rode slowly along, windows opened, and bunting hastily rolled out of them to hang in brilliant stripes down the front of the white houses; ropes flew on arrows across the streets, and trails of pennants followed; in three minutes the whole route was transformed to an avenue of dazzling colors.

By the time they had turned the corner into Ertayne Street, people had fetched out festive costumes, were running from their doors fastening red and green kerchiefs round their necks, pinning on gaudy aprons, tying streamers on their hats. Dido, looking sideways at the dancing, waving, shouting, screaming, exuberant crowds who fluttered bright handkerchiefs, blew kisses, and tossed flowers, could hardly believe that they were the same surly, scowling citizens she had encountered on her previous visit.

But there were very few children.

Now, as they turned right again and came into the big cobbled palace yard, Dido saw that as many as possible of the Thirteen Treasures of Britain had been hustled out of the museum, quickly polished up, and set on plinths: the basket, drinking horn, halter, knife, cauldron, whetstone, garment, pan, platter, chessboard, and mantle. The chariot had unfortunately fallen to pieces during its hasty removal, but the drinking horn, pan, and platter shone bravely, and somebody flung the mantle, moth-eaten but gleaming with red and gold embroidery, over the rump of Holystone's pony. He pulled out his sword and held it up in salute; it was greeted by a hushed, breathing murmur: "Caliburn! He has Caliburn!"

Somebody had also brought along the Four Ancient Creatures from the zoological garden, and there they were, blinking and yawning in wickerwork cages: the Ousel of Cilgwri, the Stag of Redynvre, the Owl of Cwm Cawlwyrd, and the Eagle of Gwern Abwy. Holystone laughed when he saw the aged creatures, and called teasingly, "Old you may be, my ancient friends, but I am older yet! Still there is work for us to do!"

Now the crowd quieted down, for in all this joyful excitement and hubbub there had been no sign from Caer Sisi, the royal palace. In fact, when Holystone turned the head of his pony in that direction, great jets of steam suddenly shot from the ground in a ring all round the palace on its island, as if to protect it from intruders.

"Dear me! That's a highly ingenious form of defense," muttered Captain Hughes, who happened to be beside Dido just then. "I must send a memorandum to the war office about it. A barricade of scalding steam—most effective. Expensive, of course . . . I am not sure that it would be practicable in His Majesty King James's dominions." He added thoughtfully, "I am afraid it gives no very encouraging clue as to Queen Ginevra's intentions."

Holystone halted his pony a safe distance from the steam jets and sat regarding them. The herald came up beside him again, blew another blast on his bocina, and declaimed, "The High King Arthur, *Rex Quondam et Futurus*, stands here outside his palace of Caer Sisi. Who bids him welcome?"

"That's a tactful way of putting it," commented Captain Hughes.

After one revolution of the rotating palace, three people emerged from the smaller door at the top of the steps: the grand inquisitor, the vicar general, and old Mrs. Morgan.

Now the jets of steam slackened down until they were only about two feet high, and the two men, Gomez and Fluellen, picked their way forward, edging between the spouts with some care, and advanced until they were within speaking distance of Holystone.

"Are you in truth Artaius Mercurius, son of Uther Pendragon?" demanded the vicar general.

"I am!" replied Holystone.

"What proof do you give in confirmation of your statement?"

"The mark of Gwydion on my arm"—he bared it—"and the sword Caliburn in my hand."

"Under whose recognizance do you come?"

"King Mabon, ruler of Lyonesse, and Caradog, son of Caradog, guardian of the Pass of Nimue."

The two men consulted together. Mrs. Morgan went back inside the castle after a very sharp scrutiny of Holystone. Gone to tell the queen, Dido guessed.

The two officials consulted together, and Gomez announced, "It is enough! We accept your recognizance, Pendragon, son of Uther. Advance to be greeted by your loving queen!"

"So I should hope!" tartly commented Captain Hughes.

Now there ensued a long pause. Dido expected that the castle would stop spinning, that the great doors would open; but neither of these things happened. Maybe they've forgotten how to stop it, she thought to herself; or more likely the machinery's gone wrong, rusted after all this time.

Whether this was the case, or whether the queen was still doubtful of her caller's legitimacy, the castle continued to revolve. However, after several more turns (and evidently with considerable difficulty, owing to her girth and lack of mobility) Queen Ginevra herself presently emerged through the rotating door and stood at the top of the black marble steps. A throne was hastily carried to the spot by several guards. She sat down on it.

Then, in a faint, high, weary, but carrying voice, she called, "Arthur, son of Uther. *Rex Quondam!* Come forward and be recognized by me!"

Holystone walked forward, crossed the bridge, and mounted the steps. Under his beard he was very pale, Dido noticed. She also noticed, with some surprise, that the queen did not seem to have made any particular alteration in her garments or coiffure. She still wore the flowing white robe, like a nightdress, and the plain circlet of diamonds over her lanky hair.

Evidently Lady Ettarde had not come up to scratch in the matter of festive robes.

For that matter, where *was* the mistress of the wardrobe?

Glancing round, as this thought occurred to her for the first time, Dido noticed Silver Taffy not far away, edging through to the front of the crowd. He was leading somebody by the arm.

A man in the crowd near Dido could be heard to mutter, "The queen looks more like his mum than his wife, don't she?"

And a woman snappishly replied, "Well, he's been reborn and she hasn't. Some people have all the luck!"

The vicar general in ringing tones proclaimed, "Welcome, Arthur, *Rex Quondam*, to your faithful, devoted, loyal, and long-suffering queen Ginevra, who has waited for you these thirteen hundred years, keeping your kingdom safe for you. Great be their reward who remain faithful in adversity!"

"What hadversity did *she* have to put up with?" somebody murmured. "*She*'s never gone hungry!"

Queen Ginevra's high voice was heard to exclaim, "Arthur! It really *is* you!" in a tone of genuine astonishment.

And he answered steadily, "Yes, it's I. Guinevere— Jenny! It's been—it was good of you to wait for me so long."

And, stepping forward, he bent down (the queen looked like a fat white dumpling beside his spare erectness) and kissed her on her broadish brow, above the pouched, poached-egg eyes, below the greasy white hair.

Dido, glancing at Elen, who was on her left-hand

side, noticed that the princess looked likely to faint. She was swaying dizzily in her saddle. Leaning across, Dido grabbed her arm. "Put your head right down on your pony's neck!" she hissed.

"Why, husband, did you stay away so long?" the queen was asking in a complaining tone. "And why, when you did come back, did you go to Lyonesse first? And then come here at the head of an armed force?"

Dido did not catch Arthur's reply. Silver Taffy had come up to Captain Hughes and greeted him with a grin and a wink.

"Got back then, I see, sir! No problems? Found the young ladies, all right and tight?"

"Certainly," said the captain coolly. "And you—what have you been doing? Where have you got that poor devil Brandywinde?"

"Oh, he's here, sir—just behind me. Well, the first thing *I* did," he laughed cheerfully, "was to put paid to my auntie Ettarde's account. *She* won't sew anybody's shroud, not ever again. She lies spitted like a partridge among her tuckers and farthingales!"

"*What,* you wretch—" began the captain, in a tone of horror. But Taffy only laughed, and moved farther toward the front of the crowd, pulling Brandywinde behind him. The latter appeared wholly confused, as if he did not know where he was, or what he was supposed to be doing.

Meanwhile, it was plain that the reunion between the queen and her husband was not going very well. Ginevra continued to scold poor Holystone for his slowness in returning to her. He looked miserably depressed. The queen's eyes had turned to their mirror-blankness, reflecting only the patchy, smoke-flecked blue sky. At this moment Catelonde gave a loud, angry rumble.

Poor Mr. Holy, Dido thought. He just can't act loving enough toward her—who could? And *that*'s what she can't stand—o' course she can see that he don't like her one bit. Anybody could see that. He can't help himself. Oh, why do I have to feel sorry for people all the time, however nasty they are?

"You are a very faithless, untrue, unkind husband!" Ginevra suddenly cried shrilly. "How do I know what you have been up to all these years?"

King Arthur's return to his wife was going horribly wrong.

Mabon called out angrily, "What about you, you miserable woman? I hadn't been going to say anything about it, if Gwydion was really fond of you—let bygones be bygones is my motto—but what about my daughter? What about Elen? You had her abducted—*twice*! You were going to murder her!"

Ginevra turned her sightless eyes in his direction.

"I had to do it," she said complainingly. "It was the will of Sul. I had to survive, for the good of the kingdom." And she repeated, "It was the will of Sul."

"Sul be blowed!"

"Oh, hush, Papa!"

Now Silver Taffy, shrewdly perceiving that the mood of the crowd was changing and turning hostile toward the queen if she was not prepared to welcome Arthur, strode out in front of the people and shouted, "Yes, and what about all our girl-children, that *she* said were taken by the aurocs! We all know what really happened to them! What about *them*, you old she-hyena?"

He turned to the crowd and shouted, "*She* had them! *She* murdered them—every one!"

There was a gasp of horror from the throng.

But at this point Elen, suddenly recognizing Silver Taffy, exclaimed, "Why, but that is the man who took me prisoner for the queen—you hateful monster! Whose side are you on, you double traitor?"

Forgetting her previous faintness, she pointed an accusing finger at Taffy. And Hapiypacha, as if he had been waiting all day for this signal, launched himself like a javelin toward the pirate. Taffy went gray with terror at sight of the snow leopard bounding toward him; he spun round, wailing, and fled along Westgate Street. Hapiypacha bounded lightly after him, and in a moment the pair were out of sight; there was not the least doubt as to what would happen.

Into the silence which followed this grim occurrence came the whining voice of Mr. Brandywinde: "And what about her wickedness and witcheries? Turned my fingers to blobs of dough, she did—look, friends"— and he exhibited them. "Can't even spread bread and butter! Compensation, there ought to be, for all she done—the tongues cut out, the shrunken heads!"

"Ay, so there ought!" shouted the crowd.

Queen Ginevra looked bitterly at the sea of faces confronting her. Incomprehension and despair were on her flabby features and in her shining, sightless eyes.

"Oh!" she cried out piercingly. "How can any of you understand me? I hate you all! But"—to Holystone— "I hate *you* worst of all!"

Holystone said hoarsely, "Guinevere, you have been a selfish, wicked woman—an unkind shepherdess, preying on your flock. I condemn your actions, and I repudiate you!"

"Oh—you brute! It was for *you*! I did it for *you*!"

With a dreadful, raging, moaning cry, a shriek that went through the hearts of her people like a saw through tissue paper, Queen Ginevra turned from Holystone and pushed her way into the revolving door, which reached the head of the steps just at that moment.

Then a portentous thing happened.

Whether because Ginevra had purposely released some control, or by simple accident, the pace of the revolving door suddenly increased to a wild whirl. It spun madly round, with the queen inside it, so that the rotating panels could only be seen as a blur. Ginevra's scream was echoed and drowned by the eerie screech of the spinning door, and then of the castle, as it, too, began to turn more quickly.

"Sir! Come back! Make haste!" Captain Hughes shouted warningly.

Holystone glanced behind him, then leapt down the steps and across the bridge. For the steam jets were beginning to grow again; in the space of forty seconds they shot up as tall as poplar trees. The crowd wailed and stumbled and stampeded in its effort to get away before anybody was scalded. Holystone, the vicar general, and the grand inquisitor just managed to dodge between the jets while it was possible to do so, before the jets became a wall of steam.

"Er—may I perhaps suggest, Your Highness, that we adjourn to the Pump Room?" suggested the vicar general, who looked badly shaken. "I think—I do not believe it possible—that Her Mercy—"

"The poor wretched woman can't possibly have survived inside *that* giddy-go-round," bluntly summed up Captain Hughes. "Nor could anybody inside the castle, for the matter of that. Human frame ain't meant for that kind of usage. Unfortunate—very; but all for the best, maybe."

"I am afraid you are right, Captain," smoothly agreed the grand inquisitor. "In which case His Highness King Artaius here is next in—"

But at this moment Captain Sextus Lucius Trevelyan came elbowing his way through the crowd with an expression of deep anxiety on his clean-cut Roman features. He bowed hastily to both King Mabon and Mr. Holystone.

"Sirs—" he began. But his voice as he spoke was drowned by a horrendous rumbling roar from Mount Catelonde. The roar went on for the space of three minutes, growing louder and louder. Captain Trevelyan's lips continued to move as he tried in vain to make himself heard.

". . . utmost urgency! Glaciers on Mount Damyake have begun to slip on account of the increased volcanic action," he was saying when the rumble died down at last. "The ice is approaching the city of Bath with—with considerable velocity from the east. And, as well, on the western side of the town, a torrent of molten lava is approaching with even greater speed. I think it my duty to suggest that you advise the citizens to gather up such household chattels as they quickly may, and remove themselves from the city within the space of one hour at longest. And you too, Your Majesty and my lady and Your Highness, if you please! The slopes of Mount Ambage would seem, at present, to offer a reasonably secure point of vantage."

"Leave the town?" said the quick-thinking King Mabon. "Right. Best tell the people. Have it proclaimed. You agree?" to Holystone, who nodded. "But

—dear me—what about Caer Sisi? What about the queen?"

The vicar general shrugged. "*Fata obstant*," he said. "She is done for. We cannot help her."

Captain Hughes was heard to remark, "I daresay the same subterranean upheaval that is affecting Damyake and Catelonde had that unexpected effect on her palace."

Holystone, who had looked white, sick, and dazed since the dreadful scene with Queen Ginevra, now visibly took command of himself.

"Send the *jefe* here," he commanded. "We must organize the removal of the citizens in an orderly manner, by streets, or there will be panic, and people will be injured and the gates blocked. Order the street watchmen to sound the alarm. Clear the town by all four gates, beginning with the citizens who live in the center. Appropriate all carts, carriages, and streetcars, all beasts of burden; inform the owners that these will be returned, and compensation paid. . . ."

In a moment he was the center of a whirl of activity; he stood calmly giving orders as messengers raced in all directions.

"Come, Miss Twite—Multiple, Windward, Gusset!" said Captain Hughes. "Since we are not natives of this town we had best get ourselves out from underfoot before the headlong rush begins. The most sensible thing we can do is make for the rack railway and go back to the *Thrush*; we certainly do not want to be cut off here in this godforsaken spot—which is all too probable if the glacier blocks the railway track, or the station is buried in lava."

"Leave *now*?" cried Dido in dismay. "Without seeing what happens?"

Without saying good-bye was what she meant.

"Cap's right, you know," Lieutenant Windward said. "No sense in hanging around where we ain't needed."

Dido glanced about her, and saw Elen mounting her pony. The princess, like Holystone, looked white, appalled, and hollow eyed.

"Papa has ordered me to go back to Lyonesse with Captain Trevelyan," she said. "He thinks it best; will you come with me, Dido?"

But Dido explained that she had to return to the *Thrush*. The two girls hugged each other rather miserably. "Here—have this," Dido said huskily, and thrust the little diamond mirror into Elen's hand.

"You *will* come and see me again sometime—visit me in Lyonesse? I'll never forget what you did—*never*! And if—and if you should see G-Gwydion before you leave"—her voice shook a little on the name—"tell him he is always welcome at my father's palace; he knows that. . . . Give him my—my affection."

"I don't suppose I *shall* see him," said Dido bluntly. "But if I do I'll tell him. Good-bye, Elen. Take care of Hapiypacha. And—you might go and play the piano to poor old Caradog now and again."

Elen nodded, ducked her head, and kicked her pony into a trot. Hapiypacha loped after her.

"*Miss Twite*! Will you please come *along*!" shouted the captain. "Windward has ascertained that a train will start from Goodridge's Corridor station in ten minutes. We must lose no time."

"I'm a-coming, I'm a-coming," Dido said. The small English party bolted for the station.

"Never mind our luggage at the Sydney," panted Captain Hughes. "They can have it in lieu of payment —if they can carry it away in time."

The streets were jammed full of carts, pushcarts, carriages, wheelbarrows, and every kind of conveyance, all crammed with domestic goods. Dido noticed the Four Ancient Creatures, looking rather bewildered, being wheeled off on children's pushchairs. Loaded llamas gazed about them tolerantly, as if wondering why everybody was making such a commotion.

When they reached the station, they found the queer little tip-tilted train already three-quarters packed with people who were using this means to escape from the threatened city; but room was kindly made for the gringos. This time there were no seats at all; Dido squatted on the floor, feeling miserably sad, remembering the ride up. Mr. Holystone had slept all the way, but at least he had been *there*; and Bran had told stories. . . .

The train gave a jerk. The engine started to shriek and shudder. But suddenly there was a disturbance on the platform; people were calling "Make way, make way!" and to the engine driver, "Don't start yet, hold your steam!" And there was Mr. Holystone. He had half a dozen men behind him, all clamoring for his attention, all asking him for instructions—but his eyes were searching through the passengers crowded together on the train.

"Couldn't let you go without bidding you good-bye, sir," he said, hurriedly wringing Captain Hughes's hand. "Thank you again for all your kindness. Tell the quartermaster to throw out the flour in the black canister, it will certainly have weevils in it by this time. Thank you for carrying me up all those plaguey mountains," he said with a grin to Multiple, Windward, and Gusset, shaking hands with each in turn. "Good-bye, Dido." He gently touched her cheek. "Don't forget how to curtsey. And remember me when you take tea—thumb and three fingers on the handle. 'We clean three tweed beads a week . . .' "

"Mr. Holy," gulped Dido. "I've a message for you." She gave it.

"Thank you," he said gravely. "And listen—will you keep Dora for me? As a gift, and a remembrance?"

Dido thought.

"I'd rather not," she said after a moment. "You won't think me rude, Mr. Holy? Dora's a person. She didn't ought to be given as a present. Someone can bring her to you."

"I know what you mean," he said. "You are right. Bran will bring Dora, with Elen's cats—Bran is going to travel down with you."

"He is?" Dido's face lit up. "Oh, I *am* glad!" as Bran climbed in. "Good-bye, good-bye, Mr. Holy—good luck!" She hung out, blowing kisses as he hurried away.

The train started with a shriek.

"None too soon," said Bran. "Look over there." They were in the boxcar which had no glass in its windows; the visibility was excellent. Dido, following the direction of his pointing finger, was just in time to see Mount Catelonde blow its top clean off; a thousand feet of mountain vanished in a great heaving spout of flame. The huge rock that had balanced on the tip of the crater for so long bounded upward like a pea and then vanished from view.

"Blocked the Pass of Nimue, likely as not," said Bran. "If this railway is cut by the glacier there will be no way into Upper Cumbria except through the mines."

"If they ain't blocked too," said Dido. "Well, it's

not much of a place, with the aurocs, and so cold, and the air so thin." And memories of Queen Ginevra and her awful end, she thought. "Maybe the folk had all better go and live in Lyonesse. Things are better there."

"Artaius is certainly going to have his work cut out for the first few years," Bran observed. "He won't have too much time to grieve for Ginevra."

"Now you don't have a steward," Dido said to Captain Hughes. "I'll do the job, if you like. I daresay I could manage; I used to help Mr. Holy a lot. I know where things are."

"Certainly not!" Captain Hughes replied disapprovingly. "You? A young lady? A passenger? That would be wholly unsuitable! No, no, I have already arranged for Brandywinde there to undertake the job. He wishes to be repatriated; he can work his passage."

"But what about his hands?"

"It seems they are on the mend."

And indeed, Mr. Brandywinde was sitting in the middle of a circle of interested auditors, waving his fingers about. "Feeling began to come back into them just like that," he was saying, "as soon as the queen rushed through that door. Oh, what respite from pain, what legerdemain, when one's fingers can do up one's buttons again! What a spasm of joy through my happy heart gambols, when a tremor of feeling returns to my fambles!"

Captain Hughes, in a corner, was busy writing up his log.

"Assistance was rendered to the Ruler of New Cumbria to reclaim the stolen lake Arianrod. The matter has been satisfactorily concluded. The water is now back in its original site, and the treaty of alliance between Great Britain and New Cumbria has been reratified. . . ."

"Geeminy," said Mr. Multiple, hanging out the window. "Will you look at that ice?"

A high white rampart was moving across the stony plain, rubbing out cactus and sigse trees as if they were mustard and cress. But the little train dashed past just in time, within a hundred yards of the approaching glacier, and rattled down the steep descent by the Severn River and its seven majestic waterfalls.

Mr. Multiple had had the forethought to provide himself with a bagful of plantains, bananas, and chirimoya, which he kindly shared with Dido.

"*You* won't suddenly turn out to be King Somebody, Mr. Mully?" Dido asked him apprehensively, munching on a plantain; and he assured her that he would not.

"Didn't I tell you that it would all come right in the end?" Bran said, sitting down beside them.

"Not for poor Queen Ginevra, it didn't."

"She had had her own way for thirteen hundred years. That is long enough."

"And what'll happen to Elen?"

"She will marry Artaius later on. And they will have three children called Llyr, Penardun, and Lud Hudibras."

"Devil take it, I have left my floater behind!" suddenly exclaimed Captain Hughes, looking up from his writing. But he added, "Never mind, I will design an improved one when I am back on board the *Thrush*."

"Would you like me to tell you a story?" asked Bran, noticing that Dido's expression was rather sad.

"Yes. Thanks, mister. I'd like that. Just a minute,

though; I want to see them again before that big wall of ice gets in the way and blocks them off."

She wriggled her way back to the window and hung out of it, looking her last at the thirteen great volcanoes, saying good-bye to them in her mind: Ambage and Arrabe, Ertayne and Elamye, Arryke, Damask, Damyake, Pounce, Pampoyle, Garesse, Galey, Calabe, and Catelonde.